THE HANGING TREE

The older postman, all col d from his face, let his sack f tated uncertainly ung vicious He scream d the oth asp.

For a tubby barrel swung to e. But no one had moved, no poke. Across the street, the florist's van started up. Grabbing a sack each, the two hooded figures turned and ran...

Triggered at a range of less than 8 feet, both barrels of the shotgun blasted...

Also in Mysterious Press by Bill Knox

THE CROSSFIRE KILLINGS
LIVE BAIT
THE INTERFACE MAN

THE
HANGING TREE

Bill Knox

MYSTERIOUS PRESS

Mysterious Press books (UK) are published
in association with Arrow Books Limited
20 Vauxhall Bridge Road, London SW1V 2SA

An imprint of Random Century Group

London Melbourne Sydney Auckland
Johannesburg and agencies throughout
the world

First published in 1983 by Hutchinson & Co. Ltd
Mysterious Press edition 1990

Printed and bound in Great Britain by
Courier International Ltd, Tiptree, Essex

ISBN 0 09 968990 1

For Myra

SCOTTISH CRIME SQUAD

QUIEN·SABE

The off-duty unofficial tie worn by members of the
real-life Scottish Crime Squad has a crest featuring
a wild goose, a red herring and a crystal ball. I'm
glad to have been trusted to wear one.

The motto beneath, 'Quien Sabe', is not always
translated literally.

B.K.

Prelude

There was more than one area like Donaldhill in the city of Glasgow. Come to that, there was more than one area like Donaldhill in any city. But it looked particularly drab that grey Scottish morning in September.

Donaldhill was streets of old tenement buildings, broken here and there by an occasional block of modern high-rise local-authority housing. The few shops kept their windows guarded by metal shutters, sometimes by day as well as night. If you lived in Donaldhill you took graffiti and broken windows for granted and used that extra lock on your door after dark. If you lived in one of the old tenements, you looked up in envy at the high-rise blocks because their people had bathrooms. If you lived in a high-rise, you looked down at the tenements and wondered if their people knew about damp that grew mould on your bedding or vandals who lit fires in the elevator shafts.

Not that many people admitted to living in Donaldhill. It helped, particularly when you applied for a job, to give a different address – a relative or a friend might oblige.

Donaldhill had the highest percentage of citizens over pension age. Apart from them, three out of every five of the adult working population were unemployed, drew some kind of social security benefit, watched TV most of the day, and clung by their fingertips to the hope that things would get better.

Somehow.

It was 8.45 a.m. and the three men in the brightly painted florist's van didn't live in Donaldhill. The van had been stolen the previous night, on the other side of the city. Two of the men were hidden in the back, one with a sawn-off shotgun cradled on his lap. He was humming nervously under his breath. His companion, more relaxed, couldn't stop sniffing and decided he had a cold coming on. The third man, the oldest, lounged openly in the driving seat. Anyone passing could see he was reading a newspaper – the sports pages.

The van was parked directly across the street from Donaldhill's post office, one of a row of small shops. The post office wouldn't open until 9 a.m. but about a score of people were waiting outside. They stood patiently, ignoring the chill wind and the puddles left by overnight rain.

It was Tuesday, the day they could draw their pension or cash their fortnightly benefit cheque.

A first sign of life showed in the post office building and the metal shutter of the door rolled up. A woman counter-clerk appeared, managed to look around yet ignore the queue, then went back inside. The glass inner door slammed shut.

The queue shuffled their feet for a moment then settled down again. A few more people arrived. One was a girl, pregnant and pushing a pram. The man just ahead of her had a mongrel dog on a lead. The girl spoke to the dog and it wagged its tail but backed away. Donaldhill dogs usually did.

A small red Royal Mail van arrived five minutes later and stopped at the kerb. There were two uniformed postmen aboard. The man in the passenger seat got out, crossed to the post office, and knocked on the door. The same woman appeared behind the glass, smiled a greeting, and nodded.

The postman turned. He was old enough to be cautious. He glanced at the queue and noticed the florist's van, the man behind its wheel still reading his newspaper. Then he tensed as a yellow Ford coupé pulled in behind the mail van. A man jumped out, hurried into one of the other shops, and emerged carrying a carton of milk.

Relaxing, the postman waited until the coupé drove off. Strolling back to the mail van, he nodded. The driver emerged. Each postman took a small canvas sack from the vehicle and they started to walk towards the post office.

The rear doors of the florist's van burst open. Two figures clad in anonymous blue overalls jumped out and sprinted over. One clutched the sawn-off shotgun, the other swung a heavy hammer. Knitted balaclava hoods totally masked their faces, apart from slits cut for the eyes.

Both postmen froze where they stood. Behind them, a woman in the queue screamed and dropped her shopping bag.

'Put down an' back off,' rapped the bandit with the shotgun. 'You're not paid hero rates.'

The older postman, all colour drained from his face, let his sack fall. His driver hesitated uncertainly and the heavy hammer swung viciously, smashing his shoulder. He screamed, staggered, almost collapsed, and the other canvas sack fell from his grasp.

For a moment the shotgun's stubby barrels swung towards the queue. But no one had moved, no one spoke. Across the street, the florist's van started up. Grabbing a sack each, the two hooded figures turned and ran.

They didn't see the motor-cyclist. He was young, he wore a white crash helmet, a white sweater, and his faded jeans were tucked into cowboy boots. He had been riding along with only half his attention on the road. The first he realized was that two running men were dead ahead of him.

He braked hard, desperately. The machine skidded and almost toppled, but he managed to stop. Then he stared, open-mouthed, an unsuspecting barrier between the men and their van.

Triggered at a range of less than 8 feet, both barrels of the shotgun blasted him out of the saddle and left him sprawled on the roadway. The motor-cycle fell across his legs.

The two bandits sprinted past and jumped into the back of the florist's van. It began accelerating, rear doors still open and swinging.

Five seconds later it vanished round a corner.

The postman driver was down on his knees, moaning, nursing his shattered arm. At the post office, the woman clerk stared out with her face pressed against the glass door. The people in the queue stayed where they were, paralysed by the sudden violence.

Moistening his lips, the unhurt postman ran to the fallen motor-cyclist. He saw what the shotgun had done and turned away, retching, closing his eyes, wanting to shut out the sight.

'Hey,' said a voice beside him. 'You all right, pal?'

The postman managed to nod. The old man who had joined him was small, white-haired, frail in appearance but totally calm. He remembered seeing him earlier, in the post office queue.

'Aye.' The old man clicked his loose dentures sadly and gestured towards the dead rider. 'Messy, eh? Still, I've seen worse – when I was in the army. First World War, the real one.' He hesitated. 'Those bags they got – was that the pension money?'

'Yes,' said the postman.

He could hear a police siren, still faint and distant. The post office door had opened and people from the queue were helping the injured companion.

'We'll need witnesses,' he said tonelessly. 'You saw it all, didn't you, dad?'

'Me?' The pensioner shook his head in alarmed innocence. 'Bad eyesight – my age. Sorry.'

'I did,' said a new, determined voice.

It was the girl with the pram. She was white-faced and still trembling, but she nodded as the postman looked at her. He sighed, hearing the siren coming nearer. She was very young and very pregnant. He thought of his own daughter.

'No, you didn't,' he said gruffly.

'But – '

'Be sensible, lassie.' He smiled bitterly, eyeing her swollen figure. 'Thanks. But get lost. There'll be others.'

He hoped to God he was right. The crowd was still growing, eager to see what would happen next. But how many had been in the post office queue, how many would admit it? Maybe murder would make a difference, but Donaldhill made a religion of not being involved.

The girl seemed ready to argue. Then she bit her lip, sighed, nodded, and wheeled the pram away.

'Hey.' It was the old man again.

'Now what do you want?' asked the postman tersely.

'How much did they get?'

'About £70,000.'

'Jeeze.' The old man clicked his dentures again, this time in near admiration. Then he scowled. 'What about my pension money?'

'There'll be another delivery,' said the postman wearily. 'Soon.'

He looked again at the toppled motor-cycle, at the dead young man in cowboy boots. There wasn't enough of his face left to know who he had been. Suddenly, the postman felt totally helpless and wanted to cry.

'Hey,' said the old man petulantly, touching his arm. 'About that money. When's soon, eh?'

1

'Superintendent, we've talked about a citizen's rights when involved with the police.' Debby Kinster, a TV news reporter who still somehow managed to look as fresh-faced and innocent as the girl next door, leaned forward a little under the studio lights. 'Do you think the average citizen knows enough about those rights?'

'Your average criminal does.' Detective Superintendent Colin Thane, joint deputy commander of the Scottish Crime Squad, shifted in the discomfort of the interview chair and tried to ignore the television camera a few feet away. 'He'll recite chapter and verse.'

Debby Kinster gave one of those slight frowns which amounted to her professional trademark.

'Everyone has rights, Superintendent. Or do the police not always see it that way?'

'Everyone has rights,' agreed Thane dryly. 'No exceptions.'

He reckoned there couldn't be more than a minute left of the agreed interview time. So far, it hadn't gone too badly. They'd talked in general terms about the police and the public, but he hadn't felt under attack. Not the way he'd been warned it might be.

'For instance, police in this country can't hold anyone for more than six hours without making a formal charge,' said Debby Kinster mildly. 'That's the law, Superintendent.' She smiled, showing perfect white teeth which might have been aimed at his jugular. 'So what happened last week, why did you hold a man for fourteen hours?'

Thane stared at her. He'd been set up, lulled along, left beautifully positioned for the kill. Worse, it was true.

'Well, Superintendent?' She was waiting.

'It happened,' admitted Thane wearily. He glanced down at the little microphone clipped to his tie and decided he could happily wring Debby Kinster's neck. 'It wasn't deliberate.'

It hadn't even been his fault, but he had been leading the investigation team. An operation lasting nearly two months had ended with ten arrests. A whole series of jewellery store robberies had been cleared up, and a small mountain of stolen jewellery had been recovered.

'Then if it wasn't deliberate, why?' demanded Debby Kinster.

He caught a glimpse of his face in the studio monitor and felt even worse.

'An administrative – uh – failure,' he said weakly. 'Nobody's perfect.'

'Not even the police?' she asked with cutting, dead-pan sarcasm.

It had been close to confusion that night. Some of the gang were talking, some were denying everything. The list of charges read like a book, people were trying to take statements, sort out that jewellery, a prisoner's wife had appeared on the scene – no one was certain how – and had gone into hysterics.

It was only when it was almost over that someone had remembered Midge Reilly. Middle-aged, small-time, mild, he'd worked as a look-out on only two of the raids and had been strictly hired help.

Midge was nobody's priority. Forgotten, he'd been found curled up asleep in his cell.

'You could have charged him, if it hadn't been for your "administrative failure"?'

'Yes.'

'But because of it, he was released?'

'That's right.'

Except it hadn't ended there. Five minutes after he'd been showed out into the street, Midge Reilly walked in again saying he wanted to surrender and plead guilty.

Otherwise, too many of his friends would decide he had been an informer and life would be extremely unpleasant.

So they'd locked him up again. Then several unfortunate cops had been roasted.

'Any final comment, Superintendent?' asked Debby Kinster gravely. Almost without pausing, she gave a sudden grin at the camera. 'Cut – he's suffered enough.'

Still grinning, she came over and helped unclip the tie microphone. Thane got out of his chair, shook his head ruefully, and drew a deep breath.

'Who the hell told you?' he demanded.

'Tell you, and I'd be in real trouble.' Her blue eyes twinkled. 'But I loved the story – all of it.'

The studio door swung open. The Scottish Police College staff officer who came in looked at Thane and gave a roar of laughter.

'You look mauled,' he declared with delight. 'Colin, that tape could set the police image back at least five years. Wait till you see the playback!'

But at least it hadn't been for real, just a closed-circuit exercise within the secure confines of the Police College, which was running a series of special one-day media seminars for senior officers from every Scottish force.

Thane's group, a dozen in all, had spent the morning being lectured on the need for better police relations with the media – and the dangers if they went too far. The closed-circuit interviews began after lunch, one person at a time being taken from the group, which wasn't allowed to see what was going on.

But the college staff didn't organize the experience for comic relief. Trusted professionals from the television world were invited along when the studio was in use. They were fed police to interview, encouraged to try any dirty trick possible.

The intended lesson was simple. Next time, the television cameras might be for real. Next time, the man or woman being interviewed would remember what might happen and think ahead. Even if that meant disappearing in the opposite direction.

'Ready for the last of them?' queried the staff officer and he turned to Thane again. 'Colin, you've to phone your boss. Use my office if you want. He called a few minutes ago, but I said you were busy.'

'He'd like that,' said Thane dryly. He gave a wry smile towards the girl. 'Thanks. What's it like when you play rough?'

'You didn't do too badly.' She winked at him, then turned to study her clipboard.

He went out of the studio. The woman coming in, the next victim, was a chief inspector from Edinburgh.

'How was it?' she muttered.

'Easy,' lied Thane.

That was what he had been told.

The staff officer's room was a short distance along a corridor. It had a large picture window with a view of cultivated lawns, disciplined shrubbery, and a backing of open parkland and distant hills.

Closing the door, perching himself on the edge of a desk, Colin Thane lifted the telephone and dialled the Scottish Crime Squad headquarters number in Glasgow.

He was a tall, grey-eyed man in his early forties. He wore a lightweight grey tweed suit with a white shirt and a plain, knitted maroon tie; his thick dark hair was in need of a trim, and the scales at home had begun telling him he was a few pounds overweight. But he still had most of the well-honed athletic build which went back to when he had been a reasonably rated entrant in the annual police boxing championships – though that had ended for him when he became tired of being knocked out in the semi-final bouts.

For the moment, he was puzzled. Waiting for the number to ring out, he remembered how he'd been despatched without any option to the one-day seminar. Jack Hart, the squad commander, had decided someone

15

had to go and had declared Thane had nothing on his plate that couldn't simmer unattended for another day.

So what had changed?

He heard the squad switchboard operator come on the line, asked for Hart's extension, and was put through.

'I appreciate you calling back,' said Hart sarcastically. 'I really do.'

Thane winced. Hart was normally a calm, quietly effective individual who didn't ruffle easily. He had been a good cop, now he was a better administrator. When he sounded on edge, something was wrong.

'Trouble?' Thane asked.

'Yes. I'm being leaned on – hard.' From Hart, it was an unusual admission. 'We've been caught early, wrong-footed, on a full target situation. It's immediate.'

Thane frowned at the mouthpiece, knowing that had to mean trouble. The way the Crime Squad normally functioned, their Criminal Intelligence section would quietly gather details on specific criminals or situations. Then, when the timing seemed right, Jack Hart would activate a target operation. But Thane couldn't think which of the current options could have firmed so rapidly.

'So –' Hart accepted his silence '– I need you back. You're handling it, with your usual team and any help you need. I've got someone from Crown Office sitting across from me.'

Thane whistled to himself. Crown Office represented the ultimate authority behind criminal prosecutions. When they stepped in, top Civil Servants with government-issue briefcases, it mattered. Even Jack Hart, who ranked as a detective chief superintendent, had to do what he was told.

'When do you want me back?' he asked.

'Now.' Hart stopped and swore. Thane heard a quick murmur of voices, then Hart came back on the line again. 'I've another call. Hold on.'

Thane waited. Outside the window, a peacock was strutting along the edge of a bank of rose bushes. A small team of gardeners was at work near an old stone stableyard.

Not many countries used a castle as their police training college. But Tulliallan Castle, a large, Victorian extravagance with a much earlier history, had been a deliberate choice. It was located in its own, considerable grounds in a quiet stretch of rural Clackmannan. It was less than an hour's travel from Glasgow and Edinburgh, reasonably convenient for most other Scottish forces, and had offered plenty of space for development.

Tulliallan Castle, with its mock turrets and battlements, elegant drawing rooms and panelled woodwork, had been in the early stages of dilapidation when the new owners took over. Dormitory blocks had been built on, a gymnasium, swimming pool and other extensions added. The vaulted main hall no longer had tapestries and paintings – instead, there were displays of ceremonial batons and old police cutlasses, showcases of police badges from all over the world.

Still waiting, able to hear the continued murmur of voices at the other end of the line but nothing more, Thane sighed and tried to stay patient.

The peacock strutted past again. He gave a half-smile at the sight.

The castle's previous owners wouldn't have appreciated the uniformed squads who now tramped its corridors to and from lectures on subjects as varied as the questioning of rape victims and the problems of juvenile offenders. They would have been aghast at the way a tarmac skid-pan for pursuit driving tuition had been laid out beside the main driveway. But they couldn't have faulted the gardens.

The gardeners were bussed in daily, picked inmates from one of Her Majesty's prisons. So far, none of the castle peacocks had gone missing.

'Sorry,' said Jack Hart abruptly, coming back on the line. 'But it mattered. There's a man arriving at the airport on the next shuttle flight from London – we're collecting.' He grunted to himself. 'He's what's called an interested party.

17

But he's also an expert – we need him.'

'For what?' demanded Thane. 'Look, I – '

'You want to know what the hell's going on,' agreed Hart dryly. 'All right; it begins with an armed hold-up over at Donaldhill this morning. A passing motor-cyclist rode into the middle of it, uninvited.' He paused, then went on, his voice flat and unemotional. 'One of the hold-up team panicked, fired a shotgun, and killed our motor-cyclist.'

'Rough,' said Thane. But he was still puzzled. Armed hold-ups weren't a usual Crime Squad interest. They went after bigger things. He frowned. 'You said "our" motor cyclist.'

'I did,' said Hart flatly. 'Forget the hold-up team. They were locked up before lunch.'

'So I've got a dead man as a target?' asked Thane incredulously.

'As a start point,' corrected Hart. He gave a wry chuckle. 'At least it's different. Ready for the details?'

'Yes.' Thane reached for the pad and pen on the staff officer's desk.

'His name, Edward Douglas. He was single, an unemployed graduate, age early twenties, home address 56 Baron Avenue. That's north of the river, Millside Division – your old territory.'

'White wine, TV snacks and all-night parties – or it used to be.' Thane scribbled quickly, tore the sheet from the pad, then glanced at his wrist-watch, thinking of the thirty-five-mile drive back to the city. 'I can be there by 4 p.m.'

'Do that,' said Hart briefly. 'Here's what it's about. Ever heard of *The Hanging Tree*?'

Thane hesitated. 'The Hollywood thing?'

'That "thing" is a damned great major-budget American blockbuster movie,' snapped Hart, giving way to his feelings. 'Still being launched in the States, winning Academy Award nominations, the lot. It shouldn't even be in Europe yet. But friend Douglas was carrying three video copies of *The Hanging Tree* in his saddlebags – pirate copies. It's the first time they've turned up anywhere.'

Things began to make sense for Thane. For several weeks, on Hart's orders, their Criminal Intelligence team had been gathering a target file on pirate video tapes and their distributors.

'We've got ourselves a front-line courier,' went on Hart bitterly. *The Hanging Tree* was being protected by the Americans like the Crown Jewels, so now total hell is breaking loose – at several levels. Interpol want in on the act, and I've even had the Foreign Office making pious noises.'

'And all we've got is Douglas?'

'Douglas and *The Hanging Tree*,' confirmed Hart. 'He hasn't yet been identified as far as the media are concerned – but we can't keep that going much longer.' He gave a growl which rasped over the line. 'Colin, I don't know if you need it, but take a warning. At street level, pirate videos probably rate about as criminal as parking tickets – and a lot more entertaining. But get to the top and you're talking about organized crime, dirty as it comes.'

There was an irony in it. Thane knew that Jack Hart was a self-confessed home-video addict – plenty of police were, because of the hours they worked. But he also knew Hart was right. He'd seen some of what was in the Criminal Intelligence file – the way in which, in a very short time, the whole illegal business of pirate video tapes had come out of nowhere to rate as one of the fastest-growing rackets in existence. The kind of racket that made fortunes for the people behind it.

'Did the Americans know *The Hanging Tree* had been copied – stolen?' he asked.

'No,' said Hart wearily. 'They thought they had it guarded round the clock.'

'Then how about Douglas – have we anything more on him?'

'No trace of any police record, nothing yet from the computer,' said Hart. 'But start at his home, get anything you can there – then I need you here for a meeting by five.

See you then.'

Hart went off the line. Thane sighed to himself, replaced the receiver, then the door opened and the college staff officer came into the room.

'We're finished,' he told Thane briskly. 'All we need is a couple of minutes to rewind the tapes, then we can start the playback session.' He nodded at the telephone. 'Get through all right?'

Thane nodded. 'I've got to leave.'

'Right now?' The staff officer's face fell. 'Hell, what about your playback?'

'My loss,' said Thane woodenly. 'But I can tell you what to do with it.'

'Very funny,' said the staff officer bleakly. 'All right, why the summons?'

'You know how it goes,' Thane grinned at him. 'My agent came up with a better offer.'

'Like what?' grunted the staff officer. 'Co-starring with Genghis Khan? You'd have made a good comedy duo.' Then he paused and nodded. 'Good luck with it – whatever it is.'

Thane left him. On the way out he stopped in one of the corridors to let a squad of recruits pass. They were all young, their uniforms still looked new, and a lean, hungry-looking sergeant instructor was barking at their heels as they marched. The sergeant instructor met Thane's eyes and gave a quick wink which spoke louder than words.

The squad disappeared from sight. Moving on, Thane passed the ceremonial batons in the main hallway, went out of the castle, and began to cross to where he'd left his car.

Another group of recruits, clad in blue tracksuits, were practising unarmed combat on a piece of open ground under the watchful glare of another sergeant instructor. The best of them was a slim girl with jet black hair. She gave a sudden twisting turn, heaved, and the lanky 6-foot male who had been her partner went straight over her shoulder. The girl laughed and stood back. The sergeant instructor took two paces, got behind her, grabbed her in an armlock, and deposited her on the ground with a thump before she realized what was happening.

'One thug down can mean his mate is still waiting,' he roared. 'I keep telling you! How about remembering it?'

It was harsh but he was right, thought Thane as he walked on.

The college had only a few short weeks in which to teach its recruit intakes a great deal on their initial training courses. Then they'd return to their various forces, still beginners, to be paired off with an experienced cop for a spell, for the next stage of the learning process – on the streets.

The ones who lasted would come back to Tulliallan Castle again and again throughout their careers, no matter what rank they achieved over the years. There was always another training course, a new lecture schedule.

Society had come to demand police who could think – even if it didn't always get them.

'Superintendent – Mr Thane – '

The shout made Thane turn. The sergeant instructor from the unarmed combat class came hurrying over and Thane recognized him. He'd been a detective constable with the squad, promoted to sergeant at the end of the usual three-year secondment and then transferred again.

'Just wanted to ask how the lads were, sir,' said the man, grinning. 'Still got Francey Dunbar as your sergeant?'

'I can't get rid of him,' said Thane dryly. 'Things haven't changed much. How are you getting along?'

'Here?' The sergeant instructor glanced over his shoulder towards the waiting recruits. 'This bunch isn't too bad and being here is pretty fair. Still – ' He looked almost wistfully at Thane. 'Anyway, give my best to the lads, will you, sir?'

'I'll do that,' promised Thane.

He watched the man trot back to his class, suddenly remembering his name was Vass. He'd left the Crime Squad within days of Thane's arrival – though that was now almost a year in the past.

Before that, Thane had ranked as a detective chief inspector, CID chief for Glasgow's Millside Division. Millside was a tough, unglamorous slice of the city's dockland and slums, with a fringe of the good life just to make things awkward. But it had been his patch, he'd run it and known it – and he'd felt strangely lost when he'd been summoned to Headquarters, promoted to detective superintendent, and told at the same time that he was being moved, seconded to the Scottish Crime Squad.

Then, it had been like being sent into exile. Now, Millside Division seemed an age away. He'd be going back as an outsider.

He reached his car, a mud-spattered Ford from the squad pool. Getting behind the wheel, he glanced at the gift-wrapped package on the passenger seat and winced to himself.

If Jack Hart's meeting went on for long, he might have a different kind of problem. Even a cop should be able to plan a night out with his wife on their wedding anniversary.

He started the Ford, and tried to think about video tapes.

The journey took just under an hour, first along minor roads to Kincardine Bridge, then over its long span across the muddy upper reaches of the River Forth, and from there to join the busy trunk M80 motorway from the north for Glasgow.

The traffic moved smoothly most of the way except at the city boundary, where a skidding truck had demolished a delivery van and wreckage blocked two whole lanes. Thane took his turn in the queue to ease past the result, then switched on the Ford's wipers as a slight drizzle of rain began falling.

Grey under the clouds, the Glasgow skyline lay ahead. It was a mixture of tall, modern office blocks and slim church spires, of dark slate tenement roofs and bleak factory chimneys. Few of the chimneys were smoking. Too many of the factories had locked gates and 'For Sale' notices.

Glasgow knew what recession meant.

The drizzle of rain faded again as Thane made a right turn at a set of lights and used a back-street route which avoided the city centre and saved time. Suburban bungalows gave way to older buildings. He drove through an industrial estate where only about half of the firms still seemed to be operating and the rest had broken windows.

Then, minutes later, he reached his destination.

It hadn't changed.

Baron Avenue had been built in the thirties, a product of the concrete shoebox school of architecture. A collection of three-storey blocks of small apartments, it had drifted down-market and become shabby. The original communal gardens had been concreted over.

But it was exactly suited to the singles and young, childless couples who had moved in. They either worked in offices or pooled student grants. They tolerated rock music at 3 a.m. and car doors banging at any hour.

Or, if they didn't, most of them left. Baron Avenue lived that way, seldom featuring in crime reports beyond the occasional brawl or burglary, and it preferred older generations to visit on Sunday afternoons.

Driving into it, Colin Thane kept the Ford's speed to a crawl and checked the numbers on the blocks. Then he saw an easier guide, a grey Mini from the Crime Squad pool parked at the kerb. He drew in behind the car and got out.

Number 56 was a few yards along. A thin, dark-haired man wearing a black leather jacket, faded jeans and a grey cotton sweatshirt leaned against the brickwork at the entrance. He straightened a little as Thane approached and gave a twist of a smile.

'Taking a break, Francey?' asked Thane with mild sarcasm.

'Hiding, sir.' Detective Sergeant Francey Dunbar thumbed towards the entrance. 'Douglas's girlfriend arrived ten minutes ago. She didn't know.'

Thane grimaced. 'Who's with her?'

'Sandra,' said Dunbar. 'She can handle it.'

Thane nodded. Sandra Craig, a detective constable on his regular team, took a normal share of whatever came along. But there were times when sex equality wasn't a two-way traffic, when a woman-to-woman situation made sense.

'Anyone else here?' he asked.

'Not right now,' answered Dunbar. He was just over medium height and in his twenties, with a thin straggle of a moustache and a strong nose. 'The Divisional CID said they'd look back again later – they had Douglas's keys but we found another set in the house.' His dark eyes showed a brief glint of amusement. 'They told a few stories about how it was when Millside was your patch.'

'Lies,' said Thane flatly. 'How about the video tapes in the apartment?'

'There were about a dozen, various titles, stacked in a cupboard,' said Dunbar with minimal enthusiasm. 'I got them ferried back to Commander Hart – he wants them checked out.'

'Nothing else?'

Dunbar shrugged. 'I double-combed the place with Sandra, but we didn't find anything. Douglas was ordinary – or that's how it looks.'

'If he was ordinary, we wouldn't be here,' reminded Thane stonily. 'I heard the shotgun team was locked up. What's the story?'

'A patrol car crew got lucky,' said Dunbar with dry satisfaction. 'They spotted the getaway van and started chasing, then the van driver lost control on a bend and hit a wall – hard. After that, it was just a mop-up. Three battered bandits, the money and the shotgun.'

'Do we know them?'

Dunbar nodded. 'They've got records, but it was their first try at an armed hold-up.' He sucked his teeth sadly. 'That was Douglas's bad luck. But at least he was carrying identification.'

'Among other things.' Thane put his hands in his pockets

24

and frowned. 'When did we hear about the video tapes?'

It had been puzzling him, one of the things he would have asked Hart if there had been more time.

'One of the sergeants on the Donaldhill case is a video fan,' said Dunbar sardonically. 'He got interested and told his divisional chief when things began to calm down. The divisional chief knew that anything involving pirate tapes has a "tell Crime Squad" sticker attached.' He stopped and scratched his neck, the heavy silver bracelet he wore on one wrist clinking gently. The bracelet's name tab was blank, but his blood group was engraved on the underside. 'My turn, sir. What the heck is going on?'

'It's a target operation.' Thane saw Dunbar's disbelief. 'Pirate videos, Francey – one in particular, and we've drawn the job.'

'You mean it?' Dunbar stared at him, open-mouthed, then almost laughed. 'What are we supposed to do – round up half the population? Anyone with a video recorder is into pirate tapes, buying them, renting them – look, I've done it!' He gestured his disgust. 'Next thing, we'll be told there's a shortage of real crime.'

'Next thing, you'll risk feeling my boot,' said Thane without humour. 'It's a target operation, there's a file – and if the orders on this one came from any higher, they'd be on tablets of stone. Try thinking, Sergeant. If Douglas was a courier, that makes him a bottom rung in one particular pirate ladder. You know he had *The Hanging Tree*?'

'Yes, but – '

'That makes it a special ladder for a lot of people. They want to know who's sitting on the top rung.'

Dunbar sighed, scowled a little, but said nothing.

Anyone in the Crime Squad would have recognized the signs. Francey Dunbar wasn't convinced, and when that happened he could be stubborn. It was one of the reasons he was the squad's delegate to the Police Federation, where he supported lost causes with a grim, regular determination. In his own time, he was unpredictable. He was equally devoted to a procession of girls and his bright red BMW motor-cycle. But sometimes he got on the motor-cycle and vanished – to surface at some weekend meditation camp.

'We'll pretend you now approve,' said Thane resignedly. 'Now, what have we got on Douglas?'

'Not a lot.' Dunbar spoke with hurt dignity. 'Neighbours say he was quiet, not a mixer – none of them knows much about him. He arrived about a year ago and lost his job soon after he moved in – the firm folded.'

'Family?'

'He's an only child – father Merchant Navy, a captain, and his mother lives up north. They're being contacted.'

'Right.' Some cop somewhere was welcome to that task. Thane continued on his mental list. 'And the girl?'

'Janice Darrow, aged twenty, a nurse.' Dunbar showed some genuine concern. 'She took it pretty badly. I – well, I don't know how she'll be now.'

'Then we'd better find out,' suggested Thane neutrally. He looked up at the building. 'Where did he live? Top floor?'

Dunbar grinned despite himself and nodded. When you were a cop, it was always top floor. Sometimes it was as if nobody ever lived lower down.

They went inside. The graffiti on the walls, Baron Avenue style, was more political than pornographic and the spray-can artist could even spell. He proclaimed in letters 2 feet high that if he couldn't Ban the Bomb then he knew Where to Put It – and his choice was exotic.

Thane let Dunbar take the lead as they climbed the stairs. They passed a smell of Indian cooking on the first landing. Further up, a sick-looking rubber plant sat on a window ledge, clinging to life in an old wooden tub. A radio was playing somewhere and Thane noticed a damp patch which stained down the wall from the roof.

Douglas's door was first of three on the top landing. Francey Dunbar thumbed the bellpush and the door opened after a moment. The girl who looked out was tall, slim, red-haired, and about the same age as Dunbar. She glared at Dunbar and then gave Thane a wry smile.

'Hello, sir.' She beckoned them in. Detective Constable Sandra Craig was wearing denim trousers and jacket over a cream roll-neck sweater. She gave Dunbar another glare as she closed the door again. 'And the rat returns to the sinking ship. Thanks, Francey – you got out fast enough.'

Dunbar shrugged. 'I know my limitations.'

'How is she?' asked Thane, ignoring the exchange.

'Talking a little, sir.' Sandra Craig gestured across the small, simply furnished hallway to one of the rooms. 'She's in there.'

'What have you got?'

'She met Douglas a few months ago, at a party.' Sandra Craig spoke quietly, precisely. 'He was supposed to collect her at home about noon today – she lives over in Monkswalk, at Watson Drive, and had the day off. When he didn't show, she tried telephoning a couple of times. Then – ' she shrugged, ' – well, she came round to find out what was wrong.'

'How was it between them?'

'He mattered.' Sandra Craig pursed her lips. 'Douglas wanted her to move in with him. She would have, but for a problem. She has a brother. He lives with her, and he was wounded in the Falklands campaign. She reckoned he needed her.'

'Maybe they need each other now,' said Thane soberly. He glanced at Dunbar. 'Where's the telephone?'

'In the kitchen.' Dunbar thumbed towards another of the doors.

'Get a Scenes of Crime team over here, Francey. Tell them I want the whole place gone over for fingerprints.'

Dunbar blinked. 'Why?'

'It's supposed to be "Why, sir?",' reminded Thane patiently. 'For whatever they damned well find, like if any of Douglas's visitors happen to be on our books.'

'I wasn't thinking,' admitted Dunbar.

'And it's getting to be a habit,' said Sandra Craig pointedly.

'Enough,' said Thane, getting between them. 'Fight in your own time.'

He let Sandra go first into the small, modestly furnished living room where Janice Darrow was waiting. She was sitting on a couch, a small, plump, fair-haired girl in a dark brown two-piece suit. As they entered, she looked up. Her face was young and attractive, but her eyes were red from earlier tears.

A framed photograph of a young, dark-haired man in graduation robes sat on a television set in one corner of the room. There was a video recorder under the set. Going over to the TV set, Thane looked at the photograph, then at Sandra Craig. She nodded, and he picked up the photograph and brought it back to the couch.

'Hello, Janice.' He sat beside the girl. 'My name is Thane.' He indicated the photograph. 'What course did he take?'

She drew a deep breath. 'Social Studies. He – he had an Honours degree.'

'I'd like to hear about him.' Thane brought out his cigarettes. She took one, and he gave her a light then put the pack away again. 'Janice, I've come a reasonable distance. I could use a cup of tea. Like one?'

The girl managed a faint smile and nodded. Thane signalled Sandra Craig and she left quietly.

'Right.' Thane put down the photograph, his manner still relaxed and gentle. 'He had a degree – but he was out of work. Well, it happens often enough.'

'That doesn't help.' The cigarette between Janice Darrow's fingers shook a little and her voice was unsteady. 'Please, Superintendent – couldn't this wait?'

Thane shrugged. 'Meaning you'd rather go into a corner and hide?'

'No. But – '

'I get paid to ask questions,' he told her quietly. 'He graduated – then what?'

'Ted told me there weren't any vacancies where he could use his degree. He worked as a clerk with a travel firm – then it closed down.'

'And afterwards?'

'Casual work, anything he could get.' She drew on the cigarette. 'That wasn't much.'

'But he kept this place.' Thane indicated the room. 'An apartment costs money.'

'Ted was careful.'

'And you met him at a party. How did that happen?'

'It was an engagement party.' She bit her lip briefly. 'The girl was a nurse I knew, Ted was her fiancé's friend. We – well, we just got together.'

Thane nodded his understanding. 'You said he took casual work. What kind?'

'Delivery driving mostly. He knew one or two firms – if someone was off sick, they'd call him and he'd stand in.' She looked at the cigarette, got up suddenly, and stubbed it out in an ashtray on a nearby table. Turning, she grimaced. 'I forgot. I've stopped smoking.'

'I'm still trying.' Thane waited until she sat down again. 'This delivery driving – was it sometimes for a video firm?'

'I – ' She stared at him, something close to panic showing for a moment in her eyes. 'Why do you ask?'

'When he was killed this morning, he was carrying video tapes,' said Thane. He let his manner harden. 'Were they for you – or do you know where they would come from?'

She didn't answer. Then, before he could ask again, the door opened. He cursed under his breath as Sandra Craig came in. She carried a tray with two cups of tea, sugar, milk, and a few biscuits on a plate.

'Here we are.' She set the tray down on the small table, and moved the table closer. Then she caught Thane's glance and understood. 'Sorry. I'll leave you alone.'

As she left, Thane added milk to one of the cups. He let Janice help herself, waiting until she'd taken a sip from her cup, then tried again.

'I need to know about those video tapes, Janice.'

'Why?' she asked in a tired voice. 'He's dead. Do they matter?'

'They do to us.' Thane nursed his cup in both hands, feeling the warmth of the liquid through the fine china, disliking what he was having to do. 'I'll have to keep asking.'

'Why? Because they were pirate tapes?' She took him by surprise by her anger. 'Yes, Ted brought some now and again. He – he knew someone who could get them. But he wasn't selling them, Superintendent. They were gifts – he knew my brother liked having them for the shop.'

'Your brother has a shop?' Thane raised an eyebrow.

'That's right.' She spoke tightly. 'My brother John. He lost an arm when his ship took an Exocet and blew up. So now he runs a shop. He sells newspapers, magazines – and he runs a little video library as a sideline.'

'And Ted brought a few free titles – to help.' Thane drew a deep breath. 'He must have said something about how he got them.'

'I told you. He said he had a friend. Sometimes you don't ask.'

'All right.' Thane nodded acceptance, fairly certain she wasn't lying. 'Where do you work, Janice?'

'At the Royal Infirmary.' She shrugged. 'I'm a surgical staff nurse, mostly on night duty.'

'So you'd be able to see a reasonable amount of Ted during the day.' He looked round the room, neat in the way no man on his own was likely to achieve, noting the way a curtain had been darned at a frayed edge and the glint of daylight on some polished brass ornaments. 'Except when he worked. Do you know any of the firms who gave him those casual driving jobs?'

'No.' She shook her head. 'Ted said they were just small firms – more or less people he knew. We – well, he preferred not to talk about it.'

'But you never wondered why?'

'Of course I did,' she said reluctantly. 'I suppose I knew that there was something crooked about it – but the way things were between us mattered more.'

He believed her. He set down his cup, got to his feet, and

stood for a moment. He could hear a child shouting somewhere outside and in a strange way the room they were in was beginning to feel cold and empty.

'Janice, a word of advice.' He waited until he was sure she was listening. 'The way Ted was killed makes him news. That means reporters, photographs. They'll get to you – that's their job and you're what they call human interest.'

She nodded, saying nothing.

'They won't know about the video tapes,' warned Thane. 'Don't tell them. It'll be easier that way, for you and your brother – and for us.'

'Whatever you want.' She looked up at him, tears in her eyes. 'I don't give a damn what this is about, Superintendent. I loved him.'

Thane left her and went back out into the hallway. Sandra Craig was there. Her face showed she'd been listening and hadn't liked it.

'Never hit them where it shows,' he told her with a defensive sarcasm. 'So I'm an animal. How did she travel here?'

'By bus, then walked, sir.'

'Make sure she gets driven home.' He paused, saw the half-eaten sandwich Sandra was holding, and shaped a wry grin. Detective Constable Craig's answer to most problems began with eating something. 'But before that, try her again. I want names – Douglas's friends, possible contacts.'

'She won't like it,' mused Sandra.

'Who does?' countered Thane.

He found Francey Dunbar in the small, surprisingly well-equipped kitchen.

'Any luck?' asked Dunbar. He was leaning against a freezer unit, drinking tea from a mug.

'Some.' Thane saw the telephone, mounted on a wall by the window. He used a handkerchief to lift the receiver, dialled his home number, and listened to it ring out. But there was no reply. Shrugging, he hung up. 'Francey – '

31

'Sir?'

'Douglas was more or less unemployed. How would you rate this place?'

'Wrong.' Dunbar opened the freezer unit and gestured. Most of the shelves were filled. 'Not your actual poverty trap. Want to see more, sir?'

Thane nodded. They went through to the only bedroom, and Dunbar opened a wardrobe. It held several suits and accessories to match. A bottle of aftershave on the dressing-table was French and expensive.

'Money, valuables?' asked Thane.

'One pair of gold cuff-links, a few pounds in cash, one bank book.' Dunbar produced them. 'Anything he had with him is still at Donaldhill.'

The cuff-links were old and initialled, the money totalled £20. Thane opened the bank book. It was a savings account, with just over £200 in credit. The last entry, a small withdrawal, had been made three months previously.

'Well?' he asked Dunbar.

'Low profile,' agreed Dunbar sadly. 'Any bills we found were marked paid. But where the money came from – ' he shrugged ' – I told you we doubled-combed this place, sir. Whatever he was doing, it was cash and careful.'

'So careful he didn't even tell his girl.' Thane went over to the window and looked out. The view was down towards the back court area. The rain had started again, heavier, darkening the concrete. The only sign of life was a large black mongrel dog, padding past a row of lock-up garages. He watched the dog for a moment then turned, frowning. 'Did Douglas keep his motor-cycle down there?'

Dunbar nodded. 'In one of the lock-ups. I checked it with one of the Millside team. But – well – ' he chewed an edge of his thin moustache in an unusual display of embarrassment. 'We were only looking for tapes. I – '

He followed Thane towards the door.

The rain was becoming heavier. They doubled across the back yard, Dunbar dragging a tagged set of keys from his pocket. The black dog padded back, barked at them a couple of times while Dunbar unlocked the door of the third lock-up in the line, then followed them in as the door swung open.

The bare brick interior and concrete floor smelled of oil, exhaust fumes and damp. Thane located a light switch, a fluorescent tube sputtered to life overhead, and he looked around. He saw a workbench and tool rack, some cans and cardboard boxes, and a set of grubby overalls hanging on a hook. The dog pawed at his trouser-leg, whined, and he bent down for a moment to scratch its head between the ears.

'Well?' He glanced at Dunbar and they set to work.

The only way to search a box was to shake it empty, then examine what had tumbled out. The only way to be sure what was in a can was to sample the contents. Fifteen minutes later, the floor of the lock-up was littered with small collections of nuts, bolts, and motor-cycle spares. Dunbar had acquired a stain of oil on his jacket and had paint on his hands. Thane had gashed a finger on a razor blade he found the hard way in one of the overall pockets and had covered the cut with a first-aid adhesive dressing from a tin in another pocket.

The dog had given up watching and was sniffing around on its own. After a moment, it began scratching at the brickwork where the overalls had been hanging.

'Give over,' Dunbar told the animal gloomily. 'If it's a rat you want, I'll give you addresses.'

The dog scraped on, ignoring him. Dunbar looked again, frowned, crouched down, elbowed the animal aside, and tapped the brickwork with his knuckles. He looked round.

'Like to hand me a screwdriver, something like that, sir?'

Thane found one on the tool rack and brought it. Carefully, Dunbar prodded the apparent mortar round two of the bricks. The tip of the screwdriver sank into soft putty and the dog shoved forward again, barking enthusiastically.

'Get the hell out of my way,' said Dunbar indignantly.

The screwdriver blade pared an edge of putty away from a section of two bricks. Dunbar used the tool again, as a lever, and the bricks came loose. Pulling them out, shoving the dog away, he reached into the exposed hole, felt around, and brought out a small, oilskin-wrapped package tied with string.

They took it over to the workbench, used the razor blade to cut the string, then unwrapped the oilskin.

'Hallelujah,' said Dunbar softly. 'No way did he get this lot from social security.'

The dog had its front paws up on the workbench as Thane spread out the contents of the package.

There was a British passport. The name on it was Paul Nord, but the photograph inside was Douglas's. Next came three thick bundles of banknotes, each secured by a rubber band.

Dunbar took one bundle and weighed it roughly in his hand.

'About a thousand in each,' he guessed.

Thane nodded. He was looking at the one thing left. It was an old .38 calibre Browning automatic and it had a full magazine.

'You two,' snapped an abrupt voice behind him. 'What are you doing with my dog?'

They turned. The woman standing at the door was small, fat, and in her thirties. She wore a loose, almost ankle-length coat and a bright green waterproof hat.

'Well?' She glared at them and took a step forward out of the rain.

'Your dog?' Thane moved to block her view of the bench. 'He just moved in – looking for company.'

'Andrew wanders.' She was still suspicious. 'But dogs get stolen.'

'You can't be too careful,' agreed Dunbar cheerfully. 'Andrew, eh? Yes, that's a good name for a – ' he broke off, swallowed, and looked down at his suddenly damp trouser-leg and the pool on the floor at his feet.

'That's rude, Andrew.' The woman came forward and attached a leather lead to the dog's collar. She smiled at Dunbar. 'Still, he only does that to people he likes.'

'That's nice,' said Dunbar with an effort.

'If you like dogs,' agreed the woman.

She turned and left them, the dog trotting at her side. Dunbar swore, softly but pungently.

'We owed him,' said Thane mildly.

He looked again at what they'd found. Ted Douglas had been ready to run, ready to carry a gun. He remembered Jack Hart's warning about what they were going into. Suddenly, it had become much more real.

They gathered up the passport, money and gun, locked the garage as they left, and went back up to Douglas's apartment. When they went in, Sandra Craig met them in the little hallway.

'We've had two phone calls,' she said quietly. 'One was from Millside Division CID. They thought you'd want to know Douglas's name has been released – it's already going out on local radio.'

Thane grimaced. 'It had to happen. And the other?'

'A funny.' She looked at them both and shrugged. 'I answered, just gave the number. Whoever was at the other end said nothing, just hung up.'

'A funny – or someone interested,' said Thane grimly. 'How about the girl?'

'She's starting to talk, sir.'

Thane nodded. 'Try and move her soon, before the vultures start gathering. And see if the name Paul Nord means anything to her.'

He waited until the red-haired girl had gone back into the front room, then turned to Dunbar.

'You stay, Francey. Take care of any mopping up here, then call it a day. We'll start again first thing to-morrow.'

'I've been thinking,' said Dunbar awkwardly.

'Again?' asked Thane stonily.

'That money – the way this is shaping,' persisted

35

Dunbar. He fingered his moustache awkwardly. 'Maybe I was wrong. It could be a nasty.'

'Yes.' Thane paused, sniffed, then looked at him deliberately. 'One other thing, Francey – that dog. You're beginning to smell.'

He left before his sergeant could reply.

2

The Scottish Crime Squad had an open listing in the Glasgow telephone directory, a token, branch-office presence to filter the unwanted calls. But its real base was a modest collection of buildings located in the comparative privacy of trees and grassland on the fringe of the city, south of the River Clyde, close to the M8 motorway.

Colin Thane took the motorway route south over the Kingston Bridge with the first of the evening homebound traffic. It was still raining and the river below looked cold and greasy. Another bulk carrier had joined the line of cargo ships berthed along the quaysides. Most of them, whatever flags they flew, had been lying there empty and unemployed for long enough to become part of the scenery. One had grass and weeds growing on her foredeck.

Until things changed, it was that kind of world.

His exit ramp came up. Thane changed lane, left the motorway traffic, and two minutes later turned in at a gate set in a high boundary fence. There was a guard and a sign which said 'Police Training Area', which was partly true. The Crime Squad's nearest neighbours were the Strathclyde force's Mounted Branch and Dog Branch training units.

Animals and humans alike seemed to have decided it was too wet to work. There was no sign of life as the Ford splashed through puddles to the Crime Squad parking lot. Thane stopped close to the headquarters building, knowing the surveillance cameras would have registered his arrival. Getting out, he hurried through the downpour, shoved his way through the glass entrance doors, then stopped in the brightly lit reception lobby to mop some of the rain from his face.

'Don't you own a coat?' asked a woman's voice.

He grinned. Maggie Fyffe, the commander's secretary, was standing at the other side of the reception counter. Middle-aged, smartly dressed, she was a cop's widow and usually knew as much as anyone about what was happening.

'I'm the drip-dry type, Maggie.' He indicated the quietly chattering telex machine at her elbow. 'Busy?'

'You damned well know I am,' she said grimly. 'You're part of it.'

She broke off to smile at two detective constables heading out into the downpour. Thane nodded as they passed. Unshaven, wearing overalls, they were almost ready to break a stolen-car ring which used an all-night garage. The owner let it happen because he didn't want his legs broken.

'Commander Hart in his office, Maggie?' queried Thane.

'Waiting,' she confirmed. 'You've to go straight through.'

'Right.' He reached for the telephone on the counter between them. 'Once I use this.'

'Keep it short,' warned Maggie Fyffe. 'He's in a mood to chew girders.'

Thane grinned and dialled his home number. It rang out and this time it was answered.

'She's not here,' said his wife's voice firmly.

'Then you'll have to do,' said Thane mildly. 'What's going on?'

'Oh, it's you.' Mary Thane laughed. 'Sorry. I've been back ten minutes and I've had four calls for Kate.'

Teenage daughters, decided Thane, kept the telephone industry in a profit situation.

'I'm back from Tulliallan,' he explained, conscious of Maggie Fyffe's quizzical interest. 'But Jack Hart has called a meeting. I could be late.'

'Tell him he can – ' she stopped and sighed. 'How soon can you get clear?'

'Within the hour,' he said hopefully. 'Through a window, if necessary. We're still eating out. I tried to call earlier.'

'I was stuck under a dryer at a hairdresser's,' she explained. 'Trying for a new me – so remember to say you like it.'

Thane chuckled, said goodbye, and hung up. Maggie Fyffe hadn't moved.

'A problem?' she asked sympathetically.

'It's called a wedding anniversary,' agreed Thane.

'Then move,' she frowned, gesturing him on his way. 'You're wasting time.'

Thane went along the corridor. Stopping at a door marked 'Commander' he pressed the button beside it. A green 'enter' light flashed and, opening the door, he went in.

Jack Hart's office was a large room, at least twice as big as Thane's, and as squad commander he rated wall-to-wall carpet. When Thane entered, he was at his desk and had just replaced the receiver of his telephone. A man in his late forties with a lined face, sad eyes and thinning grey hair, Hart sat back and greeted him with a nod.

'About time,' he declared abruptly. 'Close the door, find a chair, and meet our visitor.' He indicated the man sitting opposite him. 'This is John La Mont, our expert arrived from London.'

'We've been talking about you, Superintendent.' La Mont rose and smiled as they shook hands. His accent was firmly Canadian and he was in his thirties – a bulky bear of a man with curly brown hair, a neat beard and sharp, bright eyes. 'I work as a special counsel with the Motion Picture and Videogram Association.' He considered Thane whimsically. 'You've never heard of us, right?'

'Not till now,' admitted Thane, collecting a chair and bringing it over.

'That's usual, outside the industry.' La Mont was unperturbed. Like Hart, he wore a dark blue business suit. But the Canadian teamed it with a white roll-neck sweater and suede ankle boots, and had a thin gold chain around his neck. Lounging back, legs crossed, he shrugged. 'We're the good guys, Superintendent. We protect copyright and sink pirates – both sides of the Atlantic and into Europe.'

'Offering technical and background assistance only,' said Hart deliberately. His lined face stayed impassive. 'Mr La Mont understands his – ah – limitations.'

'They've been spelled out by your kind of people often enough,' mused La Mont. He winked at Thane. 'Which suits me, Superintendent. Don't ask me why anyone should get the idea I want to be out there having my head kicked in. I'm the peaceful type.'

Thane wasn't sure if he meant it. La Mont struck him as someone who might be tempted to trample through most things to get what he wanted.

Hart's office looked as if he already had. The desk was littered with video cassettes. The curtains at the window were drawn shut. A trestle table had been installed beside it, accommodating a television monitor set, two video recorders and a linking tangle of wires.

'We've been working,' agreed Hart, noticing his interest. 'Mr La Mont can be quite surprising.'

La Mont grinned a little. 'I'm a copyright lawyer, Superintendent. But I know a few parlour tricks with electronics.' He lifted one of the video cassettes and shook his head woefully. 'Maybe I should have stuck to plain, ordinary law. My corporate world is not a happy place right now, thanks to this. Seen it yet?'

Thane shook his head and took the cassette from the Canadian. It was in a plain black plastic case, with a simple printed label saying *The Hanging Tree* stuck to the front. Traces of grey powder at the corners showed it had been examined for fingerprints.

'You know the background?' queried La Mont.

'Only the basics,' admitted Thane.

'Then let me tell you more,' said La Mont bleakly. 'Like there's no authorized video version of that movie scheduled till next year. That it won't be shown in Europe until three months from now, when there's a Royal Command performance scheduled in London – before the Queen, with Charles and Princess Di. It's getting the full treatment.' He snorted. 'Except by then maybe a quarter of the population will have seen it at home.'

'And someone will have made a lot of money?' suggested Thane.

'A few millions.' La Mont grunted at Thane's blink of disbelief. He took back the cassette. 'I mean it, Superintendent. That's before they try dubbing it into other languages – '

'Which is someone else's worry,' said Hart pointedly. 'Let's stick with what we've got. This pirate version hasn't turned up anywhere else – '

'It will,' declared La Mont gloomily. 'Tomorrow or the day after. I know.'

'I don't – yet.' Hart silenced him with a patient frown then turned to Thane. 'What about Baron Avenue?'

Thane shook his head. 'Not a lot.'

He told them briefly about the apartment, the girl and what he and Dunbar had found in the lock-up garage. At the finish La Mont didn't appear impressed.

'We need to work on this "casual driving" angle,' he declared, slapping a hand on the desk. 'Get some names, get – ' He saw Hart's expression, stopped, and gave an apologetic grin. 'Sorry.'

'Advice is always welcome.' Hart made it plain that he meant something else.

His desk intercom buzzed. He pressed the answer key, a voice murmured, and Hart looked relieved.

'Bring it through,' he said briefly. Releasing the key, he faced La Mont again. 'We're ready. But suppose you tell Thane about the other tapes found at Baron Avenue?'

'That's simple enough,' shrugged La Mont, with little interest. 'They're a mix – a couple of home recordings, one or two legitimate titles, the rest pirate or counterfeits. Nothing I haven't seen before, thank God. *The Hanging Tree* is enough.'

They heard a light tap on the office door, then it opened. The plump, middle-aged detective constable who came in was named Joe Felix. He often worked with Thane and was also one of the squad's technical and surveillance specialists.

'Hello, sir.' He grinned at Thane, closed the door, and came over carrying two video cassettes. He looked at Hart. 'Now, Commander?'

Hart nodded and Felix went over to the trestle table. He put a video cassette in each recorder then touched switches. Both monitor sets came to life, their blank screens glowing, and indicator lights appeared on the recorders.

'Fourteen minutes in, Joe,' said La Mont helpfully.

'Fourteen minutes, seventeen seconds,' corrected Felix sturdily, without looking round.

'As you say,' La Mont grinned.

'In case you're wondering, Colin, I've only heard about this so far,' said Hart. He shifted his chair round to face the screens. 'La Mont and Joe Felix have been playing with it on their own.'

La Mont signalled and Felix pressed a switch. Immediately, the right-hand screen burst into life, shimmering images rushing and chasing as the tape whined on a vastly accelerated fast search forward. There was no sound except the whine of the reels.

'Coming up,' warned Felix.

He pressed another switch button. The images on the screen shuddered, the reels switched to normal playing speed. The picture steadied: a night scene. A car, headlights blazing, was travelling along a narrow, tree-lined road black with shadows and menace.

'Watch the top right corner,' said La Mont softly. 'Two white dots, one after the other.'

A moment later a small white dot appeared like a minor blemish in the top right corner, then vanished. The bulky Canadian began counting under his breath, and the scene changed. A girl stared directly at the camera. Her face registered fear, she took a few reluctant steps forward, then

42

her mouth opened in a silent scream of terror. Suddenly, her face filled the screen – and another white dot appeared top right, exactly as before.

'That's it,' said La Mont happily.

Joe Felix stopped the tape with the girl's image frozen on the screen and the white dot still showing.

'Interesting,' said Hart warily.

'Want to see it again, sir?' asked Felix. 'I've copied the section.'

Hart nodded. The other monitor screen came to life and they were given a slow-motion repeat of the final twenty seconds, including the white dot.

'We call them cue dots,' explained La Mont. He got to his feet and ambled over to the monitor screens. 'Every movie has them. The film laboratories add them to the final master print – they're a signal system, for when a scene change is coming up or a reel is due to run out.' Running a thumb along his bearded chin, he grinned. 'The people who put up the money for *The Hanging Tree* knew pirates would try for it. They spent a lot on security to prevent that. But just in case it did happen, they came up with something new: one extra cue dot, one that shouldn't be there, and at a different location on each print made.'

Hart frowned. 'So your people across the Atlantic can establish which print was copied?'

La Mont nodded. 'That's it, Commander. There aren't too many prints; anyone who handled them is known. They'll find a projectionist or someone along that line who was well paid to smuggle those film cans out for an overnight loan.'

'Does that help us?' demanded Thane bluntly.

'Probably not,' admitted La Mont. He hesitated, eyed Thane warily, then shrugged. 'Look, the people behind this kind of deal don't leave calling cards. I'm talking about organized crime, Mafia connections, a whole lot more.' He looked at Thane earnestly. 'I mean that. Still, at least we'll make sure someone goes to jail, and we've plugged another leak at source.'

'But not over here,' mused Thane.

'True.' La Mont grimaced. 'This end of the operation would be the standard pattern. A courier flies into London with a video copy in his – or maybe her – suitcase. It's delivered. The pirate mob starts work with its own copying set-up, its own distribution system. Hell, some of them even fix their own damned release dates for the whole of Britain.' He shrugged. 'We reckon there are maybe half a dozen major operators involved, but we can't get close to any of them.'

Jack Hart said nothing for a moment. Then he stacked some of the cassettes in front of him into a neat pile and pushed them across his desk.

'You wanted to borrow these. What about equipment?'

'Well – ' La Mont glanced towards Felix.

'I can fix it, sir,' said Felix confidently.

'I'll need a little time.' La Mont came over, and picked up the cassettes. 'You'll let me know if anything happens?'

'Yes,' promised Hart.

Joe Felix escorted the Canadian out and Hart settled back with a grunt of relief.

'That gives him something to do,' he said wearily. 'Now, what about you?'

'We may get more from Janice Darrow.' Thane paused and shook his head. 'But I don't expect much.'

'So far, it's about all we've got,' reminded Hart wryly. He glanced at his wrist-watch. 'I'll draft some of the night-shift troops on to background checks. This part-time job, names, anything else that turns up. The rest – ' he looked directly at Thane and gave a chuckle ' – Maggie phoned through. She said I wasn't to keep you long and why. On your way – there's nothing that can't wait till morning.'

'Thanks.' Thane grinned and got to his feet.

'One thing.' Hart stopped him as he reached the door. 'How did it go at Tulliallan?'

'I'm trying to forget,' said Thane wryly.

Hart laughed and waved him out.

Maggie Fyffe was still at the reception desk in the

entrance lobby. Thane had a sudden thought as he saw her, and went over.

'Maggie, about the Tulliallan seminar,' he said mildly. 'Did anyone tell you Debbie Kinster was going to be there?'

'Yes.' She eyed him with bland innocence. 'Commander Hart knew. She telephoned him and they talked for a spell. Why?'

'Nothing.' Thane swore under his breath, cursed female TV interviewers and sadistic commanders, then went out to his car.

It had stopped raining and the roads were drying on the twenty-minute journey home. There wasn't a puddle in sight as he ran the Ford into the narrow driveway outside his house.

Home was a small bungalow in a suburban street in which every house was almost identical to its neighbours down to the size of mortgage. He'd managed a fresh coat of paint on the woodwork during a week's leave in the summer, but everyone else seemed to have a neater garden. He saw some new weeds as he got out of the car and stopped to give the nearest a rueful kick.

A woman passing outside caught his eye and looked away, quickening her step. She lived at the other end of the street and her house had been burgled the previous week. She'd made it plain he should have personally prevented it.

Thane chuckled, collected the gift-wrapped package, locked the car, then saw the house door was already open. Mary kissed him more deliberately than usual before she let him in.

'Happy anniversary.' He gave her the package, then remembered. 'I like your hair.'

He wasn't too sure what was different about it, but she was wearing a blue dress he liked, and the silver Lucken-booth brooch he'd given her at Christmas. Mary Thane was a slim, attractive, dark-haired woman. She still had the kind of figure which made a nonsense of her having two teenage children – and as far as Thane was concerned, she hadn't changed in any other way either.

'Do I open this now?' She felt the package carefully.

'Not here.' He closed the door and followed her through to the living room. Clyde, their boxer dog, ambled over to give a stumpy tail-wag, then returned to the fireside rug. Watching Mary start to unwrap the package, Thane cleared his throat quickly. 'You can – uh – change it, they said.'

'I – '. she stopped, gave a gasp of pleasure, then turned, delighted, holding the froth of pink négligé against her shoulders. 'Change this? No way – I love it.'

'Good.' Thane grinned at her, partly with relief. 'Still, they had this sexy black lace number – '

'I said I love it. Come to that, I love you.' Mary put down the négligé, came over, hugged him, stood back with a mock frown. 'Unless – do you think I need black lace?'

'No.' He shook his head firmly.

'Just say that like you mean it,' she warned happily, then gestured towards the sideboard. 'These came too.'

He went over to the half-dozen red roses proudly displayed in a vase. The card said 'From Tommy and Kate'. Kate had written the card, and the flowers must have taken a chunk of their combined pocket-money. He smiled, then realized both young Thanes should be home from school.

'Where are they anyway?' he asked.

'Out.' Mary looked at him innocently. 'I said they could stay with friends overnight.'

'Did you?' Thane nodded solemnly. 'They'll like that.'

'They didn't object.' She saw his widening grin and shook her head firmly. 'I'm hungry. You said we were eating out.'

They ate at an Italian restaurant where the food and wine were good, the service superb, and the bill something customers weren't supposed to think about. Thane had booked a corner table, and there was a small dance floor and music.

But it was still before midnight when they left and went home.

It was early next morning when the bedside telephone began ringing. Thane wakened, fumbled for the receiver, and at the same time managed to focus on the luminous dial of the clock beside it. The hands showed 5.30 a.m. and he could hear Mary muttering a sleepy protest as he got the receiver to his ear.

'Thane,' he said abruptly.

'Millside CID, sir,' said a wary voice over the line. 'Sorry to trouble you.'

'That helps.' Thane fought back a yawn. 'But not a lot. Who is this?'

'Detective Constable Harris, sir. I'm – uh – new since your time out here.' The man at the other end was used to before-dawn sarcasm. 'We thought you'd want to know there's been a break-in at Douglas's place in Baron Avenue.'

'When?' Thane came up on his elbows.

'We're not sure. But it was really turned over – and they did the lock-up at the back.' Harris paused. 'We don't know if anything's missing.'

'I'll come over,' said Thane resignedly.

He hung up, swore under his breath, and switched on the bedside light. Mary had burrowed deeper under the blankets and when he said her name she barely mumbled, almost asleep again.

Getting up, Thane dressed quietly. Then he went downstairs to the kitchen, where the dog watched suspiciously from its basket while he made himself a cup of coffee. He scribbled a note for Mary and propped it against the coffee tin. Then, collecting his old sheepskin jacket from its peg in the hall, he went out to the car.

It was a cold morning, still dark, and nothing moved under the street lights. Thane used the sleeve of his jacket to scrape some of the white frost from the car's windscreen before he got aboard. Once behind the wheel, he started the engine and let it idle for a few moments while he lit a cigarette. Then he switched on the headlights and set the car moving.

He grimaced as he passed the house which had been burgled. He was driving quietly. But the woman in there would still probably complain she'd been wakened.

It was a twenty-minute drive across a city just beginning to show the first signs of stirring. There was the occasional light at a window, a few night-shift workers were heading for home, and the beginnings of the new day's traffic amounted to a few newspaper trucks making deliveries.

He reached Baron Avenue shortly after 6 a.m. There were two police cars outside Douglas's block and he parked beside them. As he got out, a man left one of the cars and came towards him.

'Hello, sir,' said a mildly amused voice. 'Sorry to drag you out like this.'

'Are you hell,' said Thane dryly. Detective Constable Beech had been a young, likeable thorn in his flesh at Millside Division. From the grin on his face, not much had changed. 'Who else is here?'

'Chief Inspector Andrews is upstairs.' Beech gave a slight grimace. 'He got here a few minutes ago – and I don't think he's too happy.'

'His privilege,' said Thane stonily. Andrews had taken over the divisional job and right from the start had made it plain he was a new broom who didn't want to know about the old. 'Anyone round the back, at the lock-ups?'

Beech nodded.

'I'll go and see your boss.' Thane lingered for a moment. 'How are those twins of yours?'

'Teething,' said Beech sadly. 'I'm glad I'm on night shift.'

Thane grinned, left him, and went into the building. When he reached Douglas's apartment, the door lay open. Broken wood on the frame beside the lock showed how it had been forced.

The lights were on inside and a uniformed constable standing in the little hallway saluted and indicated the living room. Thane went past him, then stopped and shaped a silent whistle.

The living room was a shambles. Drawers had been emptied, cushions pulled from chairs, a cupboard's contents scattered.

'And the rest is the same,' said Chief Inspector Andrews, who was standing near the window. A tall, thin man, he still looked half asleep and the collar of his pyjama jacket showed above the heavy sweater he was wearing. He came over, scowling. 'Did you expect this, Superintendent?'

'No,' said Thane wearily, 'I didn't.'

'And this division wasn't asked to provide any special watch on the apartment,' persisted Andrews.

'That's true.' Thane eyed him stonily.

'But it isn't going to look good, sir.' Andrews didn't have sense enough to leave it alone. The scowl on his thin face deepened as he gestured at the chaos. 'A murdered man's home raided – I don't like it.'

'I'm not exactly happy about it,' Thane told him bluntly.

Andrews sniffed. 'But this happens to be my division, sir. Your people are here today, gone tomorrow – that's the difference.'

The constable in the hallway was carefully looking in another direction but clearly listening. Thane went over, closed the door, then faced the Millside CID chief again.

'Do me a favour, Andrews,' he said softly, his voice cold and level. 'Stop making noises like you've got your knickers in a twist. It doesn't help.'

Andrews stiffened and flushed. 'With respect, sir – '

'Never mind the respect. We'll both live without it,' Thane cut him short, curtly. 'Just tell me what happened – or what we know.'

'The local night-beat constable found the door forced,' said Andrews sulkily. 'His shift sergeant had told him to keep a routine eye on the place because of the publicity.'

'One intelligent shift sergeant,' said Thane wryly. 'And?'

Andrews shrugged. 'He visited hourly until 3 a.m., then came back just before 5 a.m. That's when he found the door forced. He looked inside, radioed for help, and a CID duty car responded. They found the lock-up was lying open.'

'Neighbours?'

'Heard nothing, can't help – and I think that's genuine.' Andrews pursed his lips. 'I've asked for Scenes of Crime to attend. They're busy – we're in the queue behind a couple of stabbings and a warehouse robbery.'

The Scenes of Crime team, with their cameras and fingerprint brushes, their lenses and tweezers, their supplies of plastic evidence bags, were always in demand. Saying nothing, Thane looked around the room again.

Break-ins could happen when someone died, thieves had no particular scruples. Once, years back, he'd had to cope with a young couple who had come back from their sick child's hospital bedside to find their home ransacked. But this one was different – any ordinary thief, balked of anything better, would at least have carried off the television set and video recorder. Both had been left, and nothing else he could remember seemed to have been taken.

'I'll show you the rest of it,' said Andrews woodenly.

They went out, past the constable, and Thane glanced briefly at the other rooms. They had all been given the same treatment. It had been done carefully, nothing had been missed – even the freezer in the kitchen had been emptied. Moving a thawing bag of vegetables with his foot, Thane glanced at Andrews again. The man was still edgy, on his dignity. But there were tired lines round his eyes, worry behind his attitude. Divisional chief inspectors usually had enough without outsiders trampling over their patch.

He sighed. 'Andrews – '

'Sir?' The man was formally polite.

Thane shrugged. 'Sometimes I'm not at my best before dawn.'

Andrews blinked. His expression didn't change.

Thane gave up. 'I'll take a look outside. Don't bother coming down – but Commander Hart will want a copy of the incident report.'

He went out past the constable, who eyed him blandly but with interest. Senior officers having a snarling match always made good gossip at the end of a shift.

It was still cold in the open air. Frost glistened on the parked cars and Detective Constable Beech stood waiting with his hands stuffed deep into his pockets, the collar of his coat turned up. He went with Thane towards the line of lock-ups at the rear, a first hint of dawn beginning to grey the sky towards the east.

'Easy, sir,' warned Beech suddenly. He steered Thane to one side then shone a torch at the ground. 'We almost missed these at first.'

There were clear footprints on the white frost which covered the rough surface. Several footprints – but two sets of tracks had been avoided most of the way by the rest. They led towards the lock-ups then returned.

'They go down the road a spell,' volunteered Beech. 'They probably left their car down there.'

Thane nodded. The footprints were distinct enough, down to the tread-like markings on one set. He hoped they'd last until the Scenes of Crime people arrived, otherwise they'd vanish with the morning thaw.

They went on again. Another detective and a sergeant in uniform were waiting at Douglas's lock-up, stamping their feet against the cold. The lock-up door hung open, the lock forced, and Beech shone his torch into the shambles inside.

'Knew their job, these two,' muttered the sergeant, his breath misting like steam as he spoke. 'In and out, no noise, no fuss – pros, sir.'

'That narrows it down,' said Thane sardonically. 'To a few thousand.'

The sergeant grinned.

Thane had seen enough, a fresh concern now on his mind – for Janice Darrow. He indicated the personal radio slung at the sergeant's shoulder.

'Any trouble reported from Monkswalk direction, around the Watson Drive area?'

'Nothing, sir.' The man shook his head and looked puzzled.

Thane said goodbye and left them, going back to his car. Turning the heater up full, he sat for a moment while the fan churned lukewarm air. Then, knowing what he had to do next, he keyed the starter and set the Ford moving.

Monkswalk was on the other side of Millside Division, a mostly suburban fringe. It was a mix of older houses, large, with gardens to match, and smaller ones, more recent, apparently built for people who wanted to shake hands with their neighbours.

Watson Drive was off the main road, on the left. Thane turned in, then saw a shop with lighted windows ahead. He slowed his Ford and drove past at a crawl. A painted sign above the shop door said 'John Darrow' and he could see a man working behind the counter.

Newsagents opened early, but it still wasn't 7 a.m. He stopped the Ford a short distance past the shop, got out, and walked back. It was a small shop, standing on its own, with what looked like living quarters on the upper floor. Thane reached a narrow access lane which led to the rear of the little building, hesitated, then walked quietly along its unbroken white coating of frost.

The newsagent's back yard was a litter of empty boxes and packing cases, but a light shone above the rear door. It showed footprints on the frost, footprints which came from the other side of the building and stopped at the door, where the wood around the lock was splintered. Thane stopped at the footprints. One set had the same tread-like pattern he'd seen at Baron Avenue. He touched the door and it swung open a fraction.

Pushing the door open the rest of the way, Thane stepped into the back shop. A few paces more, and he was looking into the front shop. The man sorting newspapers at the counter had his back towards him, but Thane could see he was young, fair-haired, and had only one arm.

'Good morning,' said Thane quietly.

The other man dropped the newspapers with a gasp and spun round, grabbing for a heavy hammer lying beside him.

'Police,' soothed Thane. 'You're John Darrow?'

'Yes.' Darrow moistened his lips and didn't relax his grip on the hammer.

'I talked to your sister.' Thane showed his warrant card. 'That was at Ted Douglas's place.'

'She told me.' Darrow gave a sigh, let go the hammer, and forced a grin. 'You – you scared the hell out of me.'

'Sorry.' There was a stool behind the counter. Thane sat on it, unbuttoned his sheepskin jacket, and looked at Darrow for a moment.

'Had visitors?'

Darrow shrugged. His face was pale and he needed a shave. He wore an old army sweater over grey trousers, the empty left sleeve of the sweater sewn flat against its side.

'I haven't complained,' he said uneasily.

'No.' Thane waited.

'So what do you want?'

'I'm curious,' said Thane deliberately. 'Two men broke into Ted Douglas's apartment, turned it over. Then – well, I had an idea they might have come here. Looks like I was right.'

'I didn't call the police,' said Darrow stubbornly. 'Suppose I say nothing happened?'

Thane shook his head sadly and thumbed towards the telephone on the wall. The wires had been cut and hung loose.

'Not many people go around forcing their own doors, chopping their own telephone wires,' he said mildly. 'What's the matter, John? Scared?' He saw Darrow's expression and said softly. 'In my book, scared can mean sensible. You've been through a war – you probably know

53

more about that than I do.'

'Maybe.' Darrow nodded in grudging agreement, then hesitated. 'Look, I – I don't want trouble, any kind.'

'I can fix that,' said Thane. 'I want information, and it ends there. No local crime report, unless – where's Janice?'

'Upstairs, sleeping.' Darrow gave a relieved grimace. 'I gave her two sleeping pills last night. She's still out to the world.' He gestured towards the newspapers. 'Seen these?'

Thane came over. The Donaldhill shooting was page-one news for the dailies. Most had a picture of Ted Douglas, some also printed one of Janice Darrow.

'You told her they'd get to her,' said her brother bitterly. 'They did. I want her out of this.'

'I want you both out of this,' Thane told him. 'So tell me what happened.'

John Darrow chewed his lip for a moment then drew a deep breath.

'I don't sleep too well since – ' he glanced at his empty sleeve ' – since I got back. I heard them break in, at about 4.30 this morning. Then I just lay in bed and listened and hoped to God they'd leave us alone.' He gave Thane a bitter grin. 'They did. I heard them moving around for ten minutes, maybe more. Then – well, they left and I got up. If they'd come back – ' He glanced towards the hammer, but shook his head. 'I don't know.'

Thane nodded, able to imagine how it must have been for the one-armed ex-marine.

'But you know why they came?' he suggested unemotionally.

'I know all they took.' Darrow crossed to an empty display cabinet near the door. 'Every video tape I had, here and in the back shop.' He ran a finger along one of the bare shelves. 'I had about a hundred as a rental library.'

'Counting the "pirates" you got from Douglas?'

'I got rid of them, burned them last night,' said Darrow dryly. 'Maybe I should have put up a notice. But my worry was people like you arriving.' Going back behind the counter, he stooped, produced a coffee pot, and glanced at

Thane. 'I've a spare mug, if you take it as it comes.'

'Thanks.' Thane watched him bring out the mugs and pour coffee into both. Then, as Darrow slid one mug along the counter towards him, he asked, 'Did he give you *The Hanging Tree?*'

'Didn't know it existed.' Darrow looked surprised.

Thane shrugged. 'It does.'

'That figures.' Darrow sipped his coffee, then frowned. 'Maybe I wasn't too happy about him and Janice, but I didn't play big brother.' He shook his head. 'It was his idea I started the video library as a sideline, with rented stock. Then, once it was going, he appeared now and again with those tapes – for under the counter. I didn't ask where they came from.'

A fist hammered on the shop front door. A man peered in, grinning hopefully. Darrow shook his head, mouthed 'closed', and the would-be customer scowled then went away.

'What about the casual jobs he got?' probed Thane. 'Did he ever talk about them?'

'To me?' Darrow swirled the coffee in his mug. 'Just vague noises, the same as he did to Janice. But he arrived here once, driving a van; Janice was at the hospital, he wanted to let her know he was working late. The signs on the doors said Falcon Services, with a bird's head badge. The phone number was out of the city, and he had another fellow with him who just stayed aboard.'

'Can you remember anything else?' pressed Thane.

'Just one thing, because it seemed odd.' Darrow sucked his lips for a moment, frowning. 'He came one afternoon to take Janice out on that motor-cycle. She suggested they take a run Loch Lomond way, but Ted said, no thanks – that was a working trip.'

Thane raised an eyebrow. 'He didn't say why?'

Darrow shook his head. Then he had a question of his own.

'Suppose I closed the shop for a few days, took Janice away somewhere for a break?'

'Just let me know where,' Thane told him. 'And I'd say it was a good idea.'

Darrow let him out of the front door when he left. Two customers were arriving as Thane walked away. He stopped and looked back, able to see into the shop and watch Darrow serving at the counter.

Thane knew what he'd promised. Darrow and his sister deserved to stay clear of things now. But it wouldn't earn him any medals if a certain divisional CID boss ever caught a whisper of the deal he'd made.

He grinned, decided he didn't give a damn, and went on to his car.

An all-night café down in dockland served a breakfast special of greasy bacon and eggs with half-pint mugs of gritty coffee. It was as grimy and as busy as usual and it also sold newspapers. Thane bought three of them and read the front pages while he ate.

The law clamped down on just how much could be said when there were arrests in a case, but the reports did their best to get round that problem. Ted Douglas, dubbed 'the martyred motor-cyclist' by one newspaper, had given them an angle to the shooting and they'd played it for all it was worth.

Two papers had found alleged close friends from university days. All made some kind of sideways swipe at an economic situation which left an Honours graduate out of work. But, though they also featured brief interviews with Janice Darrow, none offered any real surprises – which was a relief.

He finished breakfast, lit a cigarette, and sat back. A small, wiry man at one of the other tables caught his eye and gave a slight grin. The last time Thane had seen him, a jury had found him not guilty on five counts of theft. But the jury wasn't to know he was probably the best pickpocket in the city.

Stolidly, Thane felt for his wallet, shrugged, then turned

to the sports pages. When he'd finished his cigarette he rose, leaving the newspapers on the dirty plastic table-cover.

They'd be folded and sold again. The all-night café owner managed a two-week holiday in Bermuda every winter.

It was 8 a.m. and daylight when he drove into the Scottish Crime Squad headquarters, parked his car, and went into the building.

The day shift was beginning to arrive. Thane went to his office first, hung his sheepskin jacket on the peg behind the door, took a brief glance at the overnight paperwork lying on his desk, then went through to the main Duty Room.

Francey Dunbar was already there, using a telephone at one of the desks. Thane signalled he'd wait. Around him, the men and women coming on duty yawned, gossiped, and got ready for another day. The maps on the walls covered all of Scotland, with pins marking operations under way. A large make-up mirror propped against a filing cabinet was being used by two girls who looked young enough to be at school – and meant it to be that way. A city lawyer with some unpleasant habits and a drugs connection was becoming interested in what he thought they were offering.

'Morning, sir.' Dunbar had finished his call and came over. He gave Thane a grin. 'The word is you had an early start.'

The word is right,' said Thane flatly. 'No sign of Sandra yet?'

Dunbar shook his head then eyed Thane hopefully. 'Anything worthwhile at Baron Avenue, sir?'

'Two of his friends came visiting. If you want more, don't ask Chief Inspector Maxwell. We worry him.' Thane paused as the two 'schoolgirls' went out in a waft of cheap perfume. One gave Dunbar a deliberate wink. 'Francey, I need a fast outline on a firm called Falcon Services. Where they are, who they are, what they are – Douglas worked for them.'

Dunbar blinked. 'Where did that come from?'

'John Darrow – we talked.' Thane left it at that.

'Falcon Services.' Dunbar knew he would hear the rest eventually. 'The only new thing I've got is from Scenes of Crime, the report of their first Baron Avenue visit – they haven't sorted out this morning's stuff yet.' He rammed his hands into the pockets of his faded denims and gave Thane a look of slightly bemused respect. 'You were right. Most of the fingerprints around belonged to Douglas or the girl – Sandra kept the cup she used. But they got another set from an empty beer can in the kitchen bucket.'

'Someone we know?' asked Thane with a stony lack of reaction.

'A Martin Herbert Tuce, three convictions for fraud, two for assault.' Dunbar shrugged. 'I don't know him, but I'll see what else the computer comes up with. Sandra's stuff and anything more we've got is on your desk.'

Thane left the Duty Room, and went back to his office. It was colder there and he kicked the radiator hopefully. As usual, it grunted and rumbled but didn't get warmer. His window looked out towards the parking lot, where the last of the overnight frost was still melting. The sky was clear; it might be a reasonable day.

Settling at his desk, he started with the overnight computer print-out sheets. They covered the city, a courtesy feed from Strathclyde headquarters, fifty or so of the highlights of a night's work, any of them likely to interest or matter to another cop somewhere in the system.

Thane ticked a few. A murder suspect wanted by Central Division had turned up, floating in the Clyde. No bets would be lost on that one. Northern Division were being plagued with complaints about a bogus priest with a missions collecting box. One of the vehicles in a ten-car pile-up on an icy stretch of the Glasgow-Edinburgh road had contained two safe-blowers and a load of antique silver. Special Branch wanted the divisions to ignore a man wandering around offering to sell guns. He was one of their people.

The print-out sheets and some routine surveillance reports went into one pile, for Maggie Fyffe. Most of the rest went into what she called his Tomorrow Tray.

That left the *Hanging Tree* collection, and it was thin: about a dozen of Ted Douglas's friends and a lone cousin had been traced and interviewed, mostly thanks to Janice Darrow.

The results didn't add up to much. Frowning, Thane slowly spread the typewritten sheets like a fan across his desk.

Ted Douglas's academic record had been good; he'd steered clear of student politics; he'd been popular in a low-profile way; his money problems during that time had been no worse than average. After graduation, he hadn't been alone in finding that a degree was no passport to employment in the middle of a recession. He'd seemed happy enough to get his travel-agency job.

But when that folded, Ted Douglas had gradually faded from the scene as far as his friends were concerned. Some hadn't seen him for months. None really knew exactly how he was earning money. Any who asked that directly were answered with a grin and a shrug.

No, it didn't help.

The intercom box on his desk gave a soft chime.

'Come through, Colin,' said Jack Hart. The squad commander sounded reasonably happy, though it was unusual for him to be in so early.

Thane abandoned the interview sheets and went along the corridor. Hart's office door lay open. Inside, Maggie Fyffe was sitting beside Hart with her notebook. The other man in the room was grey-haired, mild-looking, and walked with a limp as he turned and came over from the window. Detective Superintendent Maxwell was senior deputy commander, Hart's immediate deputy. He was almost a stranger – for more than two months he'd been working on a local-government corruption case in one of the northern counties.

'Just visiting,' said Maxwell cheerfully. He winked at

Thane. 'I thought I'd make sure the big city still existed. Maybe I shouldn't have bothered.'

Hart gave a sardonic grunt. He was signing his way through a sheaf of letters lying in front of him.

'Try staying quiet for a minute, both of you,' he said acidly. 'Let me finish this garbage.'

Tom Maxwell gave a mock wince, but obeyed.

Neither of them envied Hart his job, more administrator than working cop, too often having to defend their very existence against outside jealousies and political pressures.

Being unique was the Crime Squad's biggest danger: unique in the way it was financed direct by central Government, unique in the way it was free from local ties or regional boundaries, and in the way it hand-picked its men and women from every police force in the country. It used its own methods, something which didn't always win friends. It used its own selected equipment, from special low-band radio onward.

But the Scottish Crime Squad didn't possess even one lock-up cell for prisoners. They were packages to be dropped off at any convenient police station, the local force welcome to mop up the details and, if they wanted, the limelight – and the arrival of a prisoner could often be the first a bemused local constabulary knew of the fact that they had visitors. Even if their chief constable had been quietly warned.

Another grunt from Hart ended their waiting. He pushed everything across to Maggie Fyffe, looked up, and thumbed towards Maxwell.

'Tom has hit a problem,' he said. 'We're going through to Edinburgh to talk to a judge, and it'll take most of the day – Maggie knows how to contact me.' He paused and raised a deliberate eyebrow. 'Did you have to go ruffling feathers over in Millside Division? I've had a call about it from Strathclyde headquarters.'

Thane shrugged. 'Some people ruffle easily, sir.'

'Yes.' Hart laid his hands flat on the table and sighed.

'All right, I don't want to know what happened. As a diplomat, you'd be a walking disaster. How is the rest of it shaping?'

'Somebody is worried,' Thane told him. 'It wasn't just Douglas's apartment last night. They also checked on his girl.'

'I see.' Hart pursed his lips. 'Well, if you're looking for Joe Felix he won't be around for a spell. I told him to make sure our tame video expert got settled to work. Check with the Strathclyde forensic people some time today – they're handling the scientific evidence from the Donaldhill shooting, but they know our interest.' He opened a desk drawer, brought out a bulky envelope, and handed it over. 'Donaldhill have sent this – the personal effects Douglas was carrying. Don't ask me what's in it, I haven't had time to look.'

'Sir.' Maggie Fyffe made a warning noise and glanced deliberately at her watch.

'I know,' agreed Hart. 'All right, Maggie, I'm just about finished.' He turned to Thane again. 'Need any extra help?'

'Not yet,' said Thane cautiously.

Tom Maxwell chuckled. 'He's learning. Keep the options open, Colin. When things are bad, they'll probably get worse.'

'Philosophy from the north I can do without,' grunted Hart, but he gave a slight grin. 'I can tell you this. *The Hanging Tree* is worth watching. I – ah – took one of the tapes home last night, played it through.' He eyed them defensively. 'Line of duty, right?'

'Research,' agreed Thane stonily, and heard Maggie Fyffe chuckle.

He left them and went back through to his own room. Francey Dunbar and Sandra Craig were waiting outside and he beckoned them in, then waved them into chairs. Sandra was wearing a black velvet jacket and a skirt, which didn't happen too often when she was working. She also looked as though she hadn't had much sleep, but he decided not to ask why.

'Well?' He looked at Dunbar.

'Falcon Services.' Dunbar lounged back in his chair and sucked one end of his straggling black moustache for a moment. 'There are one or two firms trading with fairly similar names, all legitimate, but I think I've got the one you want. The name is Falcon Refrigeration Services. It's an agency outfit – small, but making money. Refrigeration equipment supplies, and they're out of town like you thought, sir. They're based on East Kilbride.'

Thane frowned. 'Not Loch Lomond?'

'No.' Dunbar looked puzzled. East Kilbride was south, Loch Lomond to the north.

'Who runs them?'

'The boss is an Alex Garrison, and that's about all I've got,' admitted Dunbar. 'Except that Falcon Services have a good trade reputation and operate their own vehicles. Uh – you wanted more on this character Tuce?'

'Who leaves fingerprints on beer cans.' Thane nodded.

'He's trouble,' declared Dunbar. He gave a sideways glance at Sandra, who seemed almost asleep, and grinned maliciously. 'You know, like sailors with a girl in every port – '

'Go to hell,' she said. 'He's a lieutenant commander.'

'Two in every port.' Dunbar saw Thane's patience fraying. 'Tuce is home-grown, about Douglas's age, was in the London drug scene for a spell, then got thrown out and came back to Glasgow. The frauds were the kind where old ladies got beaten up if they asked the wrong questions.'

'He sounds nice,' murmured Sandra.

'We've a possible address and a nickname – the Glass-man,' finished Dunbar. 'He likes broken bottles. Used them in both assault convictions.'

Thane nodded. 'Sandra?'

'Not much, sir.' She shook her head. 'Paul Nord, the name on the phoney passport, doesn't connect anywhere. Other contacts – ' she indicated his desk ' – you've seen the reports. Maybe if we picked up Tuce – '

'Yes.' Thane fingered the envelope he'd brought through

from Hart's office. There was another area they hadn't touched on so far. 'What about Donaldhill?' He saw it didn't register with either of them. 'Ted Douglas was there early in the morning, and that's a long way from Baron Avenue. The direction he was travelling, he could have been heading home.' Neither of the two faces opposite showed any particular understanding, and he sighed. 'He had those damned tapes. Think – maybe where he'd been was where he got them, creaming them off a brand new delivery big enough for a few not to be missed.'

'That might explain a few things.' Dunbar played with the notion, rubbing one hand against the other in a way that set the silver ID bracelet jingling. He glanced at Sandra, then added softly, soberly, 'It could have been an overnight job, and he was on his way home.'

Sandra nodded, her eyes on Thane. 'You said Loch Lomond, sir. One way back from there is through Donaldhill.'

'If we push possibility.' Thane felt it unlikely, but knew he had to keep their options wide open. Deliberately, he opened the envelope and emptied its contents on his desk. 'Let's see if we've anything else.'

It wasn't much of a collection, each item already tagged as recorded. Ted Douglas had been carrying a few pounds in cash, a small, sharp-bladed folding knife, an old St Christopher medal on a broken chain, and a small, well-worn brown leather wallet. Thane checked its contents. There were two credit cards and a bank cash card, a thin book of postage stamps, a receipted bill for a motorcycle repair and, last, puzzling, tucked in behind a torn edge of lining, a small, folded piece of stiff paper.

Thane spread it out. It was a list of numbers, running between one and forty, in no particular order and in two vertical columns.

'Some kind of code?' suggested Sandra when he pushed the slip of paper in her direction.

'Brilliant,' said Dunbar sarcastically. He took the paper, bent his dark head over it, then made his own wary suggestion. 'Something he needed, anyway, otherwise why keep it? Maybe to do with tapes he delivered – '

'We've got it, it'll keep.' Thane put the slip back with the rest of the collection. 'Francey, I want you to pick up Tuce – which means finding him first. Don't tell him why, sweat him a little, see what you can get. Sandra stays with me. We'll go out and visit Falcon Refrigeration Services.' He paused and considered them. 'Unless either of you has a better idea.'

'Sir, I – ' Sandra stopped and sighed as the telephone began ringing.

Thane answered it. The caller was John La Mont and the Canadian video expert sounded pleased with himself.

'I thought you people would want to know,' he said briskly, 'that we've got those *Hanging Tree* pirate copies traced back to the States, like I said would happen. It was a home base job – a damn projectionist at the studio theatre who didn't know about the security cue dot.' He made an apologetic noise. 'Doesn't help you too much, I suppose.'

'No.' Thane had to be honest. 'Not unless you can take it on from there.'

'We can try.' La Mont didn't sound so hopeful. 'What I'm doing now is working on those other pirate titles. Can I hang on to Felix for a spell? He's pretty useful.'

'Do that.' Thane grinned. Joe Felix would be in his element.

'Thanks.' La Mont paused and a sound like a sigh came over the line. 'Superintendent, I suppose I'd better level with you – about that projectionist.'

'Go on.' Thane sensed the uneasiness behind the Canadian's voice. 'Something happened?'

'He's dead,' said La Mont. 'Killed maybe a couple of days after the reels were probably copied.'

'How?'

'He jumped off a roof, or that's how it looked. He had alimony worries. Now – maybe it's different.'

'Like did he fall or was he pushed?' said Thane flatly.

'That's it.' La Mont spoke soberly. 'I told you, Superintendent. These people are in a million-dollar racket. They've their own brand of severance pay. I'll get back to you.'

Thane hung up.

'Bad?' asked Francey Dunbar.

Thane nodded.

The old-time pirates of the Spanish Main had been ruthless. It seemed the video pirates were keeping up some of their traditions.

'Sir.' Sandra Craig cleared her throat determinedly. 'It's just that I haven't had breakfast – '

'Hard luck,' said Thane sympathetically. 'You're going to stay hungry.'

3

East Kilbride had been a sleepy, old-fashioned country village a healthy ten or so miles beyond Glasgow. Had been – until the fifties, when a fortune in government grants came pouring in to develop it as a brand-new town.

Now it had a population of around eighty thousand, more children under the age of five than most places, and a mix of modern industries varied enough to allow it to weather the worst of the recession. One place that certainly hadn't closed was the Centre One tower block, the Inland Revenue tax computer headquarters for the entire country.

Colin Thane checked the directions he'd been given. He was in the passenger seat of Sandra Craig's black Volkswagen and she was driving. The transport pool had wanted his Ford for a couple of hours, for routine maintenance.

'Take the next on the right.' He settled back as she turned the wheel. They were on the outskirts of the town, cattle in green fields on one side, factory buildings running parallel with the road on the other. The sky was clear of cloud, the sunlight bright enough to bring a sparkle to the factory windows. 'Next on the left, and we're there.'

Sandra Craig tried to stifle a yawn and nodded. She'd yawned several times on the way out.

'How much sleep did you get last night?' asked Thane.

'Not a lot.' A rueful smile touched her lips. 'It was – well, you could call it a farewell celebration.'

'I don't want to call it anything,' Thane told her. When she wanted, Sandra was one of the best pursuit drivers in the squad. But this morning she seemed glad to have the steering wheel for support. 'Just stay awake.'

'I'm fine, sir.' She frowned indignantly, then spoiled it with another stifled yawn. 'Fine, but starving. I told you.'

Thane gave up. A few hundred yards on, they took the left turn. The Falcon Refrigeration Services building lay ahead, a long, single-storey structure topped by a falcon's head sign. Beside it, a high, wire-mesh fence enclosed a vehicle compound. Half a dozen light vans and trucks were parked close to a loading bay, where men were working.

The main gate lay open. They drove in, parked close to the office entrance, and got out.

'Look around, Sandra,' ordered Thane quietly. 'Chat up drivers, anyone friendly you find. We're out on dull, routine stuff about Ted Douglas's death – you know what to do.' He looked at her and grinned. 'I wouldn't call you bright-eyed and bushy-tailed, but pretend, dammit!'

He left her and went into the office. The young girl at the reception counter nodded quickly when he showed his warrant card and asked for Alex Garrison. She used a telephone then smiled nervously and led him along a short corridor. The door at the end was of panelled wood and marked 'Private'.

'You've to go straight in,' she said quickly, then fled.

Thane tapped on the wood, opened the door, and went in. Then he stopped, puzzled.

The room was modest in size, simply furnished, dominated by a large desk. The woman who sat behind it was in her late thirties, perhaps nudging forty, fair-haired and blue-eyed. She looked directly at him, and smiled in a way that was no ordinary welcome. Yes, he knew her. He knew her – but who was she?'

'Hello, Colin.' She got up and came round from the desk. She was tall, and she wore a tailored navy blue skirt and jacket with a white shirt-blouse. Stopping, the smile broadening and becoming amused, she spent a long moment just looking at him. Then she chuckled. 'You haven't changed much, have you?'

Her voice brought other memories together in a rush.

'Alexis?' Thane stared.

'Try something better. Like "Alexis dear, it's good to see you after all these years".' A hand touched his arm, briefly, and her blue eyes twinkled. 'Relax. I'm joking. You didn't know?'

'I came to see someone called Alex Garrison.' Thane grinned self-consciously and shook his head. 'That's you?'

She nodded. 'Most people call me Alex now.'

But years before, when he'd been a young, very green detective constable, she'd been Alexis Bolton who worked in a law office. For a spell, things had been at the stage where – but no, it hadn't happened. Gradually, without anything being said, without Thane ever being certain why, it had ended.

A few months later, he'd met Mary and been glad.

'I heard you'd married,' he said vaguely.

'And I heard the same about you.' She waved him into a chair then sat opposite him, her back to a row of filing cabinets which were topped by a display of potted plants. 'Did it work out?'

'Yes.'

'Children?'

He nodded. 'Two – a boy and a girl. You?'

'I'm a widow, no children.' She said it in a totally matter-of-fact way. 'George died about three years ago – he was my second husband. The first – ' she shaped a slight grimace ' – he took off with someone else he fancied after about a year. I think he's in the Middle East somewhere.'

'I'm sorry.' Thane mentally cursed the way Francey Dunbar had landed him unprepared.

'Don't be, Colin. It's not a total tale of woe. George and I had some good times.' She paused and her eyes twinkled again. 'You know, when I heard your name it took a moment to register.'

He nodded, making his own assessment. The good-looking girl had become a confident, totally mature and very alert woman.

'You run Falcon Services?' he asked.

'Run it and own it, lock stock and most of the barrel,' she

agreed cheerfully. 'It was George's business and I used to help him. Afterwards, I just moved in. It wasn't too difficult.' She paused again and frowned slightly. 'I suppose you'd better tell me why you came. Ted Douglas?'

'We heard he worked here,' said Thane carefully.

'He did, sometimes.' She got up, moved deliberately towards the potted plants, and stopped there with her back towards him. She touched the leaves of one for a moment. 'I heard what happened. It sounded pretty horrible. But – well, what about him?'

'Background,' said Thane simply. 'We need to know more about him.'

'I see.' Alexis Garrison moved again, went to her desk, and sat behind it. She sighed. 'And you're a detective superintendent?'

He nodded.

'I seem to remember that they were the boss breed,' she said deliberately. 'I knew a young cop once. This is the kind of job he'd have been given – unless there was a good reason.'

'There might be, somewhere,' he admitted.

'Not here,' she said firmly.

'I didn't say it had to be,' reminded Thane.

'We're a rather dull, rather ordinary little Scottish company that works hard to make a profit.' She took a cigarette from a box on her desk and used a lighter before Thane could reach for his own. Taking a first draw on the cigarette, she frowned at him. 'You know what we do?'

'Tell me,' he invited.

'We handle spares for freezer and refrigeration units – we're a central agency.' The cigarette gestured for emphasis. 'We're specialists in the industrial and catering market. Someone needs a new compressor unit or something like it in a hurry, we deliver – direct and straight away, whatever the distance.'

'So you need drivers.' Thane settled a little deeper in his chair, intent on establishing the basics. 'How many?'

'Ten on our regular payroll. Any others are like – well,

the way it was with Ted Douglas. Casuals we know and use as they're needed.'

'And the rest of it?'

'A few storemen, a foreman, and the office staff.' She gave an unconcerned shrug. 'We're not major league, Colin, but we don't do too badly. We deal with firms who want fast action – they get it, and they pay for it. We're also starting to develop into contract maintenance work.'

He brought her back to what mattered. 'When did Douglas start working for you?'

'About eight months or so ago. I – '

She stopped it there as the door flew open. The man who came in was a thin, anxious figure who didn't notice Thane at first.

'Alex, the police are here,' he said in a puzzled voice. 'They're – '

'I know.' Alexis Garrison soothed him with a smile and indicated Thane. 'We've a visitor, Detective Superintendent Thane – someone I used to know years ago. Colin, this is my brother-in-law, Jonathan Garrison.'

Garrison, in his thirties, was balding and had heavy spectacles. He wore a shabby tweed sports jacket, patched at the elbows. Blinking through the spectacles, he cleared his throat awkwardly as he shook hands with Thane.

'There's a woman outside – ' he began.

'Detective Constable Craig,' nodded Thane. 'She's with me.'

'It's about Ted Douglas,' explained Alexis Garrison patiently. She turned to Thane. 'Jonathan is the best person to ask, Colin. He runs the despatch side of things here.'

'Good.' Thane decided that Jonathan Garrison had never been called 'Jon' in his life. But his dead brother must have been very different, to have become Alexis's husband. 'It's simple enough, Mr Garrison. Just a few questions about him.'

'If it helps.' The man blinked at him again. 'I was shocked at what happened, Superintendent – genuinely shocked.' He sniffed. 'But then, there's so much crime in our streets, so much lawlessness – '

'Ted Douglas,' reminded Alexis Garrison, cutting him short. 'How long had we used him, Jonathan? About eight months, wasn't it?'

'Yes.' Garrison hesitated and looked worried again. 'But as a casual driver, Superintendent. He was always reliable, a good worker – the only odd thing was that I did suggest he could work for us full-time, that I'd recommend it to Alex, but he wasn't interested.'

Thane raised an eyebrow. 'Did he say why?'

'Well – ' Garrison looked down at his feet, embarrassed. 'Casual work pays quite well. If he was illegally drawing unemployment benefit on top of that, not declaring he was earning – that wasn't my business.'

'And it's not mine,' murmured Thane. 'How did he start with you?'

'He just appeared one day, looking for work,' said Garrison vaguely. 'I think he spoke to Alex first.'

She nodded, and stubbed her cigarette in an ashtray. 'He'd heard we sometimes used casual drivers. He had a clean licence, he seemed all right, and we needed an extra man. So I passed him on to Jonathan.'

Thane had a feeling he wasn't getting anywhere, but he had to keep trying.

'Did he have any regular route?'

Garrison looked surprised. 'No. I used him as required, anywhere.'

'Any overnight runs?'

'Once or twice, I think.' Garrison frowned uncertainly behind his spectacles. 'We sometimes do that, if something is long-distance and really urgent. But it's at least a fortnight since we used him for work – we haven't needed extra drivers lately.'

Thane pursed his lips. It was one piece of news he hadn't expected.

'Do you know any other firm he worked for?' he asked deliberately.

71

'No. I don't think he did.' Garrison glanced at his wrist-watch then moistened his lips. 'Is there much more? I've a spares order waiting to go, still to be checked.'

'I'm finished.' Thane got to his feet. 'Thanks for your help.'

Jonathan Garrison started for the door, then turned to face him again.

'Superintendent, I don't totally understand what this is about,' he declared with surprising emotion. 'But did you know that Douglas had an Honours degree? Can you imagine what that means in terms of study, achievement? He shook his head bitterly. 'But what good did it do him? He had a piece of paper – and we let him drive a van sometimes.'

'You felt sorry for him,' said Thane quietly.

'No.' Garrison paused, embarrassed but strangely determined. 'I – I felt damned angry.'

He left quickly, closing the door behind him.

'I don't believe it,' said Alexis softly. 'Our Jonathan doesn't sound off like that very often.' She spread her hands on the desk and Thane noticed that she still wore her wedding ring. 'Colin, are you going to tell me what is really going on?'

He shrugged and lied. 'Ted Douglas had some unusual friends. He could have been active on the drugs scene – we're checking it out.'

'Whatever he did, nothing happened here.' The fair-haired woman opened a desk drawer, took out an envelope, and wrote quickly. 'I want you to have my home address and phone number. Will you call me?'

'When I get the chance,' agreed Thane carefully.

'Good.' She rose, came over, and gave him the envelope. 'We could have a drink, maybe talk about old times.' A smile touched her lips and she eyed him deliberately. 'I think I'd like that.'

Thane put the envelope in an inside pocket and left. Outside the building, he looked around the loading compound and saw Sandra standing beside one of the trucks, talking to a driver. He called and she said a quick goodbye to the man and came straight over.

'Finished?' asked Thane.

'I'm not sure I got started,' she admitted. 'It seems that regulars don't speak much to casuals – it's a sort of class system. They knew Douglas, but not much more.'

'Nothing else?'

'Nothing.' She was clutching a small brown paper sack in one hand.

'What's in the bag?'

'Doughnuts, sir.' A purr of happiness entered her voice. 'They've a staff canteen – I bought half a dozen, to keep me going.' She glanced at Thane, then the car. 'I'll – uh – uh – keep the crumbs to my side.'

One hand on the steering wheel, she was on her second doughnut by the time they cleared East Kilbride and were on the main route back to the city. She saw Thane watching and nodded towards the bag.

'Like one?'

I wouldn't deprive you,' said Thane sarcastically.

'That's all right.' She finished the doughnut, wiped her hand on her skirt, then gave him another sideways glance. 'They told me Alex Garrison is a woman.'

'And a widow,' agreed Thane dryly. 'What else?'

'Just gossip, sir.' Dropping a gear, she accelerated hard, sending the Volkswagen snarling past a loitering pair of tanker trucks. 'The widow lady not only has brains – there's a steady boyfriend, though she keeps him under wraps.'

'You wouldn't have a name?' asked Thane mildly.

Sandra shook her head. 'Just the suggestion he'd have to be someone with money and that the widow lady drives north most weekends, showing up again on Monday morning.'

Thane didn't respond. But she had said north – Loch Lomond was north, but so were a lot of other places so it didn't necessarily mean anything, and how Alexis Garrison spent her private life wasn't his concern. Even if it

73

might have been once.

He drew the envelope from his pocket, and looked at her small, neat handwriting. The address was local and he knew the area, a development of small executive town houses.

'Sir?' Sandra Craig kept her eyes on the road, but seemed puzzled by his silence. Already she was brighter than she'd been all morning. 'These doughnuts – I mean, I've really plenty if you'd like one.'

He shook his head, took out his cigarettes, and had another of the day's precious quota.

Strathclyde Police headquarters is located in the heart of Glasgow, not much more than a stone's throw away from the shopping bustle of Sauchiehall Street. Home base for the largest police authority in Britain outside London, one large modern building occupies an entire block of streets. The only thing it lacks is adequate parking space.

They got there at about 11 a.m. Detective Constable Craig deliberately stopped her Volkswagen in the no waiting zone and grinned defiance at a patrolling traffic warden. The warden looked at the unmarked car, at its driver and her passenger. He didn't know who they were, but decided there might be other pickings round the next corner.

'Who squares your tickets?' asked Thane grimly.

'I never seem to get any,' she told him innocently. 'Want me to wait?'

He shook his head. There had been an occasional message on their car radio, but nothing from Francey Dunbar, nothing for their call-sign.

'Go back out and see the Darrow girl. Try her on Falcon Services again – anything more she remembers, anything we've missed.' He had another faint hope. 'Then try to get more about Douglas when he was a student – there may be something back there.'

He left the car, watched her drive away, then went in

74

through the main glass doors of the headquarters building. The scientific laboratory was on the top floor and when he got there he found Matthew Amos, the assistant director, at one of the benches in the main work area.

'Hold on, Colin.' Amos, a slim, bearded civilian who always sported a dazzling line in bow ties, greeted him with a nod. 'Almost finished this.'

He waited while Amos tapped at the keyboard of an electronic analysis unit. The unit, small in size but linked by cable to a much larger sister, reacted with a barely audible hum. An irregular graph of peaks and troughs appeared on its small display screen and Amos grunted disapprovingly.

'Wrong again,' he declared. 'Back to the drawing board.'

'For what?'

'For why,' corrected Amos. He flicked a switch and the display faded. 'That's an XRF Elemental, my fuzz friend. It scores over people – can't lie, doesn't claim overtime. I fed it a couple of paint examples and they don't match. Identical colours, yes, but different chemical compositions.'

'So?'

'It's a hit-and-run road case – paint samples from a dead girl's clothing and a vehicle.' Amos shrugged. 'Wrong vehicle. That'll make somebody's day.'

'It happens.' Thane knew the verdict wouldn't be challenged. Matt Amos was regarded as a maverick by many, a disruptive influence by some, and was renowned for his battles with any kind of rank-wielding authority. But any laboratory report initialled 'M A' was respected. If he said wrong, it was wrong. If he said right, then it was as if trumpets had sounded and any cop could go home happy.

'Matt, I need some help.'

'I heard,' nodded Amos. 'The Donaldhill shooting.'

'The Donaldhill motor-cyclist.'

'I heard that too.' Amos stuffed his hands into the pockets of his white laboratory coat. 'Want the de luxe service?'

Thane eyed him warily. 'What's the price-tag?'

Amos grinned. 'The word is your mob has a video of *The Hanging Tree*. I want an overnight loan, no queueing.'

'For research,' agreed Thane stonily. 'I'll arrange it.'

'De luxe it is.' Satisfied, grinning, Amos beckoned. 'Over here.'

The assistant director led the way across the busy laboratory area, past the white-coated figures at work on other tests. He opened a door into a smaller room, the nearest thing Matt Amos had to a private laboratory. Beneath a hand-printed banner 'Sleep Safe Tonight – Go to Bed with a Cop', a fair-haired girl looked up from a high-powered microscope.

'Are we winning?' asked Amos.

'Not yet.' She gave a frown towards the microscope. 'The separation is positive. I want to try them spectograph-ically, and with luck – '

'I've told you before, little one,' said Amos gravely. 'We don't talk about luck. We call it application. Finished the cross-section?'

She nodded.

'Then you've earned a coffee break, little one.' Amos grinned at her in a deliberately irritating way. 'And the Superintendent and I can get down to some man talk.'

'God,' she said wearily, and got to her feet. Amos's 'little one' was tall, in her early twenties, and had smoke-grey eyes. 'Don't forget that telephone message.'

'I'll tell him,' promised Amos. He shook his head as she left. 'That's Liz – I've got her on loan from one of the Ministry of Defence laboratories. We're supposed to teach her some new tricks. Teach her? Hell, I'm reading text-books at night to keep up with her.'

'Keep trying,' said Thane dryly. He knew Amos had come to the police laboratory from a high-powered uni-versity research team, dropping money to get more of what he called 'job satisfaction'. The research team still wanted him back. 'What message?'

'You've to look in on Phil Moss before you go,' said

76

Amos. 'But push some raw meat under his door first – he sounds in that kind of mood.' Perching on the edge of his desk, legs dangling, he became serious. 'This motor-cyclist, Douglas – what do you want?'

'A few small miracles.' Thane eyed him carefully. 'Maybe even some of that interchange you're always preaching.'

'Interchange.' Amos sucked his lips with something approaching satisfaction. 'That's what I expected. Just remember we don't give guarantees.'

But Thane knew he'd offered the extrovert, bearded Amos a chance to explore one of his favourite areas, an area he'd pursue with as much glee as zeal. Interchange analysis depended on the scientific precept that objects which met both received and left traces of that happening. Matt Amos related that to people. Anyone going anywhere, even just walking through a room, collected traces of where he'd been – and left other minute indications of his visit.

They had to be found, identified. They could be microscopically small. It needed skill to locate them – and it wasn't always possible. But they were there, and if they could be identified they could be built on.

'Matt, I want to know where he'd been – and anything else,' he told Amos.

'There's a possibility or two.' Amos scratched his beard for a moment, then allowed himself a slight smile. 'I think his clothes and that bike should tell you a few things. In fact, I've already put Liz to work on some of it, and a couple of my boys have the rest, but I won't say that what we've got so far makes sense.'

'Tell me,' invited Thane.

Amos came down from the desk, reached above a large glass carboy and a collection of related tubes and retorts, and brought down a bulging plastic bag from a shelf.

'His clothes.' He slapped the bag on his desk. Through the clear plastic, Thane could see the dried bloodstains on the white wool sweater. The heel of one cowboy boot protruded at an angle. 'There are some specks of candle grease – just ordinary candle grease, Colin. We've also identified a few horse hairs. Doesn't exactly connect with the video thing, does it?'

Thane shrugged. 'Not yet. That's all?'

'For now. The bike and his shoes look like telling us more.' Amos prodded the bag almost absently. 'Then there are a few other angles to try – if you give me time.' He paused. 'And, of course, you'll remember that small favour?'

'Would I forget?' asked Thane dryly. He picked up the bag and went to return it to the shelf.

'Careful!' The warning came like a yelp from Amos. 'Don't touch that gubbins underneath.'

'All right,' soothed Thane. He got the bag back in its place, then frowned at the apparatus below. 'Something special?'

'More precious than gold,' said Amos firmly. He came over, looking worried. 'Not for clumsy fuzz to mess with. That's ten litres of best home-made Chablis wine, the produce of my personal tender loving care, that – oh, to hell, just keep your hands off it. You'd probably drink it out of a mug.'

'If it works out, call it Château Glasgow,' suggested Thane helpfully. 'I'll be in touch.'

He left before Amos could do much more than snarl.

Detective Inspector Phill Moss had once been Thane's second-in-command at Millside Division. Now he was liaison officer to the Strathclyde force's assistant chief constable, Crime – which by Moss's reckoning meant being one stage above office boy. But it brought him an office of his own, even if it wasn't much bigger than a converted broom cupboard, and was located in the administration area where a white-gloved orderly and glass doors combined to keep out the unwashed and uninvited. Beyond the doors was a thickly carpeted corridor which led, eventually, to the chief constable's office.

A glum-faced Traffic Branch inspector was just leaving as Thane arrived. The man went past, muttering to himself. Whatever had happened to him along the corridor, it hadn't been good. But for the average cop a summons to any of these doors had all the attractions of an invitation to Execution Walk.

Moss's room was located next to his ACC. A small, thin man, with a wrinkled face, he gave a grin of welcome when Thane came in.

'Good to see you, Colin,' he declared with genuine pleasure, coming round from behind his desk and shaking Thane's hand. 'Still coping at the funny farm?'

'They come worse,' said Thane easily. He returned Moss's grin. They'd made a good team because of their differences. But at the same time as he'd been promoted and transferred, Moss had been hospitalized for a long-overdue stomach ulcer operation which had left him classified for light duties only. 'How about things here?'

'Me?' I could drop dead in this room and eventually someone might complain about the drains.' Moss closed the door of his little office, dumped some files off the one spare chair and waited until Thane settled into it. Then he went behind his desk again and slumped down into his own chair with a pleased grunt. 'Mary and the kids all right?'

'Doing fine,' nodded Thane. 'Why haven't you been round lately?'

'Too much of this garbage gets in the way.' Moss thumbed derisively at the other files piled in front of him. 'Half of it is unreadable, the rest is worse, but I'm supposed to know what it's all about.' His face softened. 'Say hello to them for me, and if that's an invitation, you're on.'

Thane chuckled. Wiry, with thinning, mousy hair, Phil Moss was in his late fifties and a determined bachelor. Headquarters duty hadn't particularly changed him – he still looked as if he'd slept in his clothes, and if he'd shaved that morning he hadn't got too close to the razor.

But he was still remembered on the streets, where he'd been an abrasive, acid-tongued legend with a complaining, methodical approach to everything in life. Older and more cautious, he'd provided an ideal balance to Thane's style of action. It was a balance that Thane knew he now sometimes lacked.

'So.' Moss sat back and gave a mild, relaxed belch, a pale shadow of the explosions he'd produced before the surgeon's knife had altered things. 'My boss says you're chasing video pirates.'

'Does he?' Thane was surprised. When a regional assistant chief constable became interested in a Crime Squad target operation it wasn't always welcome news.

'But he didn't know it until after he had a phone call from an old friend – which was good. Saved him from lying about it.' Moss produced a pair of heavy horn-rimmed spectacles which Thane hadn't seen before, slipped them on with a self-conscious air, then consulted one of the many slips of paper in front of him. 'The caller was a Jonathan Garrison. They used to play golf together years ago. Know him?'

Thane nodded. 'I saw him this morning.'

'You made an impression,' said Moss. 'He thought you were one of our people and he wanted to know why there was such an interest in a dead man.'

'Complaining?' frowned Thane.

''No.' Moss shook his head. 'Just asking. My ACC fed him the usual line about routine inquiries, but thought you should know.'

'I see.' Thane pursed his lips. If Alexis had made the call he would have been less surprised. But an approach from her brother-in-law was something he hadn't expected. 'That's all?'

'That's all I was told.' Moss eyed him through the unfamiliar spectacle lenses. 'Does he matter?'

'Garrison?' Thane shook his head. 'I don't know, Phil. It's too early.'

'*The Hanging Tree* – I've heard a little.' Moss scratched a patch of isolated stubble on his chin. 'Getting anywhere yet?'

'Not that you'd notice,' admitted Thane wryly.

'But I also heard you're interested in Martin Tuce – the Glassman.' Moss grinned a little. 'He reads like trouble.'

'I'll let you know when we find him.' The window behind Moss gave a view across the street to an office block. The last time Thane had visited it, it had been a busy, brightly lit place. Now it was empty, with a 'For Sale' sign across the front. There was a lot of that about. He sighed, stopped his attention wandering, and admitted, 'We're scraping around, Phil – hoping things will happen.'

'We've got a file of our own on the video trade, and it doesn't stop at tapes,' said Moss slowly. He removed the spectacles and laid them aside with a grimace. 'We've got hints of a protection racket, probably true. But any thief with sense is out there stealing recorders, cameras, hardware, software – any damn thing that is video. There's an instant market and the customer doesn't ask questions.'

'Did they ever?' asked Thane dryly. He took out his cigarettes and lit one.

'Filthy habit.' Moss scowled and pushed a grubby ashtray towards him. 'Colin, I don't often see a real, live criminal any more, but I know what's going on. Want to hear how I see it?'

Thane nodded.

'The hard men are moving in, your real pros.' Moss paused and gave another soft, deliberate belch for emphasis. 'Forget the small-timers who burgle a shop now and again. I'm talking about at least one team who hit warehouses and take stuff away by the truckload. They use split-second timing, CB radios and don't leave much to chance. If anyone gets in their way, hard luck.'

'How hard?'

'A transport yard in Northern Division was hit three weeks ago, a whole damned container-load of blank video tapes taken – over ten thousand of them, worth maybe £80,000 retail. The night-watchman got in the way, so they fractured his skull with an iron bar.' Moss pursed his lips. 'He'll live, but he won't work again.'

'No leads?'

Moss shook his head. 'No, but we've had others the same. The last was about a week ago, but misfired – an automatic alarm in a warehouse went off and they got out, fast.'

The intercom box on his desk gave two short bleeps. He looked at it and gave a resigned grimace.

'My master calls. Probably wants to know what day it is.'

'I'll move.' Thane got to his feet.

'Hold on.' Moss stayed where he was. 'Your pirate tapes – talked to any street-level dealers yet?'

Thane shrugged. 'We've people out. They haven't got anywhere.'

'Try one.' Moss wrote on a slip of paper and passed it over. 'He's not far from here.'

'Joe Daisy.' Thane raised an eyebrow. 'That's his name?'

'For real. He trades as Takki Joe,' grinned Moss.

'Friendly?'

'No, scared. He thinks we've got him cold for making obscene phone calls to female customers.' Moss gave a grin of pure goblin malevolence. 'We haven't, there isn't enough evidence, but we're letting him sweat. Try him, get the flavour for yourself.'

The intercom bleeped again, impatiently. This time Moss rose and picked up a notebook.

'I'll be in touch,' promised Thane.

'Do that.' Moss looked at him almost enviously, and seemed about to say something more.

But he didn't.

Takki Joe's video shop was located in a lane off busy St Vincent Street, only a few minutes' walk away from the headquarters building. From the outside it looked like any of the other video shops which had sprouted around the city centre. Technicolor posters of recent releases fought for space in its window display, notices by the door shouted special weekend rental offers, and there were plenty of customers coming and going.

Thane went in, threaded his way past display stands and browsing customers. He reached a counter where a 'Thieves Will Be Prosecuted' notice sat beside a video screen which was showing what looked like a mass of green sludge attacking a buxom blonde who had already lost her clothes. The sound was turned down so that the blonde's screams didn't drown a music tape being played through the overhead speakers.

There was a girl behind the counter. She was mousy-haired, wore a red jump-suit and too much eye make-up, and looked bored.

'Yes?' She gave Thane a single glance. 'If you're renting and not a member we need identification – and a deposit.'

'No deposit.' Thane showed his warrant card. 'I just want your boss.'

'That'll make his day,' she said sardonically.

Leaving the counter, she disappeared for a moment among the display stands and customers. In a few moments she returned. The man with her was middle-aged, pot-bellied, and had long, dyed black hair which showed grey at the roots. He was wearing a blue denim suit over a cowboy shirt with a string tie, and as he arrived he gave Thane a nervous, ingratiating smile.

'Joe Daisy?' asked Thane.

'Yes.' The pot-bellied man struggled to keep the smile in place. 'People – uh – call me Takki Joe.'

'I don't, Mr Daisy.' Thane showed his warrant card again. 'And people call me Superintendent.'

'All right.' Daisy swallowed hard, glanced along the counter, then gave the girl a sideways glare. 'Customers waiting. We'll be through the back.'

She shrugged and ambled over to deal with two people who were clutching tapes. Beckoning, Daisy led Thane through a curtained door into the rear of the shop. Part of it was laid out as a small office, the rest held racks of stored

83

video tapes and several stacks of anonymous cardboard cartons.

'Business pretty good?' asked Thane stonily.

'Not bad.' Daisy gestured feebly. 'We've a good location, Superintendent.'

'True.' Thane went over to the scarred wooden desk, laid his hand deliberately on the telephone for a moment, then considered him unemotionally. 'I heard that – and some other things. You've got problems, Mr Daisy – haven't you?'

The fat face paled and Daisy looked suddenly older and frightened.

'I thought – '

'That's a mistake on its own.' Thane shook his head sadly. 'As big a mistake as those phone calls. You take names and addresses before you rent out tapes, then you've got a nice little card index – '

'I haven't – '

'Admitted anything?' Thane nodded agreement.

'We've had break-ins,' said Daisy desperately. He moistened his lips. 'Someone else could have got at the index, Superintendent. It's happened before, with other shops. Maybe not phone calls, but they take names, they burgle customers' homes and know there's at least a video recorder worth stealing. I – '

'We've thought about that,' mused Thane. He paused and sighed. 'Of course, if you could help us in another direction, really help us, it might be easier to believe.'

'Help you?' Daisy grabbed at the words, looked puzzled for a moment, then thought he had the answer. 'How much would it cost?'

'About five years if you try that again.' As he spoke, Thane reached out, took the string tie in one hand, and yanked the fat man nearer. 'Dirty phone calls, attempted bribery, and maybe we really turn your place over, check every tape you've got in stock – would you like that?'

The fat face quivered. Joe Daisy was close to tears and he had bad breath. Thane let him go in near disgust.

'So we'll start again,' he said brutally. 'We'll talk about pirate tapes. Though naturally, as a totally law-abiding trader, you wouldn't stock them.'

Daisy swallowed and gave a quick nod.

'I – '

Thane cut him short. 'Just listen. I don't care if you're up to your armpits in pirate videos. I don't care if you've an old mother to support. You get offers?'

'Yes.' Daisy nursed his pot belly in his hands for a moment and looked sick. He took a stumbling step back. 'We – it happens.'

'Who makes the contact?'

Daisy shook his head. 'I – I don't know names. Two men, they just appear; they've got a batch of tapes outside, in a car.' He swallowed again. 'That's how it works, Superintendent. It's cash and carry, nothing on paper, and you're paying about half the legitimate price. Ask anyone – '

'I'm asking you,' said Thane softly. 'Suppose you want to contact them, place a rush order. What do you do?' He grinned. 'If you weren't law-abiding, of course.'

Daisy looked at him blankly. 'I couldn't. I told you, I don't know names.' He licked his lips as he saw Thane's expression. 'But – well, I suppose I could tell one or two people I know, say that if they had a delivery they could mention Takki Joe had a problem – ' His voice died away.

'He has.' Thane considered the man bleakly for a moment. 'You're lying.'

'No. It's the – the way it happens.' Joe Daisy spoke quickly, desperately. 'You don't ask names, you don't ask questions. It – you don't often see the same faces twice. But they're all your real hard men. You don't get curious because it wouldn't be healthy.'

Thane pursed his lips, then changed tack.

'What about *The Hanging Tree*?' he demanded. 'When do you expect it to arrive?'

'*The Hanging Tree*?' Daisy's mouth fell open in surprise, then he recovered. 'I didn't know. If they've got that – '

'Good business?'

The man gave a cautious grin. 'First off with that one can clean up. Is – you mean it's on the way?' He stopped and gave a quick headshake. 'I wouldn't touch it, Superintendent. My word on it.'

'Naturally,' agreed Thane dryly. He stood silent for a moment, the taped music from outside just audible. He was certain Daisy hadn't known about *The Hanging Tree*. But for the rest, he couldn't be sure, except that Daisy was scared – perhaps, if he was lying, too scared to make a choice.

He went over to the desk, picked up a pencil, and wrote the Crime Squad number on a sheet of invoice paper. Then he turned and faced Daisy again.

'Think about it,' he invited. 'You can reach me through this number any time.'

He didn't wait for an answer.

It was still dry and sunny outside, the pavements becoming busy as a first wave of office workers began heading for an early lunch. An insurance office clock showed it was twelve noon. Thane walked on, found a public telephone at a tobacconist's shop, and used it to get through to the Crime Squad number. It was answered, then Maggie Fyffe's voice came on the line.

'Where are you?' she asked without preliminaries.

'In town, St Vincent Street,' he told her. 'Just checking in. Why?'

'Francey will tell you. He's on his way in – but he thought you were at Strathclyde headquarters.' Maggie sniffed. 'We can't all be mind-readers. St Vincent Street where?'

'Near Hope Street.' Thane frowned. 'Trouble, Maggie?'

'No, a problem. I'll radio him,' she said. 'Stay there.' She hung up.

Thane left the shop and waited by the kerb. Traffic rumbled past, people went by. A group of out-of-work teenagers, girls as well as boys, jostled their way noisily along the opposite pavement. They paused briefly to shout obscenities as a Rolls-Royce purred by, then went on their way. He watched them for a moment, part of him a cop, the rest of him angry at the waste, at what was happening.

Street crime was on the upsurge; people had stopped being surprised when an old woman was mugged for her pension money. Everyone knew why, only the politicians wouldn't admit it.

The Crime Squad car, the grey Mini that Francey Dunbar liked to use, appeared out of the traffic a couple of minutes later and stopped at the kerb. Thane got aboard and Dunbar had the little car moving again as soon as he'd closed the door.

'Maggie said a problem.' Thane looked at him. 'I thought you were trying to find the Glassman.'

'He's in London – or that's the story.' Dunbar squeezed the Mini past a large bus and calmly took a traffic light as it changed to red. 'Sandra says she needs help. She's out at Donaldhill, at the local Social Work office.'

Thane grunted his surprise. 'Doing what?'

'Getting a line on Ted Douglas,' shrugged Dunbar. He gave Thane an amused, sideways glance. 'She phoned in. Seems she reckons someone out there needs booting – you know, diplomatically. She reckoned you'd manage it.'

'Thanks,' said Thane heavily. 'Anything else going on?'

'Not for us,' said Dunbar sadly, and concentrated on his driving.

The Social Work Department office for Donaldhill was a plain red-brick building built like an army blockhouse, and with about the same apparent attraction. The car park was a patch of waste ground at the rear and as they drew in and stopped, a large grey rat scuttled from under another parked vehicle and vanished among a pile of crumbled stonework.

'Nice,' said Dunbar bitterly, then swore. 'Hell, there's another.'

Thane just saw the grey shape disappear. But it happened, particularly around areas like Donaldhill. The old slum tenements still being demolished had given shelter to small armies of vermin. When the rats were made homeless they scattered and some had to come out in the open. After dark, more than one night-shift cop had ended up swinging his baton and clubbing them down while he made a swift retreat.

They left the car and entered the Social Work office by the rear door. It brought them into a waiting area, the walls lined with posters offering free milk, extra allowances, and prohibiting 'Smoking, Spitting, or the Playing of Transistor Radios'. The bench seats down the middle held a scatter of sad-faced, shabbily dressed people. The only sound came from a baby in a pram, making chuckling noises because it didn't know any better.

Sandra Craig emerged from the Inquiry Office door and came towards them, watched by several pairs of curious eyes.

'Hello, sir.' She greeted Thane with a nod and gave Dunbar a quick, rueful smile. 'I can't cope with this one.'

'Tell me,' suggested Thane.

'I got to Janice Darrow as she was packing to leave for a few days – she gave me an address where she'd be.' Sandra stuffed her hands into the pockets of the anorak jacket she was wearing, then shrugged. 'Ted Douglas hit trouble when he was doing field-work training for his degree course. He was handling some probation and discharged prisoner clients and got too friendly with them.'

'In Donaldhill?'

She nodded. 'The same Student Supervisor is still here. She agrees it happened, but says names are confidential.'

'Client relationships,' said Dunbar helpfully. He caught Thane's frown but went on unperturbed. 'That's how it goes – like a doctor and patient, right?'

'What's her name?' asked Thane wearily.

'Jean Leydon – Mrs Leydon.' Detective Constable Craig glanced uneasily at Dunbar then added, 'She's – uh – more in your age group, sir.'

'Geriatric?' suggested Thane. He nodded. 'We'll try her again.' He saw Dunbar start to move. 'Not you – that'll be one problem less.'

Sandra took him along a corridor to a glass-panelled door marked 'Student Supervisor'. She knocked on it, and they went in.

It was a bright little room with flowers in a vase, a pair of vivid Picasso-style prints on one wall, and an old teddy bear propped up on the windowsill. The woman who came round from behind her desk to greet them was in her forties with short dark hair and a thin but pleasant face.

'I know what you want, Superintendent,' she said in a crisp voice as Sandra finished the introductions. 'But the answer is no.'

Thane looked at her for a moment and knew she meant it.

'Can we talk?' he asked.

'If you don't mind wasting time.' Jean Leydon said it with a slight smile.

'Thank you.' Thane glanced at Sandra and nodded towards the door. She made a quick, throat-clearing noise and left them.

'One to one, Superintendent?' asked Jean Leydon with mild amusement. 'Why not? We can swap interview techniques.'

'On our feet?' asked Thane pointedly.

Silently, she indicated a chair, waited until he'd sat down, then went back behind her desk.

'Well?' she asked.

'Ted Douglas,' said Thane bluntly. 'You know what happened to him?'

'I read about it.' There was pain in the dark-haired woman's eyes for a moment. 'He was one of my – well, failures, I suppose. But I liked him.' She paused and drew a deep breath. 'Your Detective Constable Craig is a persuasive young officer. I've already probably said more than I should – you know that.'

Thane sighed. 'And if I want more, there are official channels – I can go climb the management ladder?'

'Yes.' She frowned. 'I still don't know why it matters now. He was here three years ago – '

'And now he's dead,' agreed Thane. He leaned forward. 'I'll give you a name, Mrs Leydon. Martin Herbert Tuce – he's known as the Glassman.'

'I don't know him. If I did – ' she gave a slight shrug. 'But I don't. All I'll say is that Ted Douglas was a young idiot when he was here. I got him another chance, with another unit – working with children. That went well.'

'But he made another mess of things later,' said Thane quietly. 'Mrs Leydon, I'm trying to find a link between an ex-student of yours and at least one known criminal. Ted Douglas was up to his neck in it when he died.'

'I heard that too, from Detective Constable Craig.' The dark-haired woman sat for a moment, her hands just touching, resting her thin chin on her fingertips. 'Maybe I'd like to help you, Superintendent. Maybe Ted Douglas became too friendly with one particular person – a discharged prisoner I'd assigned him as a client. I was Student Supervisor, I crashed down on Douglas the moment I found out. It's all on file.'

'But?' Thane saw it coming.

'Our files stay confidential. You'd need a court order to get at them.' Her mouth tightened. 'Professional ethics, Superintendent – and I happen to like my job. I'm sorry.'

Thane had heard it before, knew she was right. He nodded, got to his feet, and went over to the door. Opening it, he glanced back.

'People like you – ' He tried for the words he wanted but didn't quite get there. 'You're caught in the middle, I suppose.'

'Sometimes.' She smiled at him, oddly. 'One thing, Superintendent – it may help. I spotted Ted Douglas in Donaldhill not long ago. He wasn't alone.'

'Thanks,' said Thane wryly.

He went out, closed the door, and went back to the

reception area. Francey Dunbar and Sandra were there, waiting. He beckoned and they followed him out of the building into the parking lot.

'She wouldn't talk?' asked Dunbar.

'No,' said Thane curtly.

He saw his sergeant exchange a covert glance with Sandra Craig. Then Dunbar carefully cleared his throat.

'Sir – '

'Well?'

Dunbar grinned awkwardly. 'I got the name, and an address. He's Billy Tripp, and it's not far from here.'

Thane stared at him and Dunbar nodded.

'How?'

'One of the girls at the reception desk. She – uh – just came up and told me.' Dunbar's young, tanned face showed a degree of embarrassed bewilderment. 'Hell, I didn't even have to ask.'

'Your natural charm,' suggested Sandra dryly. She looked at Thane, a silent question in her eyes.

Thane turned slowly and looked back at the Social Work building. For a moment he thought he saw a curtain move at a window. There was an old teddy bear on the sill.

'Professional ethics,' he said softly. Then he drew a deep breath. 'Billy Tripp – let's pick him up.'

Redevelopment meant there were only a few streets like it left in the city, but even a few were too many.

The dilapidated old grey stone houses dated back to early Victorian times and faced the graffiti-covered brick walls of a shut-down factory. The roadway between them glinted with fragments of broken glass and several of the house doorways were boarded up. Children played in and around a couple of stripped, abandoned cars. There was only the corner grocery shop, where a Pakistani determined to make a living kept a ham knife beside the cash register and had a steel-mesh grille permanently over his empty display window.

But if even the air smelled stale, at least the sky was the same blue.

The two Crime Squad cars, Sandra Craig's Volkswagen in the lead with Thane aboard, crawled and crunched over some of the newer glass. Francey Dunbar kept his grey Mini a few lengths back, then, as they'd arranged, swung his steering wheel and sent the little car splashing through a puddled lane towards the rear of the houses.

Billy Tripp's address was a street-level door and the Volkswagen coasted to a halt at the kerb beside it. They got out, and Thane glanced at the slim, red-haired girl beside him.

'Ready?'

Sandra nodded calmly. Her hands were back in her anorak pockets.

They went up to the scarred door, the frame showing gaps between it and the stone, the doorbell hanging broken on its frayed wires. Thane used his fist to knock heavily on the wood.

A few moments passed. Then a lock was turned and the door opened a few inches on a chain guard. The woman who looked out was grey-haired, fat, and had a mouth like a rat-trap. The mouth fell open for a moment, she stared at Thane, then she turned quickly.

'Billy – polis!' It came like a screech. 'Move, son!'

The door started to close. Thane took one step back, kicked, and the heel of his shoe took the old wood with a noise like a drumbeat. The chain tore free and the door burst inwards.

The fat woman tried to bar his way, still screaming, dirty fingernails clawing for his face. He elbowed her hard, back against the wall, and got past, stumbling over some empty bottles and sending them clattering.

Another figure appeared in the drab, dull hallway. The man was big, bald, and in his shirt-sleeves without a collar or tie. Thane was more interested in the hatchet in his right hand. He could hear scuffling noises behind him but daren't look round.

The bald man shambled forward, then made a wild swing with the hatchet. Thane threw himself sideways, grabbed the bald man's arm before he could try again, swung him round, and slammed him head-first against the wall.

The woman screamed, the bald man howled with pain. He also dropped the hatchet and Thane slammed his fist hard behind the bald man's left ear. Giving a strangled grunt, the bald man sagged and slid down the wall to his knees.

Sandra had the fat woman face down on the hallway floor, one knee in the small of her back, handcuffing her. Thane headed for the doorway from which the bald man had emerged, reached it, then a gun barked and he hugged the wall as a bullet ripped into the wood of the door.

Behind him, the woman was shouting hysterically and the bald man was still groaning. But there was silence from the room.

Heart pounding, Thane eased forward a fraction.

Nothing happened. He inched forward again, then cursed.

The shabby room was empty. An old blanket, draped like a curtain over a large, roughly cut hole in the wall, had been torn loose and hung from a solitary nail.

A grunt came close behind him and then, as he started to turn, glass smashed. The bald man, the hatchet back in his grasp, collapsed like a sack at his feet. Sandra Craig stood over him, staring in surprise at the remnants of a bottle still clasped in her fist.

Somebody, and he knew it had to be Francey Dunbar, was kicking in the back door. Scooping up the hatchet, Thane made for the hole in the wall and went through it fast, in a fighting crouch.

Then he stopped, stared, and gave a long sigh.

He was in another room, in another house. An old woman sat in a chair beside the fireplace, grinning at him with toothless gums. He went past her, into the hallway. There was another hole. It led into yet another house, abandoned and empty. The front door lay thrown open, the street outside was deserted. Even the children who had been playing round the old cars had vanished.

Nobody, he knew, would have seen or heard anything. In streets like this one, nobody ever did.

He went back the way he had come. The old woman was still grinning.

'Did Billy get away?' she asked.

Thane nodded. She cackled and slapped her knee.

When he reached Billy Tripp's house Dunbar was there. The bald man, still dazed, was also handcuffed and now sitting on a threadbare couch beside the fat woman. Both scowled at him.

'His ma and pa,' said Dunbar tonelessly, thumbing at the couple. 'Just visiting, round for their weekly hand-out. They say they don't know anything.'

The fat woman sniffed back what was meant to be a tear.

'He's a good son,' she said defiantly. 'Looks after his folks, so he does. An' I want to complain. That red-haired wee bitch o' a policewoman attacked my poor husband.'

Thane glanced around the room. The few items of furniture were old and dilapidated. But there was a large, new, colour TV in one corner with a video recorder underneath. A CB home base radio sat on the rickety table, an aerial wire snaking up to disappear through the ceiling.

A thin wad of bank notes lay beside the radio. As Thane went to touch the money, the woman gave an indignant yelp.

'That's ours, mister,' she protested. 'It's from – '

She fell silent as her husband growled and dug her hard in the ribs.

'Where's Sandra?' asked Thane.

'Out front,' said Dunbar laconically. 'The troops have arrived.'

They came into the room a few seconds later, the uniformed crew of a patrol car. The older of the two constables looked around, saw the hole in the wall, and stifled a grin.

'Mice, sir?' he asked, then nodded at the man and woman on the couch. 'What about this pair?'

Thane looked at Dunbar. His sergeant shrugged and shook his head. Billy Tripp's parents weren't the kind who believed in conversation.

'Take them away, charge them with something – anything,' said Thane wearily. 'We'll look around this place.'

They did. In the bedroom, Billy Tripp's wardrobe showed he spent money freely – and not just on clothes. Six bottles of de luxe malt whisky sat in two neat rows, unopened, at the bottom of a cupboard.

'I got a bottle of that stuff on my birthday,' said Dunbar enviously.

Sandra came back from checking what passed as a kitchen. She beckoned Thane through.

There was a telephone on the grimy wall and Billy Tripp seemed to have some embryonic artistic ability. Various doodled drawings decorated the area around the telephone, some in pen, some in pencil. Some were female and obscene, others were violent. A few fragments of telephone numbers were scribbled around them. One drawing, more finely detailed than most, was a falcon's head with savagely accentuated beak. A telephone number filled the bird's eye.

'Get a directory,' said Thane tonelessly.

Dunbar understood. He found the telephone directory on a shelf under some girlie magazines and flicked through the pages. He ran a finger down one column of entries, paused, then nodded.

'Falcon Services,' he confirmed.

Another patrol car had arrived. Thane ordered the crew to guard the house. Then he went out to the Volkswagen with Sandra and they waited for Dunbar and his Mini.

When Dunbar appeared from the lane, he was walking. The Mini's tyres had been slashed and a brick had been heaved through the windscreen.

'Someone doesn't like us,' he concluded woodenly. 'What now, sir?'

Thane hesitated. Billy Tripp was far away. For the rest, he wanted time to think. He saw the hopeful expression on Sandra's face.

'We'll eat.' He saw her beam.

She'd earned it – and it was a very long time since he'd had breakfast in that dockside café.

4

Before they left, Thane used the VW's low-band radio and talked to the Crime Squad base. Francey Dunbar's car had to be brought in, he wanted a computer scan on Billy Tripp, and a few favours arranged from the local CID regarding the house. He knew the Donaldhill CID team. They'd cooperate, remember, and come back for some favours of their own another time.

It was 2 p.m. when they stopped at a small Italian restaurant located in a side street on the fringe of the city centre. It looked shabby from outside. Thane hadn't known it existed, but Sandra Craig was welcomed like a princess by the shirt-sleeved proprietor and his wife.

The food was good too. He allowed himself one glass of wine and finished with one of his carefully hoarded cigarettes. At the end, the bill didn't seem large enough to cover what they'd eaten and Sandra was hugged then kissed on both cheeks by the proprietor's wife.

'What the hell was that about?' demanded Dunbar suspiciously when they were back in the car.

Sandra grinned at him. 'Maybe they just like me.'

'Why?' Dunbar scowled at her.

'Stop squabbling,' said Thane wearily. His sergeant and Sandra had killed the rest of the Chianti between them and he was in no mood for one of their verbal sparring matches. 'Sandra?'

'They've a son.' She keyed the starter and the VW's air-cooled rear engine began throbbing impatiently. She winked at Dunbar. 'We nearly got engaged once. But our families said no – we were only eight years old.'

Disappointed, Dunbar grunted and settled back.

'Food,' he said sourly. 'There'd have to be a connection.' His young, strong face formed a more thoughtful frown as the car began travelling and he leaned over from the rear seat, his attention on Thane. 'What about the way the Ted Douglas connection shapes? He knew Billy Tripp, he must have wanted some easy money – '

'Tripp shows him how,' nodded Thane. He felt better for the meal, his mind was working again, but he knew they still hadn't achieved any major breakthrough.

'And Tripp draws a falcon's head on his wall,' said Sandra, her eyes on the road. 'Plus their phone number.'

'He could have been calling Ted Douglas,' suggested Dunbar doubtfully. 'Maybe when we find Billy Tripp, or the Glassman – ' He left it there.

Thane knew they were both waiting for him to point them in one direction or another. He felt a thin, acid tendril of amusement at the way they might have reacted if he'd told them how well he'd once known Alexis Garrison.

'One thing you've forgotten,' he said deliberately.

'Sir?' Dunbar was puzzled.

'I paid the bill back there,' he told them. 'We're splitting it three ways.'

It was mid-afternoon, still fine and dry, when they drove in past the Police Training Area sign. Beyond the trees, a squad of new dogs and equally new handlers were being put through their paces on the assault course. Yapping and tail-wagging, the dogs were enjoying it; but their handlers, stumbling after them over the obstacles, looked as if they'd be lucky to survive.

The assault course might have been designed by sadists for innocents. As the Volkswagen passed, one rookie stumbled and fell in the mud section. He was still holding his dog's long leather training lead and the powerful German Shepherd at the other end dragged him face-down the rest of the way.

It lightened Thane's mood as they left the Volkswagen and went into the Crime Squad building. Maggie Fyffe looked up briefly from a teleprinter keyboard and waved a greeting. Then he spotted Joe Felix ambling towards them. The middle-aged detective constable gave him a grin.

'Heard you had some fun, sir.'

'Finished playing video games?' asked Thane.

'Before lunch, sir.' Felix nodded. The grin faded and a slightly unhappy expression crossed his round face. 'La Mont gave me back the tapes he borrowed. He says he'll be in touch.'

'Did he come up with anything?'

'Not a lot, he says. I – ' Felix hesitated, then shrugged. 'He's the expert.'

'We all have our problems, Joe.' Thane nodded his understanding. Detective Constable Felix was an easygoing individual, hard to rile. Whatever had happened, he knew he'd hear eventually – either from Felix or from John La Mont. 'Have we got the computer run-down on Billy Tripp?'

'On your desk, sir,' confirmed Felix.

'Right.' He glanced at Dunbar. 'Give me ten minutes, then I want all three of you in my room.'

That gave him time to go through, get out of his sheepskin jacket, and check the small collection of messages which were waiting. The top item, with a Criminal Records Office photograph clipped to one corner, was the computer print-out on Billy Tripp. He set it aside and glanced at the rest.

Phil Moss had called, but would ring back some time. There was an underlined reminder from Maggie Fyffe that he had a witness citation to be in court the next morning, to give evidence in a fraud case. There were some expense sheets to initial, a Scottish Office circular about drug abuse figures he'd have to read later, and someone in the squad's branch section in Edinburgh had teleprinted to ask if he'd come through to their annual golf dinner. He winced at that one, remembering the last time and the hangover afterwards.

That left Billy Tripp. Elbows on the desk, he started with the CRO photograph. It showed a young, sullen-faced man with dark, close-cropped hair, a man who might have been good-looking if someone hadn't badly flattened his nose.

The print-out told its story in the usual economic wordage.

Billy Tripp was a 'ned' – Glasgow's label for a low-grade blend of layabout and thief, one of a breed likely to be spawned in any city. His criminal record began when he was a teenager. Now, at the age of twenty-three, his convictions ranged from theft and burglary to assault. His last conviction had been on a charge of mugging and robbing a doctor making night calls.

The usual physical description followed. Boiled down, it amounted to Tripp being of medium height, thin, and having 'Mother' tattooed in blue on his left wrist.

But two laconic Criminal Intelligence additions left Thane with a cynical satisfaction: Billy Tripp hadn't been in known trouble for more than a year, and the comment in the section 'Current Known Criminal Associates' was an apologetic 'not known'.

It could only mean someone was running Billy Tripp, calling just about every move he made and making sure he obeyed.

He talked it all through when the others arrived, keeping it not so much a briefing session as an open discussion on what they'd put together. It was a process that sometimes sparked an idea, an answer. This time it didn't.

'It's more what we haven't got, boss,' said Francey Dunbar sardonically. He had draped himself against the window frame and was chewing gum with a gloomy ferocity. 'You've got Billy Tripp going monastic; there's nobody out there who seems to know what the hell the Glassman has been doing lately, or where he is.' He paused, shifting his wad of gum from one cheek to the other, and grunted. 'That makes two for certain. How many more, and who's the money man?'

Joe Felix, sitting beside Sandra, nodded a mild agreement. 'I know the Glassman,' he said wryly. 'He can figure a bookie's odds on a race, but he has to get someone to read him the results.'

Thane nodded. 'Sandra?'

She looked at him almost strangely for a moment.

'Falcon Services,' she said deliberately. 'It's all we've got left, isn't it?'

'Unless there's a problem,' murmured Dunbar.

Thane looked at his sergeant. But Dunbar's face was innocent of expression; just his moustache moved steadily as he continued chewing.

'There's no problem,' said Thane curtly. 'When we have anything in that direction, I'll tell you.' He glanced at the short, written list he'd completed before they arrived. 'We stay with trying to locate Tripp and the Glassman – I don't care how. Anything on those other phone numbers on Tripp's wall?'

'Not yet,' Sandra shook her head. 'Some are only fragments.'

'Keep at it. Anything from the video trade, Francey?'

'Nothing,' said Dunbar flatly. 'We're getting the same story all round. Say "pirate tapes" and every damned trade suffers immediate loss of memory – or switches to wide-eyed innocence.' He grinned and mimicked in a squeaky voice, ' "Officer, honestly, this man just appeared and I bought from him. Naturally, I thought it was honest. Sorry, I happened to pay cash." '

'Money's what it happens to be all about,' said Thane. 'Big money.' But it brought him straight to the next item on his list. 'Widen it out.'

'Sir?' Dunbar looked puzzled.

'Anything on the grapevine about video gear being moved. Anyone waving extra money around – hold-up artists, pimps, I don't care as long as it's out of pattern.'

Thane slapped one hand flat on his desk, covering what was left on his list. 'Don't ignore the drugs scene – you take that one, Sandra. They've a ready-made dealer network and hard cash available, and anyone setting up as a pirate tapes distributor would need both.'

He finished it there, waiting until they'd left. Then, when the door had closed and he was alone again, he lifted his hand from the list.

There was one item left, Falcon Services. He thought for a moment then lifted his telephone receiver, got an outside line, and dialled the East Kilbride number. The Falcon switchboard girl answered, her voice taking on a new interest when he asked for Alexis Garrison.

'Sorry, she's out,' said the girl. Then she asked quickly, 'Who wants her? I could leave a message or – '

'How about Jonathan Garrison?' asked Thane, cutting her short.

He was in, and he came on the line a few moments later.

'What is it this time?' asked Garrison, with an unconcealed asperity when he heard who was calling. 'Look, Thane, I'm as saddened as anyone about that boy Douglas's death. But the way it happened – why come back to us?'

'I wanted to talk to Alex. It was personal,' soothed Thane, grimacing at the receiver. 'When will she be back?'

'She may be my sister-in-law, but she's also my boss,' said Garrison, in a slightly friendlier voice. 'Either way, I don't even get told when she's going out. But she'll be back before we close – she has letters to sign.'

'I'll try again.' But Thane had him and wanted to hold him. 'When I was out this morning, when we talked, you seemed to have a lot of sympathy for Ted Douglas – for anyone like him.'

'Why not?' Garrison's voice snapped back over the line with a sudden rising anger. 'He was one more educated brain being wasted. That's our trouble, Superintendent. They graduate, they say hello to the world, and the world spits in their eye. Or – or they get trapped in the system, and that's almost as bad. Because then they've got to do what the system wants and nothing more – or the system spits in their other eye.'

'Rough,' murmured Thane.

'Rough?' The man's voice trembled. 'It's butchery. I know I – believe me, I know.' Then, suddenly, Garrison was calm again. 'I've work waiting, as usual. I – I'll tell Alex you called.'

The line went dead as he hung up, and Thane cursed softly. It had ended before it'd really begun, except that Garrison – the Strathclyde's ACC's 'Jock' Garrison – had something more than ordinary anger eating at his system.

It was another question that might matter, might not.

There was someone else he had to contact. Using the telephone again, he got through to Matt Amos at the police laboratory. The assistant director was in his customary gritty but cheerful mood.

'Where's that tape of *The Hanging Tree*?' he demanded. 'I thought we had a deal.'

'I get my report, you get your tape,' Thane told him. 'Don't worry, you're on the list.'

'But?' Amos sensed a catch.

'But you'll be getting some items from a house in Donaldhill – clothing, bits and pieces.' The divisional men had been asked to concentrate on work clothes, to ignore the more exotic aspects of Billy Tripp's wardrobe. 'A pal of Ted Douglas's didn't have time to pack.'

'God,' said Amos dolefully. 'Do you know the kind of howl that goes up from the pay office if I put any of my people on overtime?' He sighed. 'All right, I'll cope – and we're starting to get places with the Douglas stuff.'

'Like?'

'Like now we know what we've got and we're having to ask someone else what it means,' said Amos cryptically. 'No sense in telling you yet – you wouldn't understand. All cops are pig ignorant.'

'But lovable with it,' said Thane dryly. 'Matt, make it as soon as you can. I'm in a hole and I need some kind of ladder to climb out.'

He hung up, glanced at his watch, then rose and reached for his sheepskin jacket.

John La Mont might be sending in that report, as Joe Felix had indicated. But it would be useful to talk to the Canadian beforehand.

Anyway, he had another reason. Thane grinned to himself as he fastened the jacket. Maybe he was being brainwashed, certainly he hadn't thought about it seriously before. But he'd been plunged up to his neck in the video world – and temptation was growing.

La Mont's hotel was close to a couple of the largest electrical discount stores in the city. His trip could include a couple of minutes window shopping. At least he could price the things.

Going through to the Duty Room, he told Dunbar where he'd be.

When he left the building, his own Ford was back in its place in the parking lot, a copy of the completed service schedule lying on the passenger seat. The transport sergeant had changed the car's registration plates, as usual. Crime Squad car registration numbers were changed as a matter of routine – keep one too long and it was noted by the opposition, noted and remembered.

Which was fine, except that Thane, like most of the squad, sometimes got equally confused in the process.

John La Mont was staying in the Albany Hotel, high-flying expense-account territory in the heart of Glasgow's business and banking centre. But he was out. He had left word at the reception desk that he'd be back by 3.30 p.m.

It was 4 p.m. on the hotel lobby clock. Thane thought of the discount store, but found himself a seat, waited, and watched the passing parade of briefcases, mink coats and expensive luggage. He knew some of the faces. One belonged to a judge, another was a man who had recently finished a prison term for tax evasion. A few of the women glanced his way with a mild interest, put a fast price-tag on his suit, and kept walking.

John La Mont arrived by taxi at 4.15 p.m. He ambled in, looking bulkier and more bear-like than ever in brown corduroy casual trousers and an open-necked sports shirt topped by a hip-length duffel jacket. He saw Thane, his bearded face twitched into an immediate grin, and he came straight over.

'Been waiting long?' He clapped Thane cheerfully on the arm. 'I had one or two people to see, places I wanted to look at. Usually, any time I've been up this way, I've been passing through. You know this city has an art gallery stacked with everything from Rembrandt to Picasso?'

'Some of us go there when it's raining,' said Thane politely.

La Mont chuckled, unabashed. 'Keep your rain – I know about that too.'

As he spoke, he led the way over to the desk, collected his key, then took Thane across to the elevators.

The bearded Canadian had a small two-room suite on one of the upper floors. When they got there, La Mont tossed his duffel jacket over a chair, took Thane's sheepskin and gave it the same treatment, then moved towards a bottle and glasses on a sideboard.

'Drink?' he asked.

Thane saw the label on the whisky bottle and nodded.

'A small one, straight.'

'Small for you, more for me. Straight for you, ice for me.' La Mont busied himself pouring. 'How's crime – or shouldn't I ask?'

'It doesn't go away.' They were in a modest-sized sitting room and, through an open door, Thane could see the bedroom with a bathroom leading off. Some of the sitting room furniture had been moved to one side to make room for an extra table. It held a tightly packed collection of electronic hardware, including two video recorders and a monitor screen, all linked by a tangle of cables.

'That's a good public relations answer.' La Mont brought

over the drinks. 'Doesn't go away – I'll remember that.'

Thane took his glass, nodded his thanks, and sipped.

If he'd wanted, he could have told La Mont exactly how crime was: that the Scottish figures for violence, burglary and theft had all come close to doubling in ten years; that in those same ten years the total number of convictions hadn't risen to match; that new laws meant the only statistic which showed a fall was the size of the prison population. But it would have sounded like a Tulliallan lecture. Anyway, wasn't it pretty well the same in most places?

'So.' Unperturbed by his silence, La Mont flopped into a chair and waved an invitation to Thane to do the same. 'What's happened? More *Hanging Trees*?'

'No.' Thane chose a small upright chair, swung its back round to face the video expert, and sat on it saddle fashion. 'Joe Felix said you'd finished.'

'And that I'd sort out a report.' La Mont rubbed his glass along his bearded chin. 'Chasing for it?'

Thane shrugged. 'I'd like to know the basics.'

'You and a lot of other people,' said La Mont sardonic-ally. 'Superintendent, some people say the biggest lie in business is "don't worry, your money is in the mail". I'll tell you a better one. It's the character who says, "I'm from head office, and I'm here to help". Right now, that's what my bosses in States are trying to do to me.' He grimaced. 'But it happens over my dead body. I've told them I don't need their office boy.'

'That report – ' murmured Thane.

'All right, I'll get there.' La Mont took a gulp from his drink. 'All those video tapes you collected were either pirate or counterfeit, top quality, as good as I've seen, not home workshop jobs. We're talking about one real profes-sional operation down south – somewhere around London. I've seen their stuff before. The way their equipment makes a copy is as good as any signature.' He paused. 'There's something else you probably haven't heard. The first copies of *The Hanging Tree* have begun turning up in

106

the London area.'

'Any chance of a lead down there?'

'Like where they're coming from?' La Mont gave a harsh laugh. 'That'll be the day. I could name you half a dozen English police forces who set up special video squads hoping to nail even one of the big operators. Now and again they catch some of the small fry, maybe even seize a load of tapes being shipped in from Europe. But they've never got near the real professionals.'

'You make it sound like a lost cause,' mused Thane.

'Maybe it is. That's what I tried to tell your boss yesterday. Want to know why?'

'I'll listen,' agreed Thane stonily. 'I heard you make noises about money and the Mafia.'

'Right.' La Mont rose, topped up his glass and offered the bottle in Thane's direction. Thane shook his head and La Mont returned to slump down in his seat again. 'Fact: just about every major film made in the last few years has been ripped off. Remember Spielberg's E.T.? Hell, there were so many pirate E.T. tapes around Britain it was like half the population saw the thing before it reached the big screen. If you want more examples, I can give you a catalogue.'

'Big money,' murmured Thane.

La Mont grunted sarcastically. 'The pirate trade is a damned industry. Look, Superintendent, consumer statistics say Britain is the most video-conscious country in the world, way ahead of the States, Japan, or anywhere. The same statistics guesstimate that recorded tape sales and rentals gross over £1,000,000 every week. I said "guesstimate" because my people say maybe four out of five of these tapes are pirates or counterfeit. How does that grab you?'

For a moment, Thane could only stare at him. Multiply that kind of turnover, calculate an average year, and La Mont was right – the video crooks were clearing more of a profit than some major industrial giants.

Clearing it in hard tax-free cash.

La Mont had said 'pirate or counterfeit'. There was a

simple difference, one he knew from the Crime Squad file. A pirate tape was a direct copy from a stolen film, a situation where no legally produced video version existed. A counterfeit tape was something different – an illegal copy of an issued video tape, with faked labels and markings cunningly printed to make it look like the original.

Pirate or counterfeit, the quality could vary from good to downright awful. But a video firm which bought either for sale or rent to regular customers could save itself a small fortune compared with the cost of legitimate stock. Pirate titles in particular, available long before any authorized version, were a new kind of licence to print money.

The Crime Squad file had a lot more about pirate video, starting with the way the law in Britain, as in most countries, had been caught wrong-footed. Fresh legislation, scrambled through, increased the previously puny penalties. But even the new fines and the prison sentences that could be handed out were ludicrously mild when faced with the size of operation that La Mont was talking about.

'And the Mafia angle?' Thane asked quietly.

'Mafia we can prove, Mafia and more. Anything new in organized crime and the vultures come flocking – you know that. There's plenty of "hot" money around to be invested, and the video world offers a damned good return on that kind of capital.' La Mont laid his glass on the carpet beside him. It was almost empty again. 'Give me $US50,000, let me make a phone call to Japan, and I can get you a machine that will turn out four reasonable copies of any video every five minutes – and do it twenty-four hours a day.'

'You're saying you can't win?'

La Mont shrugged. 'I get paid to try. To make it more difficult for the big boys, scare off the cottage-industry characters. Remember, there's a legitimate industry bleeding to death in the background.'

La Mont sat silent for a moment, then surprised Thane

with a chuckle.

'Hell, it's not all bad,' he declared. 'Give the legitimate video trade a chance to survive, to run an honest business, and that's worth while. Like last month: we nailed one operator in south London, grabbed every master tape he had and seized twenty thousand copies all wrapped up ready to go.' He sucked his teeth happily at the memory, then pointed a finger at Thane. 'You've had me do all the talking so far. Now it's your turn. What's happening?'

'Well – ' Thane hesitated.

'Do me a favour,' begged La Mont. 'Not that "routine inquiries" line, right?'

'Right.' Thane still chose his words carefully. 'We've got a lead to a couple of local villains, both in the hired-help category.'

'You've got them?' La Mont's eyes narrowed with interest.

'Not yet.' Thane gave the Canadian a lop-sided smile. 'But they'll surface.'

La Mont grunted. 'And then? Think you can sweat anything out of them?'

Thane shook his head. 'I wouldn't gamble on it – either way.'

'The man I need is their boss.' La Mont leaned forward. 'In practical terms, he's a small-timer – just your friendly local distributor. This is a London-based operation; up here is outpost of the empire stuff. But we're talking about *The Hanging Tree*, for Pete's sake.' His face shaped a grimace. 'My people want somebody's scalp.'

'Yours as a last resort?' suggested Thane woodenly.

'That could happen.' There was no humour in the man's voice. 'I need to score a few points, believe me.'

'Here, or in London?'

'London meaning the factory end?' La Mont shook his head. 'No chance – barring a miracle. One whiff of trouble and these people move somewhere new, fast. We know that much.'

They talked on, but there was nothing more that

mattered. Thane refused another offer of a drink and rose to go.

'What about your own plans?' he asked, as La Mont went with him to the door.

'Do that report for you, take care of some paperwork for the Association, then maybe drift around in Scotland for a couple of days.' La Mont saw Thane's expression and gave a reassuring chuckle. 'Don't worry, I'll stay clear of all this.'

'Shouldn't you head back to London, for the real action?' asked Thane with mild sarcasm.

La Mont shrugged. 'Hassle, Superintendent – not action. I've seen it all before, and I can get back if anything does break. But while I'm here I might as well make some courtesy calls, let some of the good guys in the video trade feel Big Brother hasn't forgotten them.'

Thane said goodbye and left.

Outside the hotel he glanced at his watch, winced at the time, but decided he could still snatch a few minutes at the discount stores.

The few minutes amounted to half an hour before he got back to his car. The parking meter had run out and there was a ticket stuffed under one of the wiper blades. He swore, stuffed the ticket into his pocket, then got in and set the car moving through the city traffic.

He hadn't learned much from La Mont, and the massed ranks of video recorders at the discount store had left him baffled. The parking ticket didn't help, but he could probably claim he'd been on operational duty – looking at video equipment was more or less background research. He could try that, at any rate.

He had to stop at the next set of traffic lights. While he waited, he thought briefly of La Mont's attitude. The Canadian was probably right and they'd only get so far then have to give up. But it didn't always have to happen that way.

The other thing on his mind was the bundle of sales brochures from the discount stores now jammed in one of his pockets. They gave the technical details but he'd been more interested in the price-tags.

Maybe he should think of renting. Maybe he should get some expert opinion – or better still, ask Mary.

The lights changed and he sighed as he set the Ford moving again.

Several fresh slips of paper were waiting on Thane's desk when he got back to the Crime Squad office. The top one said that Commander Hart was back from Edinburgh and wanted to see him.

It was nearly 5.30 p.m. He lifted the telephone, got an outside line, and dialled the Falcon Services number. When they answered, he asked for Alexis Garrison. She came on the line after a few moments.

'I heard you called earlier,' she said cheerfully. 'You nearly missed me again – I'm getting ready to leave.'

'Then I'd have tried your home number,' Thane told her.

'I see.' She was amused. 'Or do I? What's so urgent, Colin? Don't tell me it's still Ted Douglas?'

'Not particularly.'

'Then – ' she paused invitingly.

'Old times, maybe,' said Thane. He kept his manner casual. 'I thought we could meet, have a drink somewhere, talk – catch up on a few years.'

'Why not?' Alexis Garrison sounded as if she liked the idea. 'When?'

'Tonight?' suggested Thane.

'Tonight – ' she hesitated. 'No, I've something arranged, Colin. Business. I'm eating out with one of our best customers – and if I know him, I'll be picking up the bill. How about tomorrow? Make it about eight, and come round to my place?'

'Fine,' agreed Thane. 'I'll be there.'

'Good.' She chuckled. 'About young Douglas – what's happening?'

'We're putting some pieces together, finding they don't

fit,' Thane told her unemotionally. 'We may have to come out to Falcon Services again.'

'I'll tell Jonathan.' She paused, and her manner changed. 'In fact, he just walked in. So if I'm not around, he'll give you any help. Goodbye, Superintendent.'

The line went dead. Thane hung up and sat tight-lipped for a moment. He had to talk to Alexis Garrison, he had to know more about Falcon Services. But maybe he was sticking his neck out too far – and enjoying the prospect.

He made a quick check of the other message slips, saw there was nothing that couldn't wait, and went through to Jack Hart's office. When he arrived, Maggie Fyffe was just leaving with some letters Hart had signed. She gave him a quick wink and a grin but didn't stop.

The squad commander was in a good mood. Lounging behind his desk, hands stuffed into his jacket pockets, he nodded Thane into a chair.

'The Edinburgh trip went well,' said Hart without preliminaries. 'Thank the Good Lord for a judge who saw things our way – which takes Tom Maxwell off the proverbial nasty hook.' He smiled happily. 'I sent him back up north, ready to wrap up that corruption inquiry. By this time tomorrow, he'll have locked up a couple of very surprised local politicians – for starters.'

'You sound like you don't like politicians,' said Thane dryly.

'Does anyone?' Hart looked surprised. 'Any time I vote, it's to keep someone out – not to get someone in.' He ran a hand over his lined cheeks. 'Now, what about *The Hanging Tree*?'

Thane told him all that mattered. Because he was telling Jack Hart, that included Alexis Garrison. By the time he'd finished, Hart's smile had faded a little.

'I'm the boss around here, for my sins,' he said thoughtfully. 'Colin, that gives me a right to hand out warnings – and I'm going to do it now. You could be walking into trouble with the Garrison woman. Do I need to spell out why?'

'I don't think so,' said Thane soberly.

'Good.' Hart considered him through half-closed eyes for a moment and seemed satisfied. 'You've told me, we'll keep it that way for now. Watch that side of things, push on with the rest. What's your programme for tomorrow?'

Thane shrugged. 'I'm in court – probably most of the morning.'

'I forgot. Maggie mentioned it.' Hart swore under his breath. 'All right, I'll be around. Tell Francey Dunbar to report direct to me till you get back – that should guarantee he keeps the lid on things.'

The interview was over. Leaving Hart's office, Thane went along to the Duty Room. It was busy and noisy as usual. There was no sign of Sandra Craig, but Francey Dunbar and Joe Felix were talking together beside Dunbar's desk. He went over and Dunbar greeted him with something like relief.

'Joe has a notion,' said his sergeant dryly. 'Like to hear it, sir?'

Thane nodded. 'Joe?'

'It's those numbers you found in Ted Douglas's wallet,' said Felix. He paused almost apologetically. 'They're not a code, sir – if you know what I mean.'

'I don't,' said Thane bluntly.

'Sir.' Felix looked hurt. 'Francey says you found a Citizen's Band radio at Billy Tripp's place – which ties in. The numbers on Douglas's card run one to forty?'

'Yes.'

'Most CB radios are forty-channel, sir.' Joe Felix said it patiently. 'If you're a CB nut, with some breaker friends, then you all use the same "lucky number" – you keep switched to one channel in particular.'

'But?' Thane felt a faint glimmer of understanding beginning.

'But there's always a chance someone outside the group is listening,' explained Felix earnestly. 'So if it's a private conversation, some CB regulars work a twist. The first caller uses one channel, knows he'll be answered on another, and they keep it that way. Your outsider can only eavesdrop on half of what's going on.' He beamed. 'I've used the system myself – it works.'

'Hold on, Joe.' Even Dunbar had become reluctantly interested. 'Maybe I've got it now. A prearranged sequence of channels, one after another – '

'Working their way through the card,' nodded Felix. 'Or each man in the team allocated a calling and listening channel.' He looked at Thane. 'It would be complicated, but no outsider who happened on any one voice would know what there was going on.'

'Ted Douglas didn't have a CB set,' mused Dunbar. 'At least, we didn't find one.'

Thane nodded. 'But I told you to widen things out. Strathclyde are convinced the team behind some of their video warehouse raids is using CB sets.'

'Hell,' said Dunbar.

Around them the Duty Room's activity kept on. Another team was being briefed beside the main wall-map. The woman detective inspector doing the talking was petite and good-looking; her sergeant happened to be an ex-guardsman. The whole squad knew them as Beauty and the Beast. At the next desk to Dunbar's, two shirt-sleeved detectives were arguing about spelling as they put together what was meant to be a joint report. Someone else was shouting down a telephone, trying to make himself heard at the other end.

Things were normal.

But maybe Ted Douglas had been into more than just being a delivery boy. More than ever, Thane knew they needed to make more progress on the chain they were building.

'Anything new on Billy Tripp?' he asked.

'Not yet.' Dunbar sucked one edge of his moustache and scowled. 'But that story I was told about Tuce being in London was rubbish. He was seen in the city yesterday, coming out of St Enoch underground station.'

'Positive?'

'One of Sandra's girls says yes. He beat her up once,' said Dunbar laconically.

'Right.' Thane was well aware of Sandra's girls. They were mainly prostitutes and they knew their city. Most of them owed her a favour of some kind. 'Anything else?'

Dunbar and Felix exchanged a glance and shook their heads.

'Except – ' Dunbar's wide young mouth shaped an unexpected grin.

'Except what?' demanded Thane suspiciously.

'Matt Amos sent one of his lab. girls over and she picked up one of the tapes of *The Hanging Tree.*' Dunbar spread his hands in innocence. 'For research, she said – that you'd arranged it.'

'For professional services,' admitted Thane, then turned his thoughts back to the problem in hand.

There were other aspects, other areas. But they were being covered, and none of them involved him immediately. He decided he'd had enough, explained to Dunbar about the court summons, arranged for Felix to stay on for a spell, and told them to break the news to Sandra that she had the next day's early turn.

Then he left them, stopped briefly at his office to collect his sheepskin, and headed from there out to his car and home.

Tommy Thane had dark hair, a lean, sturdy build and, currently, a first crop of teenage pimples. His sister Kate was chubby, at the jeans and tee-shirt stage, but already showed every sign of inheriting her mother's good looks.

They were both home when Thane arrived, helping Mary prepare the evening meal. It had been one of the three days a week when Mary was out, working part-time as a medical receptionist. She hadn't had the job long, but she enjoyed it, and he'd noticed that both their children seemed in favour.

Tommy and Kate had their own attitudes about most things.

They sat down to eat at 7 p.m. with a TV news bulletin making soft noises in the background. Mary had produced a beef casserole, but as usual Thane found there was no chance of a second helping. Tommy and Kate had been there first, anything left over was reserved for the dog.

There were biscuits and cheese to follow. Then, while the two children cleared the table and made a noisy business of tackling the washing-up, their parents relaxed over coffee and a cigarette.

'I heard you leave this morning,' said Mary wryly. 'I thought "hard luck, Colin" and went back to sleep.'

'I'd call that sensible.' He grinned at her.

'Practical too.' Mary looked at him for a moment. 'A rough day?'

'I've had better – and worse.' Thane took a long draw on his cigarette, the last but one of his day's ration, and made up his mind. 'I met an ex-girlfriend, Alexis Bolton – her name is Garrison now. She's a widow.'

'And?' Mary raised a quizzical eyebrow.

'I wanted you to know,' said Thane awkwardly. 'She could matter in the Douglas case – I'll have to play it by ear with her.'

'Ears I don't mind.' Mary winked at him. 'Should I worry?'

'No.'

'I could always phone her,' mused Mary. 'Tell her how big a mortgage we've got on this place – that would scare her.' She chuckled. 'What else is happening?'

It was Tommy and Kate's youth club night, and it was another family's turn to give them a lift there. He waited until they'd gone before he mentioned video recorders.

'Buy or rent?' asked Mary.

'I don't know,' he admitted. 'Maybe we should ask around.'

'We could do that.' She liked the idea. 'You'd have Tommy and Kate's vote, either way. They've been making pathetic noises about one for long enough. But how about the budget?'

He'd thought about that. 'We can stand it.'

'We could go fifty-fifty,' she suggested. 'I get paid too, remember?'

The doorbell rang about half an hour later. Thane was upstairs, fixing a plug on a bedside light. He heard Mary go to the door, then the pleased surprise in her voice. She called him down.

'You said come round,' said Phil Moss, grinning in the hallway. He produced a bottle of wine from his coat pocket. 'Here – for next week's anniversary.'

'Which was yesterday,' Thane told him.

'But we'll have it anyway.' Mary took the bottle, then gave Moss a quick hug which left him embarrassed.

They went through to the living room. A drink in his hand, settled in the chair which had always been his favourite, Moss gossiped with them for a spell. He had tidied himself up for the visit. His shirt might be crumpled but it was clean. He'd shaved again and cut himself in the process. But there was a hole in the sole of his left shoe that he probably didn't know about.

'Tommy and Kate,' said Mary suddenly, getting to her feet. 'They'll be back soon, they'll need to be fed and watered. You'll stay, Phil?'

'Thanks.' Moss watched her go out, then gave a slight sigh and turned to Thane. 'There were a couple of outside reasons why I came over, Colin. Though I wanted to, anyway.' He hesitated. 'Maybe I'm just sticking my nose in, but – '

'But you're good at it,' said Thane with a grin.

Moss shrugged. 'These don't add up to much, but it maybe helps to know.'

'Then let's have them.' Thane rose, refilled their glasses, then settled again. 'Well?'

'Jonathan Garrison, the Falcon executive who complained,' said Moss, sipping his drink. 'I asked my boss what he knew about him. It seems if you go back a few years Garrison used to be a Ministry of Defence research brain. He worked on radar development – important

117

enough to be Official Secrets Act material.'

Thane raised a surprised eyebrow. 'You wouldn't guess it now. What happened?'

'He had a complete breakdown, bad enough to be hospitalized.' Moss grimaced. 'They did the usual – kept him under wraps until anything he'd been working on was stale, then pensioned him off.'

'With a chip on his shoulder,' murmured Thane. He saw Moss was puzzled. 'He doesn't like the system.'

'Who does?' grunted Moss. He allowed himself a mild belch. 'The other thing involves Martin Tuce, the Glassman. Still got him on your list?'

Thane nodded. 'And looking for him.'

'Most people think he's a freelance operator,' said Moss slowly. 'I did. Maybe that's not strictly accurate.'

'That's the story in his file, that's the story in the streets,' objected Thane sharply. 'He's a loner most of the time, Phil. He's in the city somewhere, but – '

'He could be at the North Pole for all I know,' said Moss with a hint of asperity. 'Look, this is headquarters coffee-break gossip. Two or three of us were talking, I mentioned Tuce, and that's when I heard the story. The man who told me is reliable; it's not his fault he's Discipline Branch.'

Thane grinned. Discipline Branch policed the police, called themselves unloved and unwanted, and more than a few cops would have agreed they had it just about right.

'They're human,' he agreed. 'I'm listening.'

'He's a chief inspector, used to be Fraud Squad,' said Moss doggedly. 'He remembers a run of cases a few years back – an assortment of white-collar villains who worked stock frauds then hit the insurance companies. Someone outside was helping them, but none of them ever talked. They were scared – and two who apparently didn't pay for that help got into real trouble, practically needed a sewing machine to put their faces together again.' He shrugged. 'There was no proof, nothing even halfway there. But the cops involved in it had more than a suspicion that the Glassman did the frightening.'

'You said outside help,' Thane nursed his glass in both hands, frowning, still puzzled. 'Did they have a name?'

'They had a possible.' Moss grinned at him wickedly. 'It could have been Jimbo Raddick.'

Thane swore softly. Raddick was more than a name to them both. James Cocker Raddick had to be in his mid-forties now. Several years back, as a young lawyer, he'd been disbarred and jailed for embezzling clients' money.

Raddick hadn't let that worry him. When he came out, he'd soon proved that a sound legal training could be useful to a crook. He set up deals, acted as a money man and expensive go-between, but seldom did anything in a way that left his hands directly dirty. There had been a belief that he'd dabbled in narcotics, a certainty that he had funnelled stolen antiques and jewellery abroad.

Twice Thane thought he had built a case against James Cocker Raddick. Twice, to his chagrin, Raddick had walked away grinning.

But there was one thing wrong.

'He's in Spain, Phil,' he reminded Moss bluntly. 'It must be a couple of years since he got out.'

'One step ahead of the taxman, Spain because there's no extradition treaty – I know,' agreed Moss, unperturbed. 'He owns a bar at Torremolinos or somewhere near. But he could still pull strings here, and that would mean the Glassman.'

'Why?'

'When Raddick took off for Spain, the Glassman's sister went with him.' Moss found a missed patch of stubble on his chin and scratched it happily. 'And that is on file – Raddick's file. I checked.'

'Hell,' said Thane wearily.

Coffee-break gossip – and it had brought in almost as much as the squad's activities put together, given him another whole range of possibilities to think about.

Moss wanted to hear more about what had been happening. Glad enough of the chance to talk his way through some of it, put it into words, sort out some of his own feelings in the process, Thane sketched the general picture. When he finished, Moss had some questions of his own to ask.

They stopped when Mary returned with a jug of hot chocolate and a tray of sandwiches. Moments later, Tommy and Kate arrived back. They greeted Moss, Tommy attacked the sandwiches, and Kate took a mug of chocolate out into the hallway with her to make one of her inevitable phone calls. It lasted several minutes and when she returned she bickered with Tommy over the last remaining sandwich.

'Who were you phoning anyway?' asked Thane.

'Just Lorna – ' began Kate.

'You saw Lorna at the club,' protested Tommy. 'What's left to talk to her about?'

Kate looked at him with sisterly contempt. 'Plenty of things.'

'Like who pays for the calls?' asked Thane dryly. He winced as the telephone began ringing. 'I'll get it – you might as well have an answering service.'

But the call was for him, the voice at the other end that of the Crime Squad duty officer.

'Do you know anyone called Takki Joe, sir?' asked the duty officer.

'Yes.' Thane glanced back towards the room and signalled for less noise. 'What about him?'

'He phoned looking for you, Superintendent. Said it was important – '

'When?'

'Ten, maybe fifteen minutes ago.' The duty officer anticipated possible criticism. 'I tried earlier, but your line was engaged.'

'That happens around here,' Thane told him flatly. 'What did he want?'

'You, sir. At his place, now; he says it's urgent, won't wait till morning. We told him we could send someone else, but he said no way – it has to be you.'

'Where?' asked Thane resignedly.

'The address is 242 Carcroft Road.' The duty officer paused, then added helpfully. 'That's out beyond Thornliebank, south of the river. I've an aunt near there.'

'Your aunt is your worry,' Thane told him brutally. 'Did you take the call?'

'Yes.'

'How did he sound?'

'Maybe scared, maybe excited,' said the duty officer unemotionally. 'Or both.'

'I'll go,' Thane decided. 'If there's a problem, I'll radio in.'

He thanked the man and hung up. When he turned, he discovered Moss was there.

'Trouble?' asked Moss.

'Your friend Joe Daisy.' Thane shrugged. 'He wants a meeting, now.'

'Well – ' Moss gave a quick, hopeful belch of interest ' – uh – I'm not doing anything.' He glanced back at Mary, who was listening. 'You don't mind, do you?'

'Take him, Colin,' said Mary resignedly. 'We owe him for the wine.'

They used Thane's Ford and he drove. It was a cloudy night, with enough of a hint of rain in the air to require an occasional flick of the wipers to clear the windshield glass, but the city's streets were busy with people and traffic, spangled with neon signs.

It felt strange to be driving with Phil Moss beside him again. The scrawny, untidy figure who was sprawled in the passenger seat seemed pleased, humming under his breath, making an interested inspection of the low-band radio equipment.

Thane gave Moss a sideways glance, some memories flooding back. But that was yesterday. His mouth tightened slightly, then he thought of Francey Dunbar and almost chuckled. Moss and Dunbar – they were total

121

opposites, yet he'd been lucky both times.

The car travelled on; they made good time, and the dashboard clock showed 10.45 p.m. as they reached Thornliebank. It had once been a village, but now was just an extension of the city with suburbs beyond it.

The Ford's headlights took them along an almost empty, tree-lined stretch of highway, then Carcroft Road came up next, a long, new street of smart bungalows and modern town houses. The cars along it were the latest models, and some of the houses had a boat on a trailer parked to one side of the garden. A party was in full swing in one of the town houses, the curtains left open, noise and light spilling out.

Joe Daisy's house was eleven along from the party. It was small, stood on its own with a Peugeot station-wagon in the driveway, and the front was in darkness.

Thane stopped the Ford at the entrance. Getting out, they crunched their way together over the driveway gravel and reached the porch.

The front door of the house was open a few inches. Thane touched it, and it creaked on its hinges. He exchanged a glance with Moss, pushed the door wide open, then called softly.

Nothing happened, nothing stirred. They could see an edge of light showing under another door towards the rear of the dark, shadowed hallway.

'Joe – Joe Daisy.' Thane tried again. 'It's Thane. Police.'

He heard Moss grunt under his breath. A chill sense of foreboding made his purse his lips.

They went in, walking over thick carpeting, and reached the edge of light. Thane used a handkerchief to turn the handle of the door, then let it swing open.

'God Almighty,' said Moss in a shocked whisper of a voice.

Joe Daisy lay in the middle of the brightly lit room, eyes staring blankly at the ceiling, his fleshy face bruised and bloodied, lips drawn back in a final, twisted rictus of death.

He had been gagged and bound. He was wearing a loudly patterned shirt and plum-coloured trousers, with two gold chains round his neck.

But his feet were bare, spread apart, and a broad metal nail had been driven through each of them, driven through the thick, expensive, blood-stained carpet beneath, then on down into the floor.

'Rough,' said Moss quietly, his face pale. He moistened his lips. 'Why?'

Thane didn't answer him.

5

Sudden death demanded a routine, a routine carefully orchestrated and well rehearsed. In basic terms, it wasn't particularly different from any other police investigation. There were procedures, there were forms to be filled in, and the fact that the matter at the centre of it had once been living and breathing was something not to think too much about.

Death, usually in its more unpleasant forms, was part of the job. Yet those whose job it was had to go home afterwards. It paid to develop that protective carapace, to let others do the mourning.

Alive, Joe Daisy had been Crime Squad business. Now he also belonged to Strathclyde's local divisional team. Colin Thane used his car radio to call the squad duty officer, told him to contact his Strathclyde opposite number, then stayed with the radio until the duty officer came back on the air.

'On their way, sir,' he reported.

Thane keyed his microphone. 'You logged Daisy's call?'

'At twenty-two hundred hours – 10 p.m. exactly,' confirmed the duty officer. 'I got through to you at twenty-two sixteen, sir. Anything else?'

'No, not for now.' Daisy's call would have been automatically taped, and the tape and times in the Crime Squad log would now be evidence. Thane signed off and returned to the house.

Moss had put on a few lights but was back beside Joe Daisy's body.

'I looked around,' he said laconically. 'No forced entry, nothing disturbed.'

'Just this.' Thane considered the dead man for another moment, then glanced around the room.

It was large, expensively furnished as a blend of lounge and viewing theatre. A video screen was mounted high on one wall with a rack of tapes underneath. A chair had been overturned, the glass front of a display cabinet had been smashed as if something or someone heavy had collided with it. But the display of antique silver in the cabinet hadn't been touched, and everything else seemed intact. If there had been a struggle, it had been brief.

'Better see this.' Hands in his pockets, Moss nodded towards the telephone on a small coffee table beside the fireplace.

A slip of paper, creased and folded, lay beside the telephone. Than recognized his own writing, saw his name, and the Crime Squad number.

'Must have all happened just after he called,' mused Moss. He cocked his head to one side, his thin face holding a guarded sympathy. 'He wouldn't talk when you saw him. But maybe afterwards – '

'Not good enough,' said Thane curtly. 'Who'd know?'

'All right.' Moss grimaced agreement. 'Then try this. He does some snooping on his own, comes up with something really good, and decides to try to trade with us.'

'Maybe.' Thane pursed his lips, turned and looked again at the dead video store owner, at the obscenity of the glinting metal nails driven through his feet. 'He was scared – scared of them, scared of going to jail.'

'So he made a choice, and opened the wrong box,' murmured Moss. He touched Thane's arm. 'But it shows how they'll operate. A damned sight worse than any animal. It – yes, it helps to know.'

They were in one of the far-flung outposts of Govan Division territory. The first car to arrive held a CID sergeant and two detective constables. Hard on its heels came another, bringing a detective inspector who had been more or less catapulted out from the Divisional Office. Behind them came the rest of the train – two Scenes of Crime men with their little cases and fingerprint brushes, a photographer, the duty police surgeon. A Land-Rover arrived, towing one of the white mobile incident offices, and parked at the kerb. A squad of uniformed men arrived by minibus.

Inside the house, they got to work. The photographer's motor-driven Nikon clicked and buzzed, the quick stab of his electronic flash cut across the room as he took record shots from every possible angle. Then he changed lenses for some close-ups of the nails. The Scenes of Crime twosome padded from room to room, the others went about their own methodical tasks.

The detective inspector's name was Rome. He was young, lanky, recently promoted, and wasn't used to answering calls where a detective superintendent and a headquarters staff officer were the principal witnesses. But the police surgeon, Doc Williams, was an old acquaintance who gave a wink in Thane's direction before he opened his bag and began to spread the tools of his trade on a small square of plastic sheeting.

Thane and Moss gave Rome a quick outline of what had happened and he listened with care, chewing occasionally on his lip.

'Did you touch anything?' he asked eventually, then flushed. 'Sorry, Superintendent. I – '

'You've got to ask,' agreed Thane. 'Nothing disturbed. A door handle opened with a handkerchief, a few light switches, the same. Maybe our prints on the outside door – that's all.'

'Good.' Rome showed his relief, then glanced again at Joe Daisy's body and grimaced. 'So he was – well, working for you?'

'No,' said Thane stonily. 'But he had a problem, and I'd leaned on him.'

'I see.' Rome's expression showed he didn't.

'That can wait,' suggested Moss in a dry voice. 'It's

126

complicated, son.'

'Yes.' Rome obviously didn't like being called 'son', but he nodded. 'Anyone's name on this, sir?'

'Not for sure.' Thane shook his head. 'Moss can give you some probables, in case you fall over them. But none definite.'

Detective Inspector Rome went on biting his lip. Life, so far as he was concerned, was going through a distinctly bad patch. He'd been on duty since four that afternoon. He'd dealt with an attempted rape, two armed robberies and trouble on the fringe of a Right to Work demonstration. He'd come straight from coping with a seventy-three-year-old grandmother who had gone for her seventy-year-old husband with a bread knife because he was seeing another woman. Now, this corpse with the nails job made his stomach heave every time he looked that way.

'I've got men going round the neighbours,' he said wearily, bidding a mental goodbye to any lingering notion he'd be off duty by midnight. 'We might get lucky.'

'You might,' agreed Moss with minimal enthusiasm.

But doors always had to be knocked upon, people asked if they'd heard anything, noticed strangers, seen a strange car. Thane said nothing, knowing the odds were against coming up with anything, particularly in a suburban street at peak TV viewing time. He thought of the party down the street. They probably wouldn't have noticed a bomb exploding.

'You've plenty to do, I'm in the way,' he said mildly, well aware that having him around was an embarrassment to Rome. 'I'll take a turn outside, get some air. That all right?'

'Yes, sir.' Rome tried to hide his relief. 'Uh – but if Inspector Moss likes to stay – '

'Me?' Moss grinned. 'Why not, son?'

'Good move,' said Doc Williams, still waiting in the background. 'Get him in the kitchen and he can boil some tea.' The police surgeon scowled at the photographer, who was packing his gear. 'Can I have my body now, please?'

127

Rome nodded.

'Good – and I've a new story for you,' said Doc Williams, ambling forward. 'Heard about the latest Income Tax form? Just two sections – one asks how much you earn, the other tells you where to send it.' He paused, met silence, and scowled again. 'That's it – you're supposed to laugh.'

Thane retreated, knowing there would be more. Doc Williams treasured comic-book jokes, paraded them any time he had an audience, dead or alive.

The same faint drizzle of rain was still falling outside the house. He stopped in the shelter of the porch, lit a cigarette which put him one over quota, drew on it for a moment, then walked slowly down the driveway. One of the cars parked outside was strangely familiar. There were two men aboard, just sitting, apparently doing nothing.

He went nearer, frowning. A window wound down.

'Everything OK, sir?' asked the driver, smiling out at him.

'Yes.' Thane swore under his breath. It was a Crime Squad car and the two men were from the night-shift team. 'What the hell are you doing out here?'

The driver and his passenger exchanged an embarrassed glance.

'Uh – we had a surveillance job, but it finished early,' said the driver warily. 'The duty officer reckoned – well – '

'That I might need someone to hold my hand?' asked Thane acidly.

'Something like that, sir.' The man grinned at him. 'I mean, we didn't like the idea of you alone with that Strathclyde mob.'

Thane almost told them to go to hell. Then he sighed, matched the man's grin, and nodded.

'Go home,' he advised. 'Nothing much is going to happen here – not tonight.'

He returned to the porch, finished his cigarette, then stayed where he was for a spell while other police came and went. At last, he went back inside. Doc Williams was alone, just finished working on Joe Daisy's body, deliberately wiping his hands on an antiseptic-soaked rag.

'Well?' asked Thane.

'It's different from most.' The police surgeon gave an odd chuckle to himself and tossed the rag into his bag. 'Hey, did you hear the one about the – '

'Doc.' Thane stopped him with a warning growl.

'Later, then.' Doc Williams shrugged, unperturbed. 'All right, what do you think killed him?'

'He was beaten up, nailed to the floor – you're the expert,' said Thane deliberately. 'You tell me.'

'Well, it wasn't the ironmongery.' Doc Williams shook his head firmly. 'I've seen worse cases walking again inside a couple of weeks – it's been fashionable lately. The beating he took was fairly vicious, expert – but no.' He reached into a pocket and produced a small plastic evidence bag. It held two small bottle of pills. 'Here's your answer. One of Rome's people found them in the bedroom.'

Puzzled, Thane examined the bottle. Each had a regular pharmacy label: one held a batch of small white tablets; the others were larger, yellow in colour.

'The white are Digoxin, the yellow are Bumetanide,' said Doc Williams cheerfully. 'Both are used therapeutically in congestive heart failure. He had a bad heart, Colin. I can pretty well guarantee what's going to be on the autopsy report – death due to heart failure caused by shock.'

Thane moistened his lips. 'He couldn't take what they did to him?'

The police surgeon nodded.

'And if he'd had a normal heart?'

'A healthy heart,' corrected Doc Williams mildly. 'He'd be alive, needing to be patched, but in no danger.' He rubbed a hand along his chin. 'On what's here, I'd say the fact that he died gave someone a nasty surprise – if they were still around.'

That demolished one set of possibilities, left Thane trying to find substitutes. He asked the next question almost automatically.

'Time of death?'

'About 9 p.m. tonight – give or take a minute or two,' answered Doc Williams confidently.

Thane stared at him. 'Doc, suppose I told you he called my office an hour after that?'

'Then it was a small miracle,' said the police surgeon dryly. 'First, he was dead. Second, how could he reach the phone with that ironmongery holding him down?'

'Doc – ' Thane made it a plea.

'9 p.m.,' said Doc Williams, unmoved. 'Look as sick as a parrot if you want, but our friend didn't make that phone call. I'm talking body temperatures, Colin – fact.'

Thane gave up.

'Anything else?' he asked tonelessly.

'For you?' The police surgeon shook his head. 'No. Except I presume you've noticed there's no hammer lying around. Whoever came visiting must have brought his own – and taken it when he left.' He paused, frowning. 'The problem now is moving your Mr Daisy. How do we get those damned spike-nails out of the floor?'

'Try your teeth,' suggested Thane.

He was thinking of the slip of paper with the Crime Squad number, left where it had to be found beside the telephone. Put that together with the message asking him to come over, and it was as if someone had played a deliberate, cynical game with him. Had wanted him to be the one to find Joe Daisy's body.

But there was still one tiny glimmer of relief in it all. The actual call might have been made from anywhere – and the way Kate's teenage telephone chatter had blocked the line to his home number, delaying the Crime Squad passing on the message, made no difference now.

'Don't go,' protested Doc Williams as he turned to leave. 'Do you know the one about why police should go around in threes?'

'Yes,' said Thane maliciously. 'One to read, one to write, one to look after the two intellectuals – and I know the clerk of court who says it's his copyright.'

He escaped and found Moss and Rome in the kitchen. Scenes of Crime had finished there and the two men had brewed a pot of tea and were drinking from shiny black half-pint mugs.

'Like some, sir?' asked Rome politely.

Thane shook his head. 'Spoken to Doc?'

'Yes.' Rome gave a sideways glance at Phil Moss. 'And – uh – well, Inspector Moss has told me some of the background, sir.'

'The whole damned mess,' agreed Moss with brutal candour. He considered Thane for a moment. 'I'd still call this one murder.'

'Would a jury?' Thane badly wanted a cigarette and there was one left in his pack. But he resisted the temptation. 'He had a girl working for him in the video shop.'

Rome frowned. 'I thought I'd leave her till morning, first thing – when the shop opens. That's presuming she has keys.' He hesitated and glanced at Moss again. 'This is still our patch, Superintendent. But – '

'But I've suggested our ACC Crime won't object to a joint operation,' said Moss firmly. 'Meaning we stay in our corner and let the Crime Squad get on with the rest.'

Rome nodded.

'We'll keep it that way. Make it 9 a.m. at the shop.' Thane relaxed a little. 'Any luck on the door-to-doors?'

'Three complaints about the noise from that party, one old woman who thinks she heard a car leave here – but she didn't see anything.' Rome took another gulp of tea. 'That's all, Superintendent.'

'And it's time I got home,' declared Moss. 'Do I get a lift?'

There was no reason for Thane to stay. They both said goodnight to Rome and left. Outside, the other Crime Squad car had already departed. The black shape of the mortuary van had taken its place at the kerb and a few neighbours were waiting close by, anxious not to miss anything.

'They're vulturing,' said Moss acidly. He settled back in

the passenger seat of Thane's car and gave a deliberate belch as they pulled away. 'Thanks for the night out.'

'You're welcome,' said Thane dryly.

'I mean it.' Moss scowled in the soft glow from the instrument panel. 'Because I learned something. It's called advancing years – and don't laugh. Some day it'll be your turn.'

It was 1 a.m. when Thane dropped him at his boarding house. A light was still burning. Moss's landlady was a widow with her own long-term plans for her star boarder. But when Thane reached his own home it was in darkness. He went in as quietly as he could, knowing even the dog would be fast asleep.

Upstairs, the bedside alarm next to Mary was set for 7 a.m. He sighed, but left it like that, undressed, and got between the sheets.

Mary stirred.

'Colin?' she asked, half-awake.

'No, it's the milkman,' he told her mildly.

'Goodnight, milkman.' She yawned once, and went back to sleep.

Morning brought chaos. There was something wrong about the way the sun was streaming in through the bedroom window; Mary was shaking him awake, and she was almost shouting in his ear.

'What's the matter?' He hauled himself up on his elbows, blinking.

'We've slept in. There's been a damned power cut – the clock stopped.' She was still in just her nightdress, her hair tousled. 'There's no damned electricity and it's after eight – '

It was. He dressed quickly, decided to shave later, and clattered downstairs to find Mary trying to boil a kettle on a picnic stove while Tommy and Kate scurried around getting ready for school.

'There's no breakfast,' complained Tommy. He was

drinking milk and cramming a slice of bread and jam into his mouth.

'Not my department.' Thane thumbed towards Mary. 'Tell her.'

Mary swore at him. He grinned, gave her a quick kiss, and headed for the door.

It was two minutes before 9 a.m. when he brought the Ford skidding into the Crime Squad parking lot. From there, he hurried into the building and through to the Duty Room. Sandra Craig was there, on her own. She had a thermos of coffee, and any other day he'd have asked how the hell she'd acquired a plate of hot bacon sandwiches.

'Good morning – ' she began brightly.

'It isn't,' he snarled at her. 'I'm late, I've things for you to do.'

'Yes, sir.' Calmly, she produced a notebook and pencil. 'Like what?'

'A James Cocker Raddick. There's a CRO number from a few years back and he's supposed to be in Torremolinos – '

'Spain?' Sandra became more interested.

'Spain. Get hold of anything you can on him, including whether he's still out there.' He let her pencil catch up. 'You heard about last night?'

She nodded.

'Get the tape of that call, tell Joe Felix to listen, see if he can come up with any notions.' Thane paused for breath. 'Any sign of Matt Amos's laboratory report?'

'It came with despatches.' Sandra frowned at her littered desk top, then lifted the coffee flask. She gave him the stained envelope which had been underneath and waited until he had stuffed it into his pocket. 'Anything else, sir?'

'Later – not right now.' He helped himself to one of her bacon sandwiches. 'No breakfast. Anything happening here?'

'I've finished the run-down on the other phone numbers on Billy Tripp's wall.' She shook her head. 'They seem ordinary enough. His bookie, a laundry, a carry-out restaurant – all numbers he'd maybe use regularly.'

'What else?' He cut her short. But the Falcon Services number had been there too.

'A "maybe" sighting on Billy Tripp last night, and the Millside report on that break-in at Ted Douglas's – '

'Show them to Francey. Tell him I'll be at Takki Joe's, then court.'

He gestured his thanks with the bacon sandwich, then took a first bite at it as he left.

The clock on a building opposite showed 9.20 a.m. when Thane reached Takki Joe's video shop. He parked the Ford on the double yellow lines outside, reached the shop door, saw lights inside, but found the door was locked. When he tapped on the glass a uniformed woman police constable who looked young enough to be still at school appeared on the other side. When he showed his warrant card, she let him in.

Two plain-clothes officers were idly inspecting a rack of video tapes marked 'Adult Adults Only'. One quickly nudged the other, then went into the back shop, and Detective Inspector Rome appeared from there a moment later. The lanky divisional officer greeted Thane with a barely concealed frown.

'You said 9 a.m., sir,' he reminded.

'So I'm late,' agreed Thane wearily. 'We had a power cut at home – slept in.'

'Oh.' Rome's manner changed. He grinned. 'That happened to us last week, at night, with my wife stuck in the bath.' The domestic aside ended, he nodded towards the back shop. 'The girl is Carol East. I've told her about Joe Daisy but it didn't exactly break her heart. She's more worried about her job.'

'Wouldn't you be?' asked Thane.

They went through. The mousy-haired sales assistant was sitting in what had been Joe Daisy's chair. She wore her red jump-suit and the same layers of heavy eye make-up.

134

'You again.' She gave Thane a scowl of recognition. 'Trouble himself.'

'Only for some people, Carol,' said Thane mildly. He leaned against the edge of the desk, looking down at her, while Rome stayed diplomatically in the background. 'Detective Inspector Rome told you what happened.'

'He did.' Her expression didn't alter. 'If I'd known, I'd have paid for the nails.'

Thane raised an eyebrow at the cold indifference behind her words. 'Meaning?'

'He was the original dirty old man. Any time he got me in a corner he started pawing me over. He'd try it with anything female that came in.'

'But you stayed,' mused Thane.

'He paid good wages. Dirty old basket.' She scowled. 'And a job is a job, mister.'

Thane nodded. 'What about back here, the book-keeping side?'

Carol shook her head. 'My job was out front, coping with customers, nothing else. Unless it was the real hard porn they were after, then he stepped in; he kept that kind of stuff back here, locked up.'

'But you just stayed at the counter and kept your nose clean?' suggested Rome helpfully.

She nodded.

'Tell me about yesterday,' said Thane.

'You mean after you left?' She frowned, then scratched one jump-suited thigh for a moment, not looking at him, almost grinning. 'You really put a rocket under him, telling him about *The Hanging Tree*. He'd slipped up on that one, didn't know there was a pirate around.'

Thane winced and glanced at Rome, but the divisional man's face was diplomatically wooden.

'So what did he do about it?' asked Thane.

'Made one phone call after another, then went diving out for most of the afternoon. He reckoned if he could get a few copies of *The Hanging Tree*, then with the kind of custom around here he could charge what he liked – clean up.'

135

'Did he get them?'

She shrugged. 'Not that I know about. But he got back just before we closed and seemed reasonably happy about it. He said he'd reminded one or two people that they owed him favours. Asked them if they wanted to keep their noses clean – '

'Blackmail?'

'Business,' said the girl cynically. 'What's the difference?'

Thane tried to get more from her. But she maintained the same indifferent attitude in a way he was forced to believe. She didn't know names, she knew little or nothing beyond what happened in the front shop.

At last he gave up.

'We'll need a statement, Carol. We'll also need to see the firm's books, papers.' Thane glanced at Rome, who nodded before he added, 'The shop stays closed.'

'But what about me?' For the first time, the girl showed emotion. 'I'm owed wages. Do I still have a job, or – '

'I don't know,' admitted Thane. 'But there'll be a lawyer, someone to sort that out.'

'Great,' she said sarcastically. 'Thanks.'

He left her, and Rome followed him out into the front shop, where the policewoman eased quickly away from the 'Adult Adults Only' rack.

'I can cope with here, sir,' said Rome slowly. 'Except – well, what am I looking for?'

'That depends on what you turn up,' Thane told him bleakly. 'People like Joe Daisy don't keep diaries.'

'So it could be a waste of time.' Rome nodded his acceptance. 'It's been pretty much that way at his house – he left nothing lying around. The rest is the same – no fingerprints; the rope they used could be bought anywhere; the gag was an old rag.' He chewed his lip. 'I reckon the people who hit him even brought their own hammer and nails, punishment squad style.'

It happened. According to the underworld's twisted edicts, an ideal way to deal with a potential nuisance was to terrify him into keeping quiet. One savage lesson, with word of what had happened carefully spread around, would also close other mouths.

'It wasn't your fault,' said Rome unexpectedly. He flushed. 'I mean – '

Thane nodded. But Joe Daisy's greed had made him plunge in recklessly because of what he'd learned. The rest Thane could guess. Before he died, the video shop owner had admitted his tenuous link with the Crime Squad. His attackers had found that slip of paper; then, even with a dead man on their hands, someone's macabre sense of humour had taken over.

Or had it been meant as an additional warning?

He saw the time on the clock across the street, winced, and gave up speculating.

'Best of luck,' he told Rome. 'I'm due in court.'

The city's Justiciary Buildings were old, grey, soot-stained and located close to the banks of the River Clyde. There had been a time when a High Court sitting amounted to a very special happening two or three times in a year.

In those days the Law Lords arrived with a military escort of cavalry. State trumpeters sounded fanfares, magistrates paraded with their gold chains of office, and a clergyman opened the proceedings with prayer then waited in the wings to be available if anyone was sentenced to death. Long queues always formed for seats in the public gallery, the best free entertainment in town. The press benches were full.

Now, press and public interest had waned unless a really major trial was under way. The High Court's turnover of cases had increased until they had become almost a regular part of the city scene. Economy cuts had wiped out most of the surrounding pomp. The famous black cap, which meant death, was languishing dusty and unused in a cupboard somewhere.

But the High Court could still be an awesome place, and

its witness box could be one of the loneliest spots in the world. In the two courtrooms, North and South, a judge in ermine-trimmed robes of white and crimson silk ruled supreme, as a Lord of Justiciary.

Criminal and cop alike, no one treated the High Court lightly.

Colin Thane got there with minutes to spare before the start of the day's hearing. On the way, he'd stopped to buy a disposable razor and a tube of shaving cream. Conscious of the heavy stubble on his face, he had his name ticked on the list of the day's witnesses for the North Court, then headed for the nearest washroom. When he emerged, smooth-jowled again, he took a seat in the crowded witnesses' waiting-room.

The case had been running more than a week and his evidence was going to be almost incidental. The small, meek-mannered man in the dock was an accountant who had creamed more than £200,000 from his firm. Not one penny of it had been found – which could be why the little accountant seemed to be sitting back and enjoying the whole affair.

The Crime Squad's involvement and the fact that Thane had arrested him was incidental. They'd been at Prestwick International Airport looking for someone else. The accountant had fallen into their laps as he tried to board a North West Orient flight for Boston.

He hadn't given any trouble. It had been a very civilized arrest.

Once the first few of the day's witnesses had been called, Thane found enough elbow room to take out the envelope containing Matt Amos's laboratory report. He lit a cigarette in self-defence against the stale tobacco smoke atmosphere, opened the several sheets of closely typed report, and began reading.

It took time. He finished the last page, went back to the beginning, and read it again.

Matt Amos had done his usual thorough job. Some of his report, relating to the way Ted Douglas had died, was only of interest to the Donaldhill team handling the murder case against the post-office hold-up team.

But then he came to 'other traces' found on Douglas's clothing, shoes and motor-cycle. Some he dismissed as incidental: the candle grease on his clothing and the horse hairs found on both clothes and motor-cycle were listed without comment.

That was followed by a section headed 'grit and sediments':

Grit and sediments found on the subject's shoes and embedded in the wheel treads were accompanied by flecks of straw chaff. Combined with the horse hairs mentioned earlier, this might point to a stable or similar building.

Grit and sediment included a sandwiched layer of sandy material. Laboratory examination established that this consists of three main substances, i.e. a quartz sand, a white nullipore (coralline) sand, and silicified wood grains.

These materials are of coastal shoreline as distinct from fresh-water origin. They are not commonly found together in the proportions identified. Reference then made to the National Institute for Soil Research, Aberdeen.

The Institute had come back with a list of eighteen stretches of beach where the quartz, nullipore and silicified wood make-up of Matt Amos's samples could be matched. Three were distant, tiny islands in the Hebrides and some others Thane mentally dismissed as being too far away.

He scowled at what was left. On the one hand, Matt Amos had ruled out Loch Lomond. On the other, the Aberdeen unit now gave a choice scattered round the West of Scotland's jagged, sea-loch-torn coastline. There were seven widely separated locations in that area, the smallest a two-mile stretch of shore and the largest a pocketed area of coast almost twenty miles long.

And somewhere along one of them there might be an old stable.

'Got a problem?' asked the man sitting next to him, and

grinned. 'You look the way I feel when I read my bank statement.'

Thane recognized the man. He'd been on duty at the airport's Passport Control desk.

'I asked for help with something,' Thane told him. 'I just got it.'

Puzzled, the man shrugged, then went back to dozing in his chair.

It was noon before Thane's turn came to give evidence. All he had to say, the formal evidence of arrest, took about three minutes. The judge on the bench seemed half asleep, and the accountant's defence counsel simply shook his head when asked if he wanted to cross-examine.

Excused further attendance, he left the witness box. The next witness being called was an airport police inspector, who would tell the same story and get the same treatment. But Scottish law still insisted that two witnesses were required to establish fact in all but a very few circumstances.

Clear of the courtroom, Thane started for the exit doors. A voice called his name, and, when he turned, Doc Williams was ambling towards him across the marble-pillared hallway.

'I've been waiting for you,' said the police surgeon. He thumbed over his shoulder. 'I'm on the South Court list – an attempted rape. I thought you'd like to know I've got the Joe Daisy autopsy result.'

'Already?' Thane showed his surprise.

'The pathology mob has a golf match this afternoon,' said Doc Williams dryly. 'When golf is at stake, their butcher knives work flat out. I was right – Daisy's heart was a disaster area. He knew it. His family doctor says Daisy landed up in an intensive care ward more than once.'

'Some people would still call it murder,' said Thane.

'Any half-competent defence counsel would go through that like a bulldozer,' declared Doc Williams. 'Hey, I heard a new story from one of the mortuary attendants. There

140

was this rabbit – '

'Not now, Doc.' Thane shook his head firmly.

The police surgeon sighed. 'You're missing a laugh, my friend. And you look like you could use one.'

A troop of mounted police was clattering out past the Police Training Area sign when Thane drove up. He stopped to let the bobbing line of riders pass, then set the Ford moving again up the driveway. He left the car in the parking area and went into the Crime Squad building.

Maggie Fyffe was at the reception desk. She grinned at him.

'Safe to talk to you yet?' she asked.

'Why shouldn't it be?'

She shrugged. 'From what I heard, you came and went this morning all bristles and bad temper.'

'That?' Thane nodded ruefully. 'Domestic disaster, Maggie – we had a power cut, slept in.'

'The end of the world follows shortly.' She chuckled. 'It's been happening all over. I've a cousin with the Electricity Board. He says they've one power station withdrawn for maintenance and another big one has gone sick. If you live near a hospital or something like that, they'll leave you alone. Otherwise, it's the luck of the draw.'

'Maggie.' Thane stared at her. 'These power cuts – how long have they been going on?'

'About a week. Selective load-shedding, they call it. Never hit the same place twice, so they'll have fewer moans.'

'Thanks.' A wild probability came into his mind, one outrageous enough to be possible. 'Is Francey in?'

'Somewhere.' She frowned. 'He got back about half an hour ago – said he'd wait for you, that he had a Federation problem to sort out. Sandra and Joe Felix left to get lunch – said they'd be straight back.'

He nodded. 'Do me a couple of favours. Find Francey, and I could use something to eat.'

He went through to his office, hung his sheepskin on its hook, then lifted the telephone receiver and called the Strathclyde laboratory. It took a moment or two to get hold of Matt Amos, but at last he came on the line.

'I'm in the middle of my lunch,' complained Amos. 'Look, if it's about the Douglas report, I did my best.'

'And gave me half of Scotland to worry about,' agreed Thane sarcastically. 'Matt, there was a bundle of stuff sent in yesterday – all tagged Billy Tripp.'

'Clothes, shoes – we've got them,' confirmed Amos. 'They're getting the same treatment as Douglas's things. We're not finished yet, but we've got more of that sand.'

'I want to know about candle grease.'

There was a grunt, then silence for a moment at the other end of the line.

'On Tripp's stuff?' Amos was doubtful. 'None I know about. I'll call you back.'

Thane hung up, knowing he could only wait.

Once again, a small heap of notes and messages had built up on his desk. He sorted through them quickly, discarding the routine variety.

That brought the rest down to three telephone messages and two brief, typewritten report sheets. Phil Moss had called but had left no message except that it wasn't important. John La Mont had telephoned, with word that *The Hanging Tree* was apparently turning up in more video shops in different parts of England. He'd call again later. The third phone message brought a smile to his lips. It was from Mary. Electricity had returned to the Thane household at 10 a.m. and he'd have to reset the time control on the central heating when he got home.

That left the two report sheets. The first, apologetic, was from the Scenes of Crime team at Millside Divison: they'd been busy, they were still catching up. All they'd got from the break-in at Ted Douglas's home was a photograph of one of the footprints left in the white frost outside the lock-up garage. It wasn't a particularly good photograph, but they'd send on a copy. There were no fingerprints or other apparent latents left by the raiders.

The second was shorter. The bullet fired at him in Billy Tripp's house had been recovered. Ballistic examination identified it as .38 calibre, probably from a Colt revolver.

Thane set the reports aside as he heard a light double-knock on his door. It opened and Francey Dunbar ambled in.

'From Maggie,' said his sergeant, dumping a plate of sandwiches and a mug of coffee in front of him. 'Cheese and pickles – she'll bill you later.'

Thane waved him towards a chair and Dunbar settled into it with a contented sigh. He wore a faded denim jacket over a grey wool sweater and baggy serge trousers, which were held at the waist by a broad, metal-studded belt. His feet were in badly scuffed working boots.

'Been out socializing?' asked Thane mildly, reading the signs. 'Or is that Police Federation business?'

'The Federation thing is about overtime pay, sir.' Dunbar's wide, humorous mouth shaped a grin. 'You know the old saying: crime doesn't pay enough.'

'My heart bleeds,' said Thane sourly. He indicated Dunbar's clothing. 'Been prowling?'

'You knew Billy Tripp had been sighted, sir?'

'Yes.' Thane tried one of the sandwiches. The cheese was cut thick, the pickles could have been laid on with a trowel. He munched for a moment. 'Sandra told me. Well?'

'One of the night-shift team got the tip – Billy Tripp was on the move around dockland last night. I thought I'd check it out.'

Thane nodded. Like any city, Glasgow's fading dockland area was a mixture of warehouses, slums and more slums, with a warren of back streets to match.

'And?'

'A couple of things, sir.' Dunbar ran a hand through his dark, unruly hair. 'The word is he wasn't alone, and he had wheels – big and expensive, probably a BMW. The two men with him stayed aboard, and Tripp did the legwork.'

'What kind?'

Dunbar shook his head. 'Like he was trying to find people.' He grimaced. 'He named a few names, but nobody would say who – just that they were heavies. He tried a couple of billiard halls and about half a dozen bars.'

'Which sounds like recruiting.' Thane contemplated the half-eaten sandwich in his hand. 'What about the men in the car?'

'Nobody got that curious,' said Dunbar dryly.

Thane sighed. 'You said there were a couple of things. What's the other?'

'Separate, from one of the Donaldhill CID mob.' Dunbar eyed him cautiously. 'Billy Tripp sometimes drives a van, legit., as a casual.'

'Whose van?' asked Thane softly.

'They didn't know. They've still got mother and father Tripp locked up and father Tripp let it slip – then clammed up.' Dunbar shifted in his chair. 'I'd like to have another sniff around dockland this afternoon, sir.'

Thane raised an eyebrow. 'Why?'

'A notion mainly, sir.' Dunbar grinned at him. 'He's been there, he might turn up again.'

'That's all?' Thane sensed it wasn't.

'Well – ' Dunbar sucked his thin straggle of moustache for a moment ' – I got it from a retired villain who doesn't care who buys the drinks. Our friend the Glassman has been around the same area recently, with Billy Tripp always two paces behind. Dockland isn't the Glassman's usual territory.'

'So he must have a good reason to be there.' Thane nodded a thoughtful agreement. 'Go ahead, try again. But take someone with you.'

'No thanks.' Dunbar shook his head. 'I'd be happier on my own. Down there, two strangers together might as well have a label round their necks that says "Cops".'

He was right, and Thane knew that his sergeant had a knack of blending into most backgrounds.

'All right,' he agreed slowly. 'But go carefully, stay in touch – and back off if there's trouble.' He reached for another sandwich. 'The Federation needs you, even if I don't.'

'Sir.' Dunbar chuckled, got to his feet, and left.

Fifteen minutes later, when Sandra Craig and Joe Felix arrived, the sandwiches and coffee were finished and Thane had a large-scale map of the West of Scotland spread across his desk. He'd shaded in each stretch of coastline mentioned in the list Matt Amos had obtained from the Soil Research Institute and the patchwork result made unhappy viewing.

'Going somewhere, sir?' asked Sandra in an interested voice. She came over, a folder clutched in one hand, frowned at the map, then glanced back at Felix. 'Fancy some travel, Joe?'

'Depends who's driving,' said Felix amiably.

'That can wait.' Thane swept the map to one side. 'Joe, you listened to that voice tape from last night?'

'Heard it, played around with it,' agreed Felix laconically. 'There's some muffling, which can mean a handkerchief over the mouthpiece. The phone probably wasn't in a house. My guess would be a public call-box – there's some trace of traffic noise now down in the background.' He shaped a grimace. 'The voice is ordinary enough – male, Scottish, Glasgow accent.'

'Anything more?'

'Not there.' Felix shook his head. 'I tried out that CB channel code you got from Douglas's wallet – it works all right. Then there was a phone call from La Mont, but I left you a note about it.'

'Yes.' Thane eyed him deliberately. 'You don't like La Mont. Why?'

Felix coloured. 'He talks a lot.'

'But?'

'He may have read a few books, he knows the technical chat, but he's no great video expert.' Felix moistened his lips unhappily. 'Look, sir, he says you can't trace a video

145

tape – a blank one – back to its manufacturing source. You can, if you've the right equipment. He says – ' he stopped and shrugged awkwardly. 'Hell, it doesn't matter.'

'Finish it,' ordered Thane.

Felix scowled. 'As far as he's concerned, everything is London – the pirate tapes of *The Hanging Tree* come from London, they're being made around London, the only operators who matter are down there. He says it, we're supposed to accept. I asked him to prove it, that's all. He couldn't.'

Thane sighed. 'So what do you think?'

'That there are some people you like, some you don't,' said Felix gloomily. 'Sorry, sir.'

'Good relations always help,' said Thane wryly. 'Sandra, your turn. How far have you got with Jimbo Raddick?'

'He still has that bar in Torremolinos,' she said crisply. 'But he's not there – not according to the Spanish police.'

Thane stiffened. 'They're sure?'

'That's what the Interpol telex says.' She didn't try to hide the satisfaction in her voice. 'Our James Cocker Raddick has been the original absentee landlord lately. He turns up for a few days then disappears for weeks; the Spanish believe he's spending the rest of his time over here.'

The telephone rang. Thane ignored it, staring at her. 'What else?'

'Just what's in his file, sir. Home video wasn't really part of the scene when he got out for Spain – but he has strong connections with some of the dockland rackets, was suspected of handling stolen shipments from there.' She paused deliberately, 'There's a mention that when it came to cars he usually drove a BMW.'

'Does Francey know?'

She nodded.

The telephone was still ringing. Thane lifted the receiver, thinking quickly. If Jimbo Raddick was back, if he was using the Glassman as an enforcer, if he'd recruited some of his old contacts, the pirate video racket could have been made for him – just as the way Joe Daisy had been tormented till he died fitted the Glassman's style.

Maybe, at last, he could stop chasing shadows.

He answered the call.

'You took long enough, damn you,' said Matt Amos indignantly from the other end of the line. 'Still want to know about your candle grease?'

'More than ever,' Thane told him.

'You're out of luck,' said Amos flatly. 'No trace of candle grease on Tripp's stuff.' Then he chuckled. 'But I think I know what you've got in mind. Would you settle for battery acid? There are stains down the front of a jersey, a pair of trousers, and on the same shoes which had the sand. It's like he'd been lugging spare batteries around in a hurry, in the dark, and they spilled.'

'Thanks, Matt.' Thane added a silent prayer of thanks that Billy Tripp had left his work clothes behind when he made his hole-in-the-wall escape. 'I owe you again.'

'Everybody does,' said Amos. 'And I'll give you another tip. If Doc Williams tries to tell you his rabbit joke, run for cover. It's the worst yet.'

'I'll remember,' promised Thane, and hung up.

Sandra and Felix were watching him. He drew a deep breath, pulled the map towards him, and indicated the shaded areas.

'Sandra, your job: one of these areas should have had a power cut in the last few days. Find out which.'

Sandra Craig looked puzzled. 'Why, sir?'

'Because it looks like Ted Douglas and his pal Tripp had problems that way. Maybe the last time Douglas was out of town.' He saw she was still clutching the folder. 'What's in that?'

'Photographs.' She opened the folder, which held a thick bundle of prints, and spread a set of three in front of him. 'Raddick, Martin Tuce the Glassman, and Billy Tripp – I ordered a batch of each.'

Thane looked down at the three faces, each photograph a police record shot, harshly lit, the photographer not giving a damn about his subject's mood.

Jimbo Raddick, his face fat with good living, his greying hair smartly cut, had been caught with a slight disparaging smile twisting his lips. Next to him, the photograph of the Glassman showed a thin-featured individual with mousy hair, prominent eyes, and a thin, tight mouth. Then Billy Tripp, by far the youngest of the trio, with his sullen face, flattened nose and short dark hair.

They were out there, somewhere.

But who else was sheltering behind them?

He drew a deep breath, knowing what he had to do. Picking up the set of photographs, he slipped them into a pocket.

'You and I, Joe,' he told Felix, 'are going to Falcon Services. Sandra – '

'Sir?'

'If Francey calls in, contact me – no delays.'

She understood and looked troubled.

But she nodded.

6

The afternoon was grey, with a wind blustering from the west in a way that sent leaves scattering and overhead wires quivering. Thane was driving, the weather matched his mood, and Joe Felix was content to doze most of the way.

They reached East Kilbride before 3 p.m. and arrived at the Falcon Services depot a few minutes later. Driving into the depot yard, Thane parked beside an old but immaculate Volvo coupé. It was sand-coloured, the interior seemed filled with fishing gear, and a long, thin, whip-like radio aerial sat exactly centred on the roof.

'That's Citizens' Band equipment,' murmured Felix as they left the Ford. 'Magnetic mount antenna – ' he gave another interested, slightly puzzled glance at the aerial ' – could be home-made. But someone knows what he's doing.'

'Let's hope we do,' said Thane grimly. A man was coming across the yard from the loading bay area, where three vans with the Falcon Services crest were being worked on. He watched the man head towards them, then added, 'Keep everything happy – for now, anyway.'

Felix's broad face grinned and he nodded.

'Police, aren't you?' said the man, reaching them. He frowned at Thane. 'You were here last time – with the girl.'

'That's right,' agreed Thane easily.

'Like to talk to you, then.' The man was in his thirties, stockily built, and wore overalls. Shoving his hands in his pockets, a fresh gust of wind clutching at his long, fair hair, he looked them over with suspicion. 'My lads want to know what's goin' on. I'm here to find out – I'm Bert

149

O'Connell, the shop steward here.'

'We've got one of those too,' murmured Felix.

'Ignore him,' said Thane dryly. 'What's the problem, Mr O'Connell?'

'I told you.' O'Connell thumbed over his shoulder towards the loading bay. 'We work here, right? The bosses told us it was to do with that kid Douglas, that he'd maybe been involved in something crooked.'

'That's how it looks,' agreed Thane. He waited while the union man muttered a curse and used a hand to brush some of that long, fair hair away from his eyes. 'That's also why we're back. You knew Ted Douglas?'

'He was a casual.' O'Connell shrugged. 'The firm hires them; we don't have to like them. They should get rid of the casuals, hire a few more full-timers.'

'Tried telling that to management?' queried Thane.

'A few times.' O'Connell pursed his lips. 'They wouldn't wear the idea – the Garrison woman told us it would cost more. That was that. These days, if you've a job and the pay is reasonable, you don't push your luck. Say "industrial action" an' most of my lads would run for cover.'

'Know anyone named Billy Tripp?' asked Thane mildly.

The man frowned then nodded. 'He's another casual – haven't seen him around for a while.'

Thane took the three photographs from his pocket, holding them with both hands as the wind tried to snatch them.

'Which?'

'The young one.' O'Connell tapped Billy Tripp's photograph with a grimy fingernail.

'How about the other two?'

'No, sorry.' O'Connell paused at the Glassman's photograph. 'But the one in the middle looks nasty.'

'He is,' said Thane flatly.

'Is that the lot?'

'Yes – and thanks for your help.'

'Right, then.' The man sounded disappointed. 'So I tell

my lads it's a couple o' the casuals in trouble on the outside?'

'That's about right,' agreed Joe Felix cheerfully. He nodded towards the Volvo. 'Who owns the Jodrell Bank rig?'

'The boss's brother-in-law.' O'Connell thawed a little. 'He's all right – reasonable, even. But she can be a hard bitch, believe me.'

Hands back in his pockets, he headed back towards the loading bay.

Skirting round the Volvo, pushing their way in through the main door of the Falcon building, Thane and Felix reached the reception counter. The same girl who had greeted Thane on his previous visit came forward with the same slightly nervous smile.

'Sorry, Superintendent,' she began. 'Mrs Garrison is out and – '

'Jonathan Garrison will do,' Thane told her.

She hesitated. 'I'll see if he's in.'

'He'd better be.' Joe Felix gave her a friendly wink. 'His car's outside, lassie.'

The girl giggled and used an internal phone. Then she came back and led them through a corridor towards the rear of the building.

Garrison's office was a back room, only half the size of the one occupied by his sister-in-law. When their guide showed Thane and Felix in, he stayed seated behind his desk.

'Thank you, Jean.' He gave a slight smile of dismissal, waited until she had gone and the door was closed, then let the smile fade. He frowned at his visitors through his spectacles and his voice became frosty. 'What is it this time, Superintendent?'

'A problem, Mr Garrison.' Thane made it a flat, unemotional statement of fact. 'One we're going to have to talk about.'

'I see.' The thin, balding figure in the patched tweed jacket stiffened a little. 'Will it take long?'

'Probably not.' There was only one spare chair. Seeing there would be no invitation, Thane took it and sat down. Joe Felix stayed where he was.

Most of one wall of the room was occupied by a large delivery-schedules chart. The furnishings were basic and the shade on the overhead light was cracked. But everything, down to the papers on Garrison's desk, was scrupulously ordered. Thane had the feeling that the man could have told him the number of paper-clips in his desk-tidy.

'I'd like you to explain something.' Thane produced Billy Tripp's photograph from his pocket and laid it on the desk, facing Garrison. 'Do you know this man?'

'I – ' Garrison chewed briefly on his upper lip. 'Yes, I might.'

'You should,' Thane said wearily. 'Isn't he Billy Tripp, one of your casual drivers?'

'Yes.' Garrison flushed. 'You're right – I'm sorry.'

'And wasn't it Tripp who brought Ted Douglas here, looking for work?'

'I'm not sure.' Garrison gestured vaguely. 'It could have been that way. Young Douglas just applied in the normal fashion.'

Thane shrugged. 'But they knew each other?'

'I believe so. It didn't concern – ' Garrison stopped and stiffened, looking past Thane. 'You! Don't touch that!'

'Sorry.' Joe Felix nodded amiably.

He had gone towards a shelf in one corner of the room and was examining a small glass sculpture. It was a model of an angler, complete with rod and line, the rod bent, and a large hooked fish rising from a rippling base.

'It's fragile.' Garrison moistened his lips as Felix stepped back. 'I – well, I warn everybody.'

'We saw the fishing gear in your car,' said Thane. He relaxed back in his chair and smiled at the man. 'I heard golf was your game.'

'It was – for a time.' Garrison gave a short, forced laugh. 'Then I gave it up, when I gave up some other things. A rod and line is more relaxing. I enjoy being on my own.'

152

Pausing, he glanced at his wrist-watch. 'That's my pro-gramme, leaving here as soon as I can. Tomorrow is Friday and I'm due some time off, so I'm adding it on to the weekend. I'll have three full days fishing.'

Felix grinned. 'I've got a trout rod at home. When I was a kid, I used to tie my own flies.' He paused then asked casually, 'Where are you heading?'

'Somewhere north – I'll see how conditions are.' Garri-son's manner changed again and he faced Thane. 'Why these questions about Tripp?'

'We're looking for him,' said Thane dryly. 'For the same reasons we're interested in what Ted Douglas was doing.' He tapped the photograph lying between them. 'How much do you know about your casual workers?'

'Only what they choose to tell us. My interest is whether they do the job,' Garrison answered him stiffly. 'I knew Tripp had been in some trouble in the past, in prison. He told me.'

'You make a habit of hiring ex-prisoners?' asked Thane deliberately.

'I don't look for them,' snapped Garrison. He removed his spectacles and began polishing their lenses with a handker-chief, his fingers shaking a little. 'Anyone can have a bad experience and put it behind them.'

'I know that,' said Thane wearily. 'But there are a couple of things you're going to have to do, Mr Garrison. I want a full list of your casual drivers – names, addresses, how you contact them. Then I want a list of every delivery job assigned to Douglas or Tripp over the past three months.'

'You – ' Garrison froze for a moment, then replaced his spectacles and stared at Thane. 'You're serious?'

Thane nodded

'Suppose I refuse?'

'Then I'd expect a good reason,' said Thane bluntly. 'And you'd better have a good lawyer.'

Garrison swallowed, sat silent for a moment, then gave a reluctant nod.

'I'll have the main office give you the list of casuals. But the deliveries – no, that's impossible. I'm sorry.'

Thane raised an eyebrow. 'You don't keep records?'

'I don't mean that.' Garrison got to his feet. 'But it would take time, days – '

'And you're going fishing,' murmured Thane. He shrugged, picked up the photograph, and put it in his pocket. 'We won't spoil your weekend. The delivery list can wait.'

The names could be important. The delivery lists were unlikely to matter, and he wasn't sure how far he wanted to push Garrison – how much more the thin, bald figure could take without some kind of an explosion. For the moment, that was the last thing Thane wanted.

Garrison was at the door of his room, standing impatiently. Thane rose, signalled Felix, and they followed the man out into the corridor.

There was a waiting-room separated from the main office by a thin partition. Garrison installed them there, then left the door open while he went over and talked to one of the secretaries. He returned and looked in.

'It'll take a few minutes,' he said curtly.

The door closed on them.

There were the usual old magazines in the waiting-room. They settled down, thumbed at the magazines, and the minutes crept past. Thane could hear typewriters rattling in the office. Telephones rang and were answered. But no one came near them. Twice he checked his wrist-watch, then glanced at Joe Felix, who was reading.

At last, patience exhausted, he got to his feet. Before he could get to the door, it opened and the same secretary he'd seen Garrison with came in.

'I'm sorry I took so long, Superintendent.' She held out a folded sheet of paper. 'This is what you wanted.'

He took the paper, opened it out, and scanned the typewritten column of names. There were more than he'd expected, each with an address, most with a telephone number.

'Thank you,' he said.

'You're welcome.' The secretary, a pleasant-faced

brunette in her twenties, hesitated awkwardly. 'I – Mr Garrison said I was to tell you he couldn't wait.'

Thane stared at her, then went over to the window and looked out.

Garrison's car was gone.

'He said you'd understand,' said the girl weakly.

Joe Felix gave a cynical grunt.

'It doesn't matter,' said Thane wryly.

Another car was driving in, another Volvo, a large red station-wagon. It parked and he watched Alexis Garrison get out from behind the wheel, grab at the loose edges of her coat, then hurry into the building.

He pushed past the startled secretary and met Alexis Garrison in the corridor.

'Hello, Colin.' She gave him a smile, her blue eyes twinkling. 'You'll need to stop walking all over my brother-in-law every time you meet.'

'You've seen him?' he asked.

Alexis Garrison chuckled and smoothed back some of her wind-blown hair.

'Seen him? He was driving out of here like someone was chasing him – but he stopped when he saw my car.' She frowned a little. 'I got this garbled story about another of our drivers, police brutality, and that the end of the world was at hand. Then he was off again. What's going on?'

'I asked for some help,' said Thane woodenly.

'Great.' She looked past him. Joe Felix and the secretary were both standing listening. 'I want a moment with you anyway – alone.'

Taking Thane's arm, she guided him past their audience, back into the waiting-room, and closed the door.

'Well?' she asked in a sigh. 'What really happened?'

Thane shrugged. 'I told you Ted Douglas was into something crooked. We've tied in another of your casuals, Billy Tripp.'

'I know him.' There was more impatience than surprise in her voice. 'This "something crooked" – you hinted at drugs before, and I still don't believe it. What's the real reason?'

He shook his head. 'There's getting to be a list, maybe including murder.'

She stared at him, then moistened her lips with the tip of her tongue.

'You mean that?' Her voice was surprisingly steady.

Thane nodded.

'Damn. Will – does Falcon have to be involved?' Alexis paused and pursed her lips. 'No, you can't answer that. That's the way it used to be, any time I asked an awkward one.'

'Every time,' said Thane gravely.

'Damn,' she said again, then grimaced. 'I'm still glad it's you. And there's that other reason why I wanted to see you – it was about this evening.'

'I can still make it,' declared Thane warily.

'But I can't – not for eight. I was going to phone.' She laid a hand on his arm. 'Colin, it's a leftover from the meeting I had last night. Business – the kind I can't ignore. But – well, how about still looking in, for a quick drink? If you made it around seven – '

'And the curfew tolls at eight?' Thane nodded. 'I'll be there.'

He opened the waiting-room door and they went out. Joe Felix and the secretary were still in the corridor.

'Thank you, Superintendent,' said Alexis Garrison briskly. 'I'm glad we sorted out that difficulty.'

Then she turned and left them.

'Do I ask what that was all about?' queried Joe Felix with a dry edge of mischief in his voice.

It was several minutes later. East Kilbride was behind them and the Glasgow skyline was growing near.

Thane fed the Ford more accelerator, overtook two large trucks lumbering in convoy, then let the car ease back into the traffic flow.

'Meaning what?' he asked.

'You and that woman.' Twenty years' service and no particular ambitions beyond his specialist rating meant that Joe Felix was liable to say nothing or come out with the totally unexpected. 'I got the feeling you knew her from somewhere.'

'Sometime,' corrected Thane.

'Sir.' Felix gave a grin and considered the traffic ahead for a moment. 'Reasonable mileage but good bodywork – this car, I mean.'

'And what else?' Thane gave him a brief, caustic glance.

'I still don't like the set-up back there.' Felix scowled and rubbed a hand along his chin. 'That list of names we got from Garrison – suppose we find a few more like Billy Tripp crawling out of the woodwork?'

'Then we haul them in, if we can find them,' said Thane dryly. 'But more likely they've had time to get far away.'

'Ever do any fishing, sir?'

'Not a lot.' Millside Division had run an annual angling outing. Thane remembered a bus, several crates of beer, and a late-night sing-song. 'Why?'

Felix sighed. 'The fishing gear I saw in Garrison's car was heavy tackle, for sea angling. He didn't mention it, but I thought you'd like to know.'

'Thanks,' said Thane bitterly.

They were in the city, less than a mile from base, when the car's radio muttered their call-sign. Felix scooped up the microphone, answered, and Crime Squad Control came back.

'From DS Dunbar. A thirteen forty-three, his location Riverview Street at Anstruther Lane. No back-up requested meantime.'

Thane set the speedometer needle climbing, mentally plotting the most direct route. Francey Dunbar wasn't in an emergency situation, but he wanted assistance, wanted it soon, and was having to leave his vehicle.

'What's Francey driving?' he asked, as Felix finished an acknowledgement.

'Sandra's VW.' Felix grabbed for support and blinked as they cut a corner in a way that made the Ford's tyres squeal. 'She created hell about it, but he said it blended best – and the transport boys are still patching his Mini.'

Thane grunted and concentrated on the road.

Despite its name, Riverview Street didn't feature in the tourist guides. There were one or two places along its winding length where it was possible to get a glimpse of a greasy stretch of the River Clyde – if anyone was determined enough to climb to a rooftop when the visibility was good.

The truth was a derelict dockland road, a mix of crumbling buildings, abandoned warehouses and weed-choked gap sites. There were beds by the night in a Salvation Army hostel for women. There were two scrap-metal yards, plus a scatter of other occupants from down-and-outs and runaways to businesses that could open one month and vanish the next. The gap sites were useful places where stolen cars were abandoned or wandering teenagers went glue-sniffing. Occasionally a vagrant would be found dead and the cops who discovered him simply hoped he wasn't too ripe.

Riverview Street, in short, had a role to play.

Colin Thane slowed the Ford to a respectable crawl when they reached the street. Bouncing over the pot-holed surface, they passed one of the scrap-yards and the women's hostel, scattered a handful of stray dogs, investigating something animal and dead, and then saw where the Volkswagen was parked.

It was empty. They drew in behind it, got out, and found the doors were locked.

Thane looked around. Anstruther Lane was almost directly across the street.

'Sir.' Felix nudged him.

Two young boys, thin-faced and sharp-eyed, were sheltering from the blustery wind in a doorway. They were about ten years old, wore grubby denims and old baseball boots, and one of them was grinning.

'Lookin' for someone, mister?' asked the tallest carelessly as Thane went over.

'Maybe.' Thane nodded towards the Volkswagen. 'The driver – know where he went?'

'You're cops, aren't you?' asked the other. He had the face of a young angel, but the tell-tale sores around his upper lip spelled solvent-sniffing sessions. 'You look like cops.'

'That's right, son,' said Joe Felix, coming round on the other side to cut off any escape. 'Nasty ones. So where did he go?'

'We're thinkin',' said the tallest. He had carrot-red hair, cut short against his skull. He exchanged a glance with his companion. 'Want your car watched, mister? We'll keep it safe, cost you half a note, that's all.'

Thane glanced back at the Volkswagen. Both boys sniggered. The car was unmarked.

'He paid,' confirmed the young angel. 'Left a message for you too.'

Silently, Thane dug into his pocket and gave them some change.

'Well?'

'He went up the lane; we'd to tell you he had to see a man about some glass.' Thin shoulders shaped an imitation of a shrug. 'Daft.'

Joe Felix swore under his breath.

'Anyone else go up there?' demanded Thane.

'Just a bloke in a van,' said the youngster with minimal interest.

'Tell Control.' Thane tossed the Ford's keys to Felix. 'I want local back-up on standby.'

He crossed the road and plunged into the lane, moving at a fast jog-trot. The buildings on either side were derelict or abandoned, windows devoid of glass, doorways bricked up or black, empty holes.

The lane took a turn and became a funnel for the wind. A

gust sent pieces of old cardboard cartons and torn plastic cartwheeling towards him, and gritty dust stung his eyes. Round another turn and he stopped, tight-lipped, looking at another long, debris-littered but otherwise empty stretch of the same.

Yet Francey Dunbar was there somewhere, in search of the Glassman.

'You're too late,' croaked a voice that seemed to come out of thin air. 'Aye, they're gone.'

Startled, he swung round. Something moved inside the dilapidated remains of a wooden packing case. Then an old woman stuck her head out. She was wearing several ragged coats, one on top of the other, the outer layer fastened round her by a piece of string. She had a greasy scarf round her head, her feet were in cut-down rubber boots, and both blackened hands gripped a bulging, grubby plastic bag.

'What the hell are you doing in there, ma?' he asked sharply.

She showed her gums in a grin which twisted her wrinkled face. 'This is my wee house, son. Temp – ' she frowned and tried again ' – temporararily, like.' Pleased at herself, she nodded. 'But they've gone, like.'

'Who've gone ma?' Thane spoke with an iron, desperate patience. 'What happened?'

'The shouts an' everything.' She shifted her feet inside the packing case and an empty wine bottle rolled into view. 'Woke me up, they did, noisy devils – an' I don't care if they're friends of yours. Then it's all banging doors and starting engines – and they're away.'

'In a van?'

'There was a car too, son.' She shivered and huddled deeper into her coats, her voice suddenly wistful. 'A big car – nice big seats. It would cost money, a car like that.'

'Where from, ma?' He was conscious of Joe Felix panting up and joining them, but didn't look round. 'You remember that, don't you?'

'Along there.' She nodded further down the lane. 'Those

big green doors – '

They started running. Her voice called after them.

'An' you tell them to make less noise next time, you hear me?'

The green doors, vehicle width, were in a high brick wall topped by rusting strands of barbed wire. They lay open, giving a view of a small warehouse yard. Littered with debris, the rear of the compound was a long, low, single-storey building as dilapidated as its surroundings.

Nothing moved.

They went in carefully, Joe Felix whistling softly through his teeth. He had drawn his personal substitute for a baton, a stubby length of lead piping with a rope wrist-loop attached to one end. A ned had tried to beat his head in with it once. He'd carried it, totally illegally, ever since.

They found Francey Dunbar near the entrance to the building, one foot protuding from a sheet of corrugated iron which had been thrown on top of him. Thane dragged the sheet clear then dropped on his knees beside his young sergeant.

Blood matted the mop of dark hair and had trickled down most of one side of his face. There was a long gash in his scalp and another, spreading stains of blood lower down, where the denim jacket had been ripped.

But there was a faint pulse and he was breathing. Cursing with relief, Thane tried to ease Dunbar into a more comfortable position and heard a faint groan.

'Thank Christ,' said Felix, and it was no blasphemy. 'You want to stay?'

Thane nodded and Felix set off at a shambling run.

By the time he panted back, with a message through to Crime Squad Control, an ambulance on its way, the standby back-up team called in, Thane had used his sheepskin jacket to make a temporary pillow for Dunbar's head. Dunbar's pulse-beat was still faint, but his breathing seemed better and his eye-lids made an occasional attempt at a flicker.

'What do you think?' asked Felix anxiously.

Thane didn't answer. Leaving Felix to stand guard, he went into the building.

Someone who must have had plenty of experience of getting into other people's buildings had put a reasonable amount of thought, effort and money into making sure that it didn't happen at his place.

The front door, when closed, would have been protected by two heavy double-action locks backed by a solid steel plate. The windows, grimy and cracked on the outside, were also backed by steel plate with only a few small slits to let in daylight. A trap door leading in from the flat roof had been sealed by a series of parallel steel bars.

But it had all been abandoned, and in a rush. He saw two sleeping bags spread out in one dilapidated room. A kettle, an electric boiling ring, empty food cans and dirty crockery littered a filthy table.

Most of the rooms – offices, whatever they had been – were empty. But he found one which had been used as a store. It held cans of fuel and oil, some small drums of paint and a portable paint spray.

That left just one door. It was in the middle of the building, was of sheet steel, and was secured by two heavy bolts top and bottom, each protected by a glinting metal padlock.

Thane kicked at it experimentally. As he'd expected, it didn't budge.

He turned on his heels and went back outside. Joe Felix was squatting beside Dunbar.

'Left in a hurry, did they?' asked Felix, looking up.

Thane nodded.

'Good,' said Felix. 'Then they'll have made some mistakes.' He glanced down at Dunbar's bloodstained face and added softly. 'Like this one, for a start.'

The first Crime Squad back-up car arrived less than a minute later. Another pulled into the yard soon afterwards, followed by an ambulance and then more police vehicles.

Thane gave the few orders that were necessary, then stood back from the organized bustle. Francey Dunbar was carefully carried on a stretcher into the ambulance, and it departed with lights flashing and siren shrieking. The back-up team was led by Hugh Campbell, a stocky, balding, Gaelic-speaking detective inspector whose cross in life was a sergeant named Donald MacDonald. Campbell posted his men, made his own perfunctory search of the building, then came back to Thane.

'That locked door, sir –' He raised a questioning eyebrow. 'Do we wait for the fingerprint mob?'

'Get it open,' Thane told him curtly.

'Clean?'

Thane looked at him. 'It's not my door. Any damned way you want.'.

'Aye.' Campbell twisted a grin. 'That useless devil MacDonald has a trick he plays with a car jack. It's about all he's good for.'

He turned away, shouting for his sergeant.

Thane walked across the yard, looking for Joe Felix. A uniformed constable on duty at the gates directed him out into the lane.

He found Felix back at the broken packing case, talking amiably to the old woman still sheltering inside it.

'Any luck?' asked Thane.

'Not a lot.' Felix took a step back and shook his head. 'Her name is Aggie; she's been sleeping here about a week now – she thinks.' He grimaced. 'Seems the local cops know her. So does the Sally Army hostel down the road. Give her a bottle and she doesn't trouble anyone.'

'An' what's wrong with that?' asked the old woman suspiciously, peering out at them. 'None o' your business, is it?'

'None, Aggie,' agreed Thane, with deliberate amiability. He thumbed along the lane. 'Our business is back there.'

'Noisy devils.' She shuffled out into the open a little and sniffed her disgust. 'No peace for anyone, comin' and goin' at all hours – day and night.'

'Would you recognize any of them again?' asked Thane patiently.

'With my eyesight, son?' She gave a cackle of laughter. 'No chance.'

'How about their transport?'

'Different vans, that big car. Then once or twice there was a damn motor-cycle.' She shivered in the wind. 'Noisy, all of them – but I wouldn't know one from another.' Leaning forward, clutching her coats together, she gave Thane a conspiratorial grin. 'That ambulance – your friend says it was a polis that got hurt, hurt bad. Is that right?'

'Yes.'

'Ach, he'll be fine,' she consoled. 'You'll see. Nobody wants to kill a polis – think o' the bother it causes.'

Nodding to herself, she retreated back into the packing case.

Thane exchanged a shrug with Felix. Their only real witness could be written off as a lost cause.

'What do we do about her?' Felix stuffed his hands into his pockets and scowled. 'I suppose the hostel; she told me to go to hell.'

'Tell them anyway – and put a bomb under the local beatmen,' said Thane.

Felix followed him back to the yard and into the building. Detective Inspector Campbell greeted them with a nod.

'Almost through,' he said laconically.

The upper padlock on the inner metal door hung loose, already broken. His sergeant was kneeling beside the remaining padlock, a flat steel bar through the hasp, a car jack jammed between the bar and the metal of the door.

'Hurry it up, man,' said Campbell brutally. 'You're keeping folk waiting.'

His sergeant glared at him, gave the car jack another two full turns, and the padlock groaned. The man spat on his hands, gave the jack another swift turn, and there was a loud snap.

The padlock tumbled, the two bolts were slid back, and Campbell bundled the sergeant to one side then pushed the door open. The room was in total darkness.

'I'll get a torch,' declared Campbell briskly.

Silently, his sergeant felt inside the door, clicked a switch, and an overhead light blazed to life.

'Hell,' said Joe Felix softly.

The room was long, narrow, and lined with metal storage racks. About half were empty but the rest were filled with plastic-wrapped video tapes, several hundred of them – or more.

'Aladdin eat your heart out,' said Campbell's sergeant wryly. 'Keep your cave.' He glanced at Thane. 'It's what you wanted, isn't it, sir?'

'Maybe.' Thane walked slowly round the racks. Every stack was titled, most of the tapes were complete with their counterfeit labels. There were musicals and westerns, horror shows and sex outings, a batch of children's cartoons, and titles he knew were among the latest releases.

But there was one missing – *The Hanging Tree*.

He felt a sick sense of failure, yet it was one he could almost have anticipated without being totally certain why. Thanks to Francey Dunbar, they'd found the pirate team's distribution depot.

But that was all.

'Joe.' He signalled Felix over. 'Soon as you can, take some samples and find La Mont.' He saw Felix's expression. 'Just do it – keep your feuding till later. Take him over to my office and wait there till I get back.'

'Right.' Felix nodded resignedly. 'If we need you – '

'Francey,' said Thane simply.

He walked back to Riverview Street. The two boys had gone. But someone had used a knife-point to dig a long, deep gouge along both sides of the Ford's paintwork.

★

Francey Dunbar had been taken to the Western Infirmary for the simple reason it was the nearest casualty receiving unit. It was big, basically old, but rebuilt and well equipped. The mere fact he was still there when Thane arrived was a pointer in itself: any patient with a critical head injury would have been turned around as soon as possible, ferried over to the Southern General, where one of the best neurosurgical teams in the business was in permanent residence.

Thursday afternoons were a slack time for casualty departments, the relative calm before the usual evening rush, in itself a mere limbering-up for what the weekends could bring. A couple of road accident victims, one of them a child, and a construction worker who had fallen off a roof were creating their own isolated pools of activity. But a girl at the receiving desk took time off from dealing with the queue of lesser walking wounded and gave Thane directions.

He went along a corridor into the usual hospital smells of people and disinfectant, then reached a small waiting-area.

Jack Hart was there. The squad commander was sitting gloomily under a 'No Smoking' sign and gave a grunt of relief when he saw Thane approach.

'How is he?' asked Thane.

'They've had him through X-ray.' Hart shaped a disgusted shrug. 'More than that, I don't know. Sandra brought me over – I sent her to find some coffee.'

The squad commander's lined face was tired, his voice was flat and unemotional, but when one of his officers was injured it was a point of honour with Hart to get there – no matter where 'there' might be. He thumbed Thane into the seat beside him.

'So what happened?' he demanded.

Thane told him, as briefly as he could. At the finish, Hart gave a pensive scowl and rubbed a hand along his chin.

'There are more and more things about this I don't like,' he said softly. 'I get a feeling – ' he stopped and shook his

166

head. 'Dunbar's parents – where do they live?'

'They've a farm, a few miles out of Edinburgh.'

Hart grunted. 'No sense in worrying them – yet. For the rest, you stay with the main situation. I'll take care of the loose ends.'

He left it there as Sandra Craig appeared. Clutching two plastic cups of coffee, she gave Thane a slight, wry smile.

'God,' said Hart in disgust, tasting the contents of the cup she handed him. 'That's worse than our own stuff. Here – ' He gave it to Thane.

It was warm and it was wet. Thane sipped the hospital coffee and all three of them sat in silence for a few moments.

A door opened. They had a brief glimpse of white coats and nursing uniforms, then a middle-aged woman doctor emerged and walked towards them.

'Sergeant Dunbar's friends?' A faint reassuring twinkle showed in her eyes as they got to their feet. 'I'm Doctor Graham, in charge of his case.'

'How is he, Doctor?' asked Hart.

'Remarkably intact,' she told him. 'He's also fairly interesting, from a medical viewpoint. Sergeant Dunbar has the good fortune to have a surprisingly thick skull.'

'I could have told you that!' Hart almost grinned his relief. 'Then he's all right?'

'Let's say, he'll mend.' Doctor Graham hitched her thumbs into the pockets of her white coat. 'There's no sign of a skull fracture, no apparent internal bleeding. But he's suffering from concussion, and has that head wound, two broken ribs and some minor injuries. You'll have to do without him for a spell.'

'Is he conscious?'

'Yes, but not exactly making sense yet.' She shook her head, anticipating Hart's next question. 'I can't let you talk to him – not yet. We're dealing with concussion, and we can't take chances – I'm having him sedated. Perhaps some time tomorrow – '

Hart didn't argue.

'I'd like to have someone stay with him,' he suggested.

'Yes.' Her eyes strayed to Sandra. 'That might be a good idea.'

'And that blow to the head?' Hart looked at her hopefully.

'Caused by a blunt instrument.' She glanced at the fob watch on her lapel. 'Now, I've patients waiting. Let's just say your Mr Dunbar is a lucky young man.'

She left, and Hart made a self-conscious business of clearing his throat. Thane drew a deep breath, with the same feeling of relief.

'No sense in us staying,' said Hart, glancing at Thane. 'Not when the medics have pulled up the drawbridge. We'll leave Sandra here – I'll get someone along to relieve her later.'

Thane nodded and heard Sandra Craig chuckle to herself.

'Thick-skulled,' she said softly. 'Yes, I'll remember that.'

Hart rode with him on the journey back to Crime Squad headquarters, and had more questions about what had happened. Then, almost at their destination, Hart spoke again.

'Still seeing the Garrison woman tonight?'

'Yes.' Thane kept his eyes on the road. 'But she changed the time.'

'Do you know why?'

'Not yet.'

Hart sucked his teeth, but left it at that.

Maggie Fyffe intercepted them the moment they entered the Crime Squad building.

'How is he?' she asked anxiously.

'He'll survive,' said Hart, and winked at her. 'Get your notebook – I'm behind schedule.'

'And I'm on my coffee break,' she said tartly, then grinned at Thane. 'You've a visitor.'

'La Mont?'

She nodded. 'Joe Felix just arrived with him. Neither of them looked very happy.'

Thane went through to the Duty Room. Felix and La Mont were both there, La Mont seated, Felix several feet away and studiously looking out of a window. But they both came towards him as he entered.

'He'll mend, Joe,' said Thane before Felix could ask.

'Good,' said Felix fervently. He indicated La Mont. 'I found him.'

'Meaning he hauled me out of a meeting.' La Mont's broad, bearded face almost quivered with anger. 'Look, Superintendent, I've heard what has been happening. I'm glad your sergeant is OK – '

'I don't think that's how he'd describe it,' said Thane stonily.

'Sorry. But I still don't like being dragged out to a car like I was under arrest. Hell, Superintendent – '

'Detective Constable Felix may have been forceful,' soothed Thane, 'I'll talk to him about it – later. You know why you're here?'

'This new batch of tapes.' La Mont gave a grudging nod. 'I've had a glance at them.'

'Forty-three different titles,' said Felix cheerfully. 'I took one of each in that storeroom.'

'It's a wholesaler's stock – it has to be.' La Mont gave a gloomy shrug. 'Nice work. A lot of people are going to be happy – but it's going to take me all night sorting out what you've got.'

Felix gave an unsympathetic grunt. 'Hard luck.'

'That does it,' snarled La Mont, jumping to his feet.

'Sit down,' said Thane wearily. He waited until the bulky Canadian obeyed. 'Now listen, both of you. You don't have to like each other, but that's going to have to wait.' He faced La Mont. 'Can you do it if I give you till morning?'

La Mont scowled, but nodded.

'Thank you,' said Thane. 'Joe – '

'Sir?' Felix eyed him resignedly.

'Organize any help he wants. When that's done, see me. I – ' He paused, then committed himself, 'Yes, I need you for something else.'

The telephone was ringing as he reached his office. When he answered, Mary was on the line.

'I heard about Francey,' she said, without preliminaries. She didn't say how and Thane knew better than to ask – police wives had their own bush telegraph. 'Maggie says he'll be all right. True?'

'That's what the hospital says,' he agreed.

'I wanted to make sure.' She didn't hide her relief. 'What about you?'

'I'm fine, but I'm working late again,' Thane told her. 'I've – well, someone to see.'

'The widow what's-her-name – your one-time?'

'Yes.'

'Good luck,' said Mary cheerfully. 'I'll wait up and hear about it.'

'Go to hell,' he told her gloomily.

She laughed and hung up.

7

Dusk brought a change in the weather's mood. By 7 p.m. when Thane arrived in East Kilbride, it was a calm, pleasant night with a clear, star-lit sky and a first hint of frost sharpening the air.

He stopped his car at Alexis Garrison's address, got out, and glanced briefly at the row of small but expensive town houses. He was definitely in executive territory.

A light was on outside her door. Thane went along a slabbed path, touched the bell-push, and the door opened a moment later.

'Colin.' Alexis Garrison welcomed him with a warm smile, closed the door again as he entered, then leaned back against it for a moment, the smile still lingering. 'I'll be honest. I wasn't totally sure you'd come.'

'That used to be my line,' he said dryly.

In the soft glow of the hallway light it was easy to forget the years. Alexis Garrison, her fair hair brushed back and secured by a wisp of ribbon, wore a champagne-coloured dress with a low collar and a fitted waistline. A small diamond pendant sparkled at her throat, the setting hand-beaten gold. But one thing had changed. The woman behind the smile had a mature air of confident assurance.

'Haven't you got a coat?' she asked unexpectedly.

'I left it in the car,' he lied.

It brought Thane back to reality with a jerk. The last he'd seen of his old sheepskin, it had still been pillowing Francey Dunbar's head. Tomorrow he'd need to check with the hospital.

'We can't just stay here looking at each other.' Taking his arm, Alexis led the way through to a room where the

171

furnishings were teak or leather and the carpeting was deep and cream. She waved him into one of the deep armchairs which flanked a quarried-stone fireplace. 'What do you drink these days? Whisky?'

'When it's on offer,' he agreed.

'It used to be beer – except on paydays.' She chuckled, went over to a small, well-stocked bar, busied herself for a moment, then came back with their drinks in heavy, cut-crystal glasses. She gave him one, then raised her own. 'Happy days.'

'They were – most of them,' he agreed, and sipped his drink.

She settled in the other armchair, legs tucked beneath her like a schoolgirl.

'I didn't feel so friendly this afternoon, after your visit to the plant,' she said unexpectedly.

'Why?' He raised an eyebrow. 'What happened?'

'We had more people gossiping than working.' She shaped a scowl. 'They were too busy swopping rumours to bother about deliveries.'

'What kind of rumours?' asked Thane mildly.

'The kind that started because you asked about Billy Tripp – and Ted Douglas.' She tasted her drink, eyeing him over the rim of the glass. 'Admit it, Colin. That story you told me the first time – the one about the drug scene – was a load of police rubbish.'

'You've got a better one?' queried Thane.

'The one around the depot is that the pair of them had a heavy sideline in pirate video tapes.' She waited, apparently hopefully, for his reaction, shrugged, and went on. 'At least, it seems Billy Tripp could produce a few – and, as Ted Douglas went around with him, some people are putting two and two together.'

'I can show you a computer game,' said Thane unemotionally. 'How to ask a computer to add two and two and have it print out the answer "three" every time.'

'To hell with computers,' she said. 'What about video tapes?'

172

'Maybe.' Thane smiled, but sensed a lot depended on how he answered – and that behind the warmth and friendliness Alexis Garrison was waiting, calculating. She had trailed an innocent-sounding bait, now he was expected to take it. He nodded. 'Yes.'

'We have breakthrough!' She leaned forward a little, the diamond pendant sparkling again. 'Well, go on – are you getting anywhere with it?'

He had to play the same game, had to be sure. By now, if Alexis Garrison was part of it all, she had to know about the Riverview Street raid.

'We managed to seize a load of tapes this afternoon. But the rest of it misfired – we're still not much further than Billy Tripp.'

'Hard luck.' For a fraction of a second, a flicker of relief showed in Alexis's eyes, then disappeared. But it had been there, it was enough, even though it was immediately replaced with a relaxed, almost amused sympathy. 'What started it all – can you tell me that?'

It was a natural enough thing to ask, and again she had to know already.

'Some tapes we found after Ted Douglas was killed. We've been going one step forward, two steps back ever since.' Thane thought of La Mont, sweating over the latest samples they'd recovered, and added deliberately, 'It's a big-money racket – we're out on the fringe. The experts say it's London-based, but get to the top and there's someone raking in a fortune.'

'Then if this is the fringe, why so much fuss?' she demanded.

'Fuss?' He tightened his lips without meaning to do it. 'I don't see it that way – not when I know a man died because of the way he was treated, not when I've a sergeant in hospital, injured.'

She moistened her lips. 'I didn't know. Your sergeant – how is he?'

'We won't be sure for a spell,' he said brutally.

'I'm sorry.' Alexis Garrison sighed. 'Colin, let's – well,

forget it. I asked you here so we could remember the old days.'

Thane went along with her. They talked, about names they'd known, places they'd been to together. More than once Thane tried to extend beyond that, to learn more about her life after they'd parted. But each time Alexis smoothly eased away from the subject, back to the original ground.

Along the way, she offered him another drink but he shook his head. At last, she stopped and looked deliberately at the clock on the mantelshelf.

'Almost eight,' agreed Thane.

'And I'm going to have to throw you out,' she apologized as he got to his feet. 'Sorry, but I've a living to earn.'

'You can recover over the weekend,' said Thane casually. 'What have you got in mind? I can't see you going off to join Jonathan and his fishing rods.'

'No.' She laughed at the notion. 'I get away from things, as fast as I can.'

'Straight after work?' suggested Thane.

'Tomorrow afternoon, as soon as my desk is clear.' She looked at Thane and gave a slight wink. 'Whatever you're thinking, don't ask. What I do is nobody's damned business as long as I can crawl back into the Falcon office on Mondays. I may be a widow, but I still like to live.'

She went with him through the hallway to the front door, opened it, then kissed him lightly on the cheek.

'Next time,' she promised, 'we'll have the evening to ourselves – I guarantee it.'

Thane went down the pathway, reached his car, and looked back. She waved goodbye, went inside, and the door closed.

He got into the Ford, started the engine, and let it tick over for a moment. Maybe he still didn't have proof, but every instinct told him any remaining hopes were gone. Alexis Garrison had to be involved. For once, she had just been too clever, had fallen into her own trap.

But it didn't make him feel any better when he thought

of what he'd done. It also meant he had no choice now.

He set the car moving. About 100 yards along, the Ford's headlights briefly lit a small, blue, motor caravan. It had been there when he arrived, one of several vehicles parked along the roadside.

Reaching down, still driving, he flicked on the car's radio, picked up the microphone, and pressed its switch.

'Yours now, Joe,' he said quietly.

Crouched out of sight in the rear of the motor caravan, Joe Felix radioed an acknowledgement. Grunting, he heaved himself round, nodded to the Crime Squad driver squatting beside him, then checked the camera he had ready. It had a bulky projection attached to the lens, an infra-red light intensifier which had started life as an army night-fighting gun sight.

Twenty minutes passed, then a large black BMW coupé drove sedately past the motor caravan. It vanished from sight. A few minutes later it returned again and repeated the performance.

But on its third appearance it stopped outside Alexis Garrison's house.

The driver, the only occupant, got out and went straight to her door. It opened, Alexis Garrison greeted him, and the door closed again as they went in together.

Inside the motor caravan, Joe Felix lowered the camera, checked the number of exposures he'd used, then reached for his microphone again.

He gave his call-sign.

From his own car, waiting a few streets away, Thane answered.

'Who was it, Joe?' he asked.

'Jimbo Raddick,' murmured Felix's voice from the car's speaker. 'Positive – and we've got the pictures to prove it.'

'All right.' Thane pursed his lips. They had nothing on Raddick; they could only lose by grabbing him. 'Stay with it.'

'This could be a long night,' grumbled Felix.

Thane didn't answer him.

It was another hour before the radio came to life again.

'I was wrong,' reported Felix. 'He's leaving. Do we follow?'

'From well back,' ordered Thane. 'I'll be behind you. Let me know when you're moving.'

He started the Ford, let it idle, and waited.

A full four minutes passed, then Joe Felix came on the air once more. He sounded flustered and penitent.

'We lost him, boss,' he admitted unhappily.

'How?'

'First the Garrison woman stayed watching at her door until he was well away. Then – hell, we got boxed in by traffic at the first road junction.' Felix made an apologetic noise. 'What now? We've got his vehicle number.'

'Give me the number then head back, Joe,' said Thane wearily. 'I'll see you in the morning.'

He did the only thing left. Switching channels, he radioed Strathclyde Police Control and requested that their traffic-patrol cars kept a look-out for Raddick's BMW on a non-interception basis.

But even as the Strathclyde operator obliged and the message began going out, Thane knew it was a waste of time.

He was glad to get home. Almost the first thing he did was make a phone call to the Western Infirmary. A ward sister told him Francey Dunbar was totally comfortable and sleeping peacefully. Then Tommy and Kate were waiting to pounce. They had got hold of more video recorder literature and bombarded him with ideas they'd gathered.

It was the last thing he wanted to think about, but that wasn't their fault. Mary joined in the discussion, talking as interestedly as any of them, but Thane knew she was watching him.

At last, Tommy and Kate went to bed and they were left alone.

'I'm not going to ask,' she said quietly. 'But the way you

176

look, I can guess.'

'She's up to her neck in it,' said Thane sadly.

'I'm sorry.' She reached for his hand. 'But damn her for a stupid bitch.'

Thane loved her for that.

It happened shortly after 2 a.m. near junction 4 on the M74 London-Glasgow motorway – the home stretch for any Glasgow-based trucker on the overnight trunk haulage route. But it was about twenty minutes later when the first call reached police from one of the motorway emergency telephones. Q Division at Hamilton caught it first, P Division was immediately involved, and it spread from there.

The cryptic telex incident log filled up quickly:

SER. NO. 1193CR1 0223 DIV – AS

CODE (1) 20 00 00 CODE (2) 05 00 00

LOCATION M74 SOUTH OF JUNCT. 4

MESSAGE. REPORTER HELD UP, FOUR PLUS MEN, ARMED HANDGUNS AND SHOTGUN. SHOTGUN DISCHARGED. CONTAINER ARTIC. MERCEDES MAKE REG. NO. BHP 720 T STOLEN. LAST SEEN EXITING M74 AT JUNCT. 4 BELIEVED HEADING EAST. NO PERSON INJURED.

REPORTER – MR ROBIN BANKS, ARTIC. DRIVER.

ACTION BY CR Q6 – V53 CR Q11 – V82 CR P41 – 82

CR P9 – 74 CR14 – H53. ADDITIONAL UNITS ADVISED.

0227	CR Q6 BM2 0000 0000
0228	BROADCAST ON AS
0228	TM2
0230	AM4 0000 AM2 0000 AM4 0000
0242	CR Q6 SPECIAL SEARCH REQUESTED GREY TRANSIT VAN, DAMAGED REAR. BLUE BEDFORD VAN, WHITE STRIPES. REG. NOS. UNKNOWN. NFD. BOTH HAVE ARMED MEN ABOARD.
0245	CR Q11 ARTIC BHP 720 T MAY HAVE DAMAGED HEADLAMP NEARSIDE.
0247	CR P4. DAMAGED TRANSIT VAN FOUND ABANDONED. NO

TRACE OF OCCUPANTS.

0249   CR P9 VM12 0000 0000

RESULT —
0250   CR Q6 — V 53
AMB. NOT REQUIRED. NO PERSON INJURED. MERCEDES
ARTIC. FORCED TO STOP. SHOTGUN DISCHARGED IN AIR,
REPORTER/DRIVER ORDERED OUT. ASSAULTED THEN
THROWN INTO DITCH. MERCEDES DRIVEN AWAY, BOTH
VANS ACCOMPANYING. ALL ASSAILANTS MASKED, NO ID
POSSIBLE. VAN REG. NOS. OBSCURED. CID IN ATTEND-
ANCE.

0252   CR Q6 — V53. MERCEDES CARRYING PARTIAL LOAD 50
CARTONS BY 100 BLANK FORMAT VIDEO TAPES.

0253   CR P4. DAMAGED TRANSIT VAN IDENTIFIED AS FGG 678 X
PREVIOUSLY STOLEN GLASGOW. BEING RETAINED FOR
FORENSIC AND FP EXAMINATION. CID IN ATTENDANCE.
TOW WILL BE REQUIRED THIS VEHICLE DUE TO REAR END
DAMAGE.

0256   CR Q6. CID NOW MAKING FURTHER INQUIRIES.
ARRESTS — 00 SUMMONS — 00

Four hours later and fifteen miles away, in neighbouring
Central Region, the early-morning shift arriving to start
work at a small, isolated chemical plant found the
Mercedes truck and the blue Bedford van lying abandoned
side by side in their transport yard. Twenty cartons of
video tapes were missing from the Mercedes's container,
which had been forced open. The Bedford van had been set
on fire and had burned out, although the registration
plates matched another van stolen in Glasgow.

But the men who had brought them there had vanished.

Colin Thane heard about it at 8 a.m. when Jack Hart
telephoned him at home. The Crime Squad commander
was already at his desk, in a snarling mood.

'The method, everything else, matches up,' he rasped
over the line. 'It's the same team as before – it has to be,
and you know what that means. If that damned fool driver
with Joe Felix last night hadn't lost Raddick's car – ' he

gave up with a grunt of despair. 'Look, get hold of that Canadian – '

'La Mont?'

'Is there another one?' asked Hart sarcastically. 'Have him in your office by 9 a.m., even if you've got to drag him in. Squeeze any sense you can out of him about the tapes we got yesterday. Then you and I have an up-date meeting at 9.30 a.m. I want us moving before the damned pin-striped bureaucrats get through doing their morning cross-words and deciding what they'll have for lunch.'

'Any word on Francey?' asked Thane as the tirade ended.

'Yes.' Jack Hart became fractionally happier. 'The night shift checked before they packed in. No fresh problems, thank God; that female doctor is scheduled to see Francey again this morning, then we should be able to talk to him.'

Hart hung up. Thane said a wry 'goodbye' to the purring line, then replaced his own receiver

He went through to the kitchen, where Mary was already beginning to clear up after breakfast. It was another of her part-time job days, with everyone in the house, even the dog, geared to an early start.

'Who was it?' she asked, dumping some unused toast in the kitchen bin.

'Jack Hart, spitting nails.' Thane managed to get another cup of coffee from the pot before the rest of the dregs went down the sink. He could hear Tommy and Kate clumping around upstairs, getting ready for school. 'But Francey's doing fine.'

He took his coffee back through to the phone, checked the Albany Hotel number, then sipped while he dialled.

The Albany switchboard had trouble getting a reply from the Canadian's room. But at last John La Mont's sleepy voice came on the line.

'You want me by 9 a.m.?' La Mont's voice rose in indignant protest as he listened. 'Look, Superintendent, I was up half the damned night watching those crummy videos. I'm not a cop. I like a civilized start to my mornings – '

'Your choice,' said Thane stonily. 'What size do you take in handcuffs?'

'Sweet Jesus!' La Mont spluttered. 'Now listen – '

Thane cut him short.

'Just be there.' He grinned at the mouthpiece. 'And thanks for your cooperation.'

It was a bright, sunny day with only a few wisps of cloud around; the kind of day when it would have been fairly easy to find little wrong with the world.

North of the river, a stranger who had offered a piece of chocolate to a child was being beaten up by half a dozen angry, coldly determined mothers. Three children had been molested in the same street in the past ten days. South of the river, firemen were cutting away the wreckage of a car to free the driver, a young salesman. It was his twenty-first birthday, he was dying, and he'd swerved to avoid a dog. On the river itself, the body of a woman was being recovered near the Suspension Bridge. She had been missing for two weeks, had been a volunteer welfare worker, and later in the day an autopsy would decide she had been strangled.

But these things happened.

For Colin Thane, it was simply the kind of day when he drove to work knowing for certain that very little, if anything, was likely to go smoothly.

His regular parking space had been stolen when he reached Crime Squad headquarters. A big blue police bus, lying empty, left in a way that took up several spaces, was the culprit. Shrugging, he abandoned his car in someone else's slot and went into the building. The main Duty Room was already becoming busy, but he located Sandra Craig first, then Joe Felix, and thumbed them through to his office.

Once he had them there, the door closed, he lit his first cigarette of the day.

'Francey Dunbar seems on the mend,' he told them.

180

They had heard.

'Our Sergeant Stoneskull,' murmured Sandra. 'I was ready to bet he'd be all right.'

'So that was why you went back to the hospital last night?' queried Felix sardonically. He grimaced at Thane. 'While I was being just about as useful – losing Raddick.'

'He'll turn up,' shrugged Thane. 'If you want to do penance, don't stray. La Mont is on his way in.'

Felix sighed, but nodded.

'After that, I've a session with Commander Hart.' Thane eyed them both. 'So what have we got from overnight? Those photographs?'

'Commander Hart has them,' said Felix. 'He's been – well, gathering things.'

Thane pursed his lips, but nodded.

'Your turn, Sandra. Power cuts?'

'We've got the full list, and dates.' She picked up the map lying on his desk, opening it out as she spoke. 'It narrows down to two of your coastal locations – I've marked them.'

Thane saw for himself. The first stretch was one he knew well, a five-mile curve of shoreline, where the long, narrow finger of Loch Fyne stabbed in from the sea. Frowning, he considered the other possibility. It was lonelier, further north, a ten-mile stretch of the west coast of Argyll, near Oban.

'Loch Fyne was a daytime power cut,' said Sandra quietly. 'Oban area was for four hours during the night – the night before Ted Douglas was killed.'

'Then it's Oban.' Thane studied the map again, more closely. The ten-mile sweep that mattered was a clutter of small bays and sea-lochs, with few roads and only a thin scatter of place names. But ten miles as a straight-line measurement was probably twice that length of actual shore. 'Does Commander Hart know?'

'Yes, sir.' She gave him a sympathetic grin.

'Anything we have that he doesn't?' asked Thane sarcastically.

'One thing.' Joe Felix paused, scratching his chest

through his shirt for a moment, frowning. 'That check on the list of casual drivers we got from Falcon Services. Two are on CRO's books, but one is in jail, doing six months for wife assault, so he doesn't count.'

'And the other?'

Felix shrugged. 'Hasn't been seen anywhere for a couple of days. He's an ordinary four-by-two ned named Maxie Brown – a few convictions for vehicle theft. Is he worth chasing?'

'Not if we've anything better to do.' Thane glanced at his watch and saw it was almost 9 a.m. He remembered something else as he looked up. 'Campbell and MacDonald were to sort out who owns that yard in Anstruther Lane.' He saw Felix exchange a glance with Sandra and guessed. 'Commander Hart has it?'

They nodded.

He sighed. Jack Hart was weighing in, determined to help. But that didn't necessarily make life easier for anyone.

John La Mont arrived ten minutes late. Joe Felix brought him into Thane's office and straight away the bearded Canadian put on a display of indignant truculence.

'Have you forgotten I'm supposed to be on your side, Superintendent?' he snapped, dumping his bulk into a chair. 'I'll tell you this for free. I don't like being ordered around like the office boy – and that goes double when I'm still damn only half awake.'

'Tell Commander Hart,' suggested Thane, unmoved. 'It was his idea. I thought it was a good one.'

'Hart gave the order?' La Mont blinked in surprise. 'Is this some kind of joke?'

'Do you see anyone laughing?' asked Joe Felix.

La Mont glared at him.

'Be polite to our visitor,' chided Thane gently. 'In fact, find him some coffee – I could use some too.'

'But go easy on the arsenic with mine,' suggested La Mont acidly as Felix left. He scowled as the door closed. 'What's got into that character? I could work with him at first. Now, it's like I was a social disease – why the change?'

'Ask him,' suggested Thane without humour. 'I'm more interested in those tapes we found yesterday.'

'From that warehouse collection?' La Mont grunted. 'Just another batch of pirates and counterfeits, different sources, different recording qualities. A few are from the same stable as *The Hanging Tree*, the rest could have come from anywhere.' He paused, puzzled. 'You brought me here just to ask that?'

'No.' said Thane quietly.

'So what else is on the list?'

'About 2 a.m. this morning a container truck from London was hijacked. The gang involved was armed, and the truck's cargo was blank video tapes.'

La Mont winced. 'How many?'

'Several thousand.' Thane eyed him grimly. 'You're the video expert – tell me why it keeps happening.'

'Well – ' La Mont moistened his lips ' – uh – there's a market. Video stores might take some, back-door style. Or – or – '

'There's somewhere else?'

La Mont nodded reluctantly.

'Where?'

'It could be a contract job for a pirate outfit,' said La Mont slowly. 'They need big, regular supplies of blank tapes for recording. They can't buy in bulk – too many questions. Small lots are awkward, a nuisance. But if they can buy the stolen variety, cut price, it's ideal – keeps down the hassle, and the overheads.' He gestured vaguely. 'Maybe this local hijack mob knows someone down south.'

'Why down south?' Thane got to his feet and came round to stand over the Canadian. He said it again, unemotionally. 'Why down south? Does everything have to be in London?'

'I – ' La Mont stared up at him. 'Meaning what?'

'That I'd like some proof,' said Thane remorselessly.

La Mont's broad face shaped an uneasy grin. 'Impossible. You're beginning to sound like Joe Felix.'

'Detective Constable Felix,' corrected Thane. 'Who may not know much about video law but happens to be a damned good technician.' He went to the window, then spoke again without looking round. 'How about you, La Mont? Maybe you know every crinkle of legislation in the video business. But how do you rate in Joe Felix's world?'

He waited, looking out at the vehicles in the parking area, ignoring the man behind him. There was a long silence, then he heard a sigh.

'I don't,' said La Mont unhappily.

Thane turned. The Canadian was on his feet, hands stuffed in his pockets.

'Level with you?'

Thane nodded.

'First time we met, I told you I was a copyright lawyer.' La Mont considered his feet, looking more bear-like than ever – but a shame-faced, embarrassed bear. 'I am – and a pretty good one. I wanted this job, I bluffed the rest.'

'And the technical side?'

'I've picked up some of the basics – well, maybe less than some.' La Mont looked up and chewed a stray tendril of beard for a moment. 'How much have I fouled things up?'

'That depends,' said Thane bluntly.

'Anything I've told you about the tapes you've given me has been genuine,' said La Mont wearily. 'That much, I guarantee.'

'And London?'

La Mont shrugged. 'When you're the expert, you've got to make positive noises. *The Hanging Tree* stable could be a London operation, might not. There's gossip, there's rumour. Some of the pirate trade is multi-national – there's a whisper that one of the new boys keeps himself based in Spain.'

Thane stared, then grabbed him almost roughly by the arm.

'La Mont,' he said softly, 'I'm not dealing in fantasy. Try pulling something on me, now – '

'Spain,' insisted La Mont. He straightened his shoulders

and scowled. 'It's a whisper, nothing more – no names. But the source is good. It should be – I pay him enough. Why? Does it matter?'

'You've maybe just hauled yourself out of the muck heap,' said Thane fervently.

He released La Mont's arm, a whole tangled confusion of possibility and fact beginning to come together with sudden clarity.

'I don't understand,' said La Mont, relieved but puzzled.

'You don't have to – yet,' said Thane. He grinned, leaving La Mont even more bewildered. 'About sixty seconds ago, I was ready to kick your fat backside out of here. Now – maybe you'll be able to tell your bosses you helped smash one of the best pirate operations in existence!'

La Mont swallowed, speechless.

The door opened. Joe Felix came in, carrying two mugs of coffee. He looked at La Mont then at Thane, sensing something had happened.

'Our friend wants to talk to you, Joe,' said Thane mildly. 'He wants to put a few things right, and he could use some advice.' He glanced at La Mont. 'An apology – isn't it?'

La Mont nodded.

'From him?' Felix scowled his disbelief.

'From him,' agreed Thane. He glanced at his watch. It was exactly 9.30 a.m. 'Sorry I can't stay, but I've a meeting.'

He made the fourth person round the table in the Crime Squad commander's room. Phil Moss was on Hart's left, and gave a grin and a wink. The chair on Hart's right was vacant, waiting for Thane, and the lanky Detective Inspector Rome from Govan Division filled the other place.

'So, let's begin,' said Jack Hart briskly. 'I've told Maggie to pull up the drawbridge till we're finished. Phil Moss is here as liaison officer from Strathclyde, otherwise we may stand on a few toes. But – ' he pointed a warning finger in

Moss's direction ' – that's all. It's a desk job. I've already had your boss spell that out to me. In the same way, Rome is here only because he's still running the investigation into Joe Daisy's death. That's clear to you both?'

The two men nodded, Moss with a slight scowl, Rome's thin young face suitably solemn.

'Right.' Hart glanced at the notepad in front of him. 'I've got an outline agenda; we're going to stick to it.' He paused, put a pencil tick at the first item, then glanced at Thane. 'What did you get out of La Mont?'

'More than I expected,' said Thane briskly.

'Like what?' Hart sat back, surprised. 'And don't look so damned pleased with yourself – just tell it.'

'Those pirate copies of *The Hanging Tree* should be marked "Made in Scotland". We've been after the right people for the wrong reason; they're not just peddling these tapes, they're making them.' Thane met Hart's startled gaze and allowed himself a twist of a smile. 'That's how it looks. They may ship everything down south and use London as their distribution centre, but the tapes are recorded here, in Scotland. The best pirate video factory in Europe is probably on our doorstep.'

Hart swallowed. 'Explain.'

He did, and his audience heard him through to the finish in total, attentive silence.

'It all fits,' said Hart slowly. 'Moss?'

Phil Moss nodded. 'It fits, sir. It also makes sense out of the weight of muscle they've been ready to throw around.'

'I think – ' began Rome. He left it there, and shook his head. Nobody asked him to expand.

'So Jimbo Raddick sets this up from Spain, with a little help from his friends. Or was it the other way round?' Hart scowled, flicked open a folder lying at his elbow, lifted a photograph, and slid it across to Thane. 'Seen these yet?'

'No.' Thane's mouth tightened a little as he glanced at the print. Joe Felix's camera and its light intensifier had taken it with pin-sharp clarity. Raddick was standing with Alexis Garrison at her door. His arm was round her waist.

'The others will keep.' Hart cleared his throat with sudden embarrassment. 'We'll – u n – stick to the agenda.' He glanced down and ticked again. 'The truck hijack next. That's Strathclyde's baby. Moss?'

'Not a lot,' reported Moss unemotionally. 'They weren't amateurs. We've been working with Central Region on it; nothing significant left in the truck or the first van. Anything left in the other van was burned to a crisp.'

'Fingerprints, anything?' persisted Hart.

'A possible smudge or two, that's all. But it was the same bunch as before. They used CB radios.' Moss glanced at Thane. 'Probably on that code sequence you found. One of our people dug up a local breaker who calls herself Passion Flower. She's frustrated, forty, and likes to talk with CB males late at night. She was picking up strange one-way conversations on several channels for more than an hour last night.'

'Passion Flower – dear God,' grunted Hart. 'All right; CB radios, and they're pros. Any bright ideas about why they only took about half of these tapes?'

'Not enough transport,' suggested Moss.

'With their organization?' Hart shook his head in disbelief and frowned at his agenda again. 'Next – yes, it's your turn, Rome. Anything more on the Joe Daisy end of things?'

'No,' said Rome sadly. 'It's – well, proving difficult, sir.'

'I can believe it.' Hart surprised him with a sympathetic nod. 'Keep trying.' Another tick went on the list. 'Moss, your Scenes of Crime people were tackling the Anstruther Lane depot.'

'They're still putting it together.' Moss sat back, happier. 'But it looks good – better than that. We caught them off balance there. It looks like we'll have a catalogue of fingerprints – so far, that includes Raddick, Tripp, the Glassman, and even Ted Douglas.' He grinned. 'Somebody even left the best set of teeth marks I've ever seen on a cheese sandwich.'

'What about papers, pointers?'

'Not yet,' admitted Moss. 'But we're not finished.' He

glanced across at Thane. 'Maybe Francey – '

Thane nodded.

'Once the medics lower their force field,' said Hart acidly. 'That's not a profession, it's a conspiracy. Now, I've got some bits and pieces. Like – '

He stopped short, eyes widening, as a strange wailing began somewhere outside, a noise that grew and strengthened, punctuated by occasional drumbeats.

'I'm supposed to work against that?' Swearing indignantly, Hart rose and stormed over to his partly open window. 'Look at them – damn them!'

His audience of three came over, and Thane suddenly remembered the bus he'd seen earlier.

On the grass lawn outside, kilts swinging, feather bonnets quivering in the breeze, a pipe band was forming up. They wore full Highland dress in Royal Stewart tartan. They belonged to Strathclyde, were several times over World Champions, and regularly travelled the world. They also came out to the Training Area once a month for special rehearsals.

'Noisy devils,' snarled Hart, and slammed the window shut. The sounds diminished a little and he gestured the other three back to the table. 'Let's get on with it.'

His 'bits and pieces' were just that, small additions to the picture.

Traced by its registration plates, Jimbo Raddick's BMW had been bought from a dealer for cash – but no new owner had been recorded.

A separate probe had located the owner of the depot in Anstruther Lane, but with less useful results.

'Somebody paid him two years' rent in advance, cash again, and that's all he knows or cares,' said Hart caustically. He winced as the pipes outside skirled into a full-bore version of 'Highland Laddie', but went on grimly. 'The paperwork was on behalf of a firm which called itself Calasan and which you'll be surprised to hear doesn't seem to exist.'

'Who paid him?' asked Thane.

'A woman,' said Hart flatly. 'Blonde, late thirties or older, blue eyes. Do I have to ask who that might be?'

Thane shook his head.

'And that brings us up to right now, and what we're going to do,' said Hart. He sat back, his lined face hard to read, his eyes on Thane. 'As a target, this is about to get messy. Still want to run it?'

'Yes,' said Thane simply.

'Good.' Hart muttered something else under his breath, but looked relieved. 'You'll need some extra bodies. I'm giving you Campbell and MacDonald and anyone else we've got spare. What's your first priority?'

'That coastal strip. The factory base.'

'All right.' Hart nodded. 'We'll presume it's there. Boot Campbell and MacDonald on their way, tell them to liaise with the local constabulary, and for God's sake warn them it's low-profile stuff till we're sure.' He paused, the pipe music filling the room again. 'What else – apart from Francey?'

It was deliberate. Thane knew it and why.

'Alexis Garrison.'

'And her damned brother-in-law – wherever he is,' agreed Hart. He scowled. 'Don't underestimate the brother-in-law bit. A half-cracked electronic genius could slot nicely into this little scenario.' He paused again. 'She's at her office. I put a tail on her this morning. Didn't think you'd mind.'

'No.' Thane gave the squad commander a slightly bitter grin. 'Maybe we could do better. If Sandra and Joe Felix went out to Falcon again, on some pretext, Joe could tag her car.'

'Plant a homer device on it?' Hart liked the idea. 'Why not? Then we'd really keep track of her. Yes, do it.'

The meeting was over. Phil Moss and Rome left; Thane stayed behind and discussed details for a few minutes with Hart.

'That's it.' At last, Hart crumpled his agenda sheet and tossed it at the waste basket. 'Except that your people go armed, Colin. I don't like police widows getting medals.'

Thane had expected it.

The traditional British bobby, carrying nothing more lethal than a wooden baton, was still the accepted norm. But too many British criminals now carried guns and used them, too many traditional British bobbies had been killed or maimed.

More and more police now had firearms training to marksman standard. The rules had altered. If the opposition might be armed, then weapons were issued.

For self-defence – or circumstance.

He nodded. 'Anything else, sir?'

'No.' Hart reached across his desk and pressed his intercom key. 'Maggie – '

'Sir?'

'Lower the drawbridge. Meeting over.' Hart released the key and glanced shrewdly at Thane. 'On your way. Get it done.'

La Mont had gone when Thane returned to his office. He saw Joe Felix, but the latter simply smiled and nodded, saying nothing about what had happened between the two men.

Thane had other things to think about, to plan, to organize. It meant telephone calls and quick briefing sessions, taking men and women off cases they were already handling, spreading duties for others to provide cover. The Armoury sergeant had already been warned by Hart but still wanted to check details. Detective Inspector Hugh Campbell and Sergeant Donald MacDonald came next.

To get them up north to Oban and on to the coastal area that mattered would take more than two hours by road. But the airport was only a few minutes away by motorway, and a helicopter would get them from there to Oban and a link-up with the local police. It would take less than half an hour's flying time.

He briefed both men carefully, then sent them on their way. Soon afterwards, four more Crime Squad men set off for the north by road, taking two cars.

Next in line came Sandra and Joe Felix. They listened to what he wanted; but when he finished they exchanged a glance and Sandra frowned.

'What happens once we get the homer on her car?' she demanded. 'Do we stay stuck out there?'

Felix nodded agreement. 'We've been in this from the beginning, boss. Don't leave us out now.'

Thane saw they were prepared to be stubborn.

'Another car will take over,' he promised. 'But get that Volvo tagged, one way or another.'

There were more telephone calls to make. One was to the Western Infirmary. When he spoke to Doctor Graham, he found her in a cheerful mood.

'I've seen Sergeant Dunbar,' she confirmed, then chuckled. 'He's well enough to be causing havoc with the nursing staff. But I still want to keep him in for another day or so – and I don't care how much he howls.'

'When can I talk to him?' asked Thane.

'That's no particular problem.' She paused, and he heard a rustle of paper. 'I've ordered some new X-rays and tests – purely routine. We'll need until after noon. Could you leave it until one o'clock?'

Thane thanked her and hung up.

The Armoury sergeant returned. He laid a ·38 Smith and Wesson and a box of cartridges on Thane's desk, then flourished forms, wanting signatures.

The Smith and Wesson revolver was the squad's standard handgun, not as compact as an automatic but rated more reliable. In addition to Smith and Wessons, the team heading north had taken gas grenades and smoke canisters, four Savage shotguns and a brace of the 'qualified marksman only' 7·62 Enforcer rifles.

The Savage, a pump-action twelve-bore weapon, was used with solid shot as a vehicle stopper. The Enforcer rifles, in the right hands, had acquired an awesome reputation for accuracy and effect.

Thane initialled the forms. Afterwards, each weapon, each round of ammunition issued would have to be accounted for with more paperwork.

'I don't plan on fighting a war,' he said gloomily.

'No, sir.' The Armoury sergeant had heard it all before. 'But you never know, do you?'

An incoming call from Oban told him that Campbell and MacDonald's helicopter had arrived and that they had linked up with the local police.

A surprisingly short time after that, Maggie Fyffe came through with a radio message from Sandra. The homer device had been attached to Alexis Garrison's car. Felix and Sandra were heading back from East Kilbride.

He glanced at his desk, then at his wrist-watch. It was already past noon. For the moment there was nothing more he could do.

'I'll let things tick over for a spell, Maggie.' He got to his feet. 'I'll head for the Western Infirmary, get something to eat on the way, then see Francey.'

'You'll keep your ears on?' she asked.

'Yes.' He grinned at the Citizen's Band jargon.

'Then give my love to Francey.' She winked. 'Tell him he has a new nickname – Iron Top.'

There were traffic delays in the city, all rippling out from a protest march. Part of a jam of vehicles stopped at a junction; Thane watched the last of the demonstrators amble past. They were good-humoured, mostly young, and one was blowing a bugle. Their banners declared they wanted to change the Government, ban the Bomb, and end cuts on student grants – but not particularly in that order. Two comedians in the rear ranks carried placards demanding equal rights for men.

Thane watched them pass with a bemused sympathy, wondering how most of them would feel in another few years. Then, suddenly, the traffic was flowing again.

He stopped close to the Western Infirmary and had a sandwich and a beer in a small bar where most of the custom seemed to be off-duty hospital staff. There were some shops nearby and, when he left, he visited two and emerged with some magazines and a half-bottle of white wine.

At the hospital he went in with the bottle concealed inside the rolled-up magazines. Francey Dunbar had been given a side room in one of the casualty wards and Thane arrived to find his sergeant lying propped up on pillows. Dunbar already had company. A slim, good-looking staff nurse with red hair and long legs sat on the edge of his bed, chuckling as she listened to him.

'Hello, sir.' Dunbar broke off, looked at the redhead, then sadly patted her thigh. 'He's my boss. Sorry.'

She smiled at Thane and left them.

'Maybe I should have come later,' said Thane dryly. He looked at Dunbar for a moment. His head was bandaged, only a few locks of his dark hair escaping at the edges. The young, confident face was still paler than usual and he saw the wince when his sergeant moved a little. 'Feeling better?'

'I've had worse hangovers,' claimed Dunbar. He eyed Thane hopefully. 'Any chance you can get me out of here?'

'No.' Thane gave him the magazines and wine.

'I had that feeling.' Dunbar nodded his appreciation of the magazines, checked the wine label, and raised an eyebrow. 'Who chose this?'

'I did.'

'Thanks anyway.' Dunbar thumbed towards his locker cupboard. 'There's something of yours in there. Thanks for that too, sir.'

Thane opened the cupboard. His sheepskin jacket was on a hanger. The bloodstains had been sponged out, though a few faint traces remained.

'I'm sorry about – well, what happened yesterday,' said Dunbar. He grimaced. 'I didn't handle it too well.'

'That depends how it happened.' Thane came over and

sat on the bed. 'Tell me.'

Dunbar sighed. 'I picked up a story that the Glassman was working from a location somewhere off Riverview Street. So I went there. I was sniffing around, and next thing, I saw him going into Anstruther Lane.'

'So you followed?'

'I'd already called in.' Dunbar paused ruefully. 'And I left a message with a couple of kids.'

'We met them,' agreed Thane neutrally. 'Then?'

'I found that damned yard.' Dunbar eased into a more comfortable position under the sheets and clenched his teeth for a moment at what it cost him. 'Anyway, that's when I did the idiot bit. The yard was empty, except for the van and black BMW. I reckoned I could sneak in, see who was in the building, and get out again.'

'But you didn't. When we found you, Joe Felix wasn't sure whether to get an ambulance or order a wreath,' Thane told him bluntly.

'What does Joe know about flowers?' Dunbar gave a lop-sided grin at the thought. 'They must have spotted me. One moment I was trying to look in a damned blocked-up window, the next I heard a noise and someone was coming at me.' He shrugged. 'But someone else got me. I didn't even see him – or, if I did, I can't remember. It was like being hit with a telegraph pole.'

'You were lucky,' said Thane quietly.

Dunbar nodded. 'They keep telling me.'

'Did you see Raddick there?'

'I think so, I'm not sure.' Dunbar scowled his annoyance. 'I've a couple of minutes that just stay hazy.' He sighed. 'That's my lot, sir. How does the rest of it stand?'

Thane told him.

'And I'm stuck in this damned place.' Dunbar scowled at the bed sheets. 'One thing is odd, isn't it?'

'Just one?' asked Thane sarcastically.

'These blank tapes,' persisted Dunbar. 'Why only hijack half of them? It doesn't make sense.'

'They'd have a reason. They've had a reason for everything.' Thane got to his feet. 'Shall I chase your nurse back in – tell her you need a bedpan or something?'

'She knows where I am.' Dunbar watched him pick up the sheepskin jacket. 'But you can do me a favour. I'd like that wine chilled. There's a refrigerator outside, marked "Pathology Specimens". If you could slot it in there – '

The pathology refrigerator was at the entrance to the ward. It was filled with a variety of specimen jars and other unpleasant items, but Thane found a corner for the wine bottle.

Closing the refrigerator, he turned to go.

'Visiting the sick?' asked a voice.

Doc Williams was standing a few paces away. The police surgeon thumbed at the refrigerator.

'I used that trick when I was a student,' he said with a reminiscent chuckle. 'Bright boy, our Francey. I thought I'd look in, tell him a few jokes, cheer him up a little.'

'He'd like that,' agreed Thane maliciously.

'Yes.' Doc Williams frowned. 'Which reminds me: that rabbit joke I started telling you. You see, there was this rabbit, an old and wise rabbit, and he was out for a walk with this young rabbit and – '

'Doc, I'm in a rush,' said Thane quickly. 'It'll have to wait.'

He was on his way before the police surgeon could draw breath.

The early afternoon sun was bright; there was even a degree of warmth in the air as Thane left the hospital and walked to where he'd left his car.

Someone was already there. He found Detective Inspector Rome draped against the driver's door.

'I was told I'd find you here, sir.' The divisional man straightened quickly and greeted him with enthusiasm. 'I've turned up something I thought you'd want to know about.'

'That depends what it is,' said Thane.

'Yes, sir.' Rome smiled dutifully. 'It's Calasan – I know what it means.' He saw Thane's lack of reaction. 'Commander Hart mentioned Calasan this morning – the company name Raddick's people used.'

'The company that doesn't exist.' Thane remembered.

'But it does – at least the name does,' said Rome earnestly. 'I stayed quiet because I wanted to be sure. Then I was delayed; I got caught up in a stabbing – just a domestic thing.' He paused. 'But I was right. Calasan is the name on some of the posters in Joe Daisy's shop, so I asked that girl Carol. She knew.'

'Well?' asked Thane, trying to stay patient.

'It's a one-man printing shop Daisy sometimes used; a man named Pann Kinton runs it and has Calasan as his unofficial trademark. Kinton strays into porn work if the price is right.'

'Does Carol know where he's located?'

'Clava Square, off George Street. She picked up packages there a couple of times.' Rome hesitated. 'I thought you'd maybe want to come along, sir.'

'I would,' said Thane softly. 'Do you need a lift?'

'No.' Rome thumbed further along the parking area. He had a car and driver waiting.

'Then you lead, I'll follow,' Thane told him.

8

Clava Square was just east of the city centre and had once been new, elegant and fashionable. But that had been when Glasgow's tobacco lords were just beginning to realize they had been ruined by those damned North American colonists and their War of Independence.

Now it was old, run-down, grimy, and a warren of small businesses. The garden in the middle had become a parking area, and the church which had dominated most of one side had been converted into a storage warehouse for plumbers' supplies.

The only parking space available was outside the warehouse loading bay. The two police cars nosed in, stopped, and Rome's driver was left to take care of any protests.

Pann Kinton's printing shop was on the opposite side of the square. Thane and Rome walked across to it, a narrow, two-storey building with a basement separately occupied by a second-hand clothes dealer. Spiked iron railings guarded the front and stone boundary walls topped with broken glass set in cement separated it from its neighbours.

A buzzer sounded as they pushed open the door and went in. The outer office was small, little more than a counter with a hinged flap. The floor was bare, warped wood, and the walls were covered with a haphazard display of posters, printed lettering, and other samples of Kinton's work.

A swing door flew open and a man wearing a printer's apron bustled in behind the counter. He was in his thirties, sallow-faced, small, and prematurely bald.

'Pann Kinton?' asked Rome, while the door quivered shut again.

'That's right.' The smile on the printer's lips faded as he took a second look at them. 'Uh – '

'Police.' Rome showed his warrant card briefly. 'Mr Kinton, do you sometimes use the name Calasan?'

'Sometimes,' Kinton seemed suddenly frightened. He wiped his hands on the front of his apron. 'It's – well, a sort of trademark. Not registered or anything, but – '

'Sir?' Rome glanced at Thane for approval.

'Go ahead,' murmured Thane. 'He's yours.'

'Mr Kinton.' Rome's voice took on a cutting edge. 'You had a customer named Joe Daisy.'

'I – ' Kinton stared at him, then gripped the counter as if to stop his hands from shaking. 'Yes, I – '

He stopped short as the door behind him swung open again. The man who barged through was of medium height, with mousy hair, and wore an old leather jacket over a sweater and slacks.

'That's fixed, Pann,' he began curtly, then stared.

'They're police,' said Kinton, his voice a high despairing wail.

Martin Tuce, the Glassman, might have stepped straight out of his CRO photographs. He stood for a moment, his thin, tight mouth hanging open, his prominent eyes bulging, then he cursed and hurled himself backwards through the swing door at the same instant as Thane vaulted the counter.

Kinton was in the way. Thane shoved him aside, slammed through the wildly flapping door, and found himself in among the machinery of the printing shop.

He caught a movement out of the corner of one eye then ducked as a heavy metal block hurled towards him, missed his head by little more than a hair's breadth and smashed against a cabinet. Tuce burst from behind the shelter of a typesetting machine, running towards the rear.

There was a door. He reached it, wrestled with the handle, but it didn't budge. Snarling, the Glassman swung round as Thane charged towards him. One hand fumbled under the leather jacket then appeared again. A knife-blade, narrow and needle-pointed, glinted as it slashed for Thane's throat and ripped the collar of his sheepskin.

Tuce steadied, crouching a little, the knife held blade uppermost, those strange eyes narrowed, edging forward a little while he muttered to himself.

Thane retreated a step, found himself against a table littered with half-set type, then grabbed a heavy metal page rule. Grunting, Tuce tried another stabbing lunge and, as he did, Thane used the rule like a sword, slamming it down on the other man's knife-wrist with all the force he could muster.

Tuce screamed. The knife clattered to the floor, and the Glassman dived away again.

Rome was running through from the front shop. Thane ignored him, tossed the rule aside, and went after the escaping man. There was a flight of stairs; Tuce was scrambling up them with his right arm hugged protectively against his side, and at the top they were in a photographic area.

Glancing back, Tuce used his good arm to topple a large easel and make-up board into Thane's path. Thane tripped and went down briefly, and as he got on his feet again he saw Tuce reach another door, one that opened, and go through.

Rome was at his heels. They emerged into the open, on a small area of flat roof. Tuce was just ahead. He glanced back at the two men desperately, looked ahead at the gap between him and the next building, then seemed to make up his mind.

'Don't be a fool – ' yelled Rome.

Tuce was already running. He had only about four steps before the jump, and even as he made the leap Thane knew the Glassman wouldn't make it. He crashed against the edge of the other building, grabbed desperately with both hands, and his injured right arm clawed uselessly.

For a long moment Martin Tuce hung one-handed on to the low parapet opposite. He looked back at the two detectives, his thin face twisted in horror. Then his fingers lost their grip and he fell. The beginnings of a scream ended in a thud.

They went to the edge, looked down, and Thane felt sick.

Martin Tuce, the Glassman, the enforcer who had terrorized so many, hung draped like a limp, lifeless sack over the boundary wall between the buildings.

They went back down the stairs, paused long enough to handcuff Kinton to a radiator pipe, then went outside to the wall.

The sunlight glinted on the sharp shards of glass set along its top, the same glass Tuce had been impaled on when he landed. He was dead; a few thin trickles of blood were running down the stonework, and some small, buzzing flies had already arrived out of nowhere.

They turned away. Rome's driver came running over to join them and other people were beginning to appear.

'Take care of things,' said Thane tonelessly.

He went back into the printer's shop and Pann Kinton stared at him apprehensively.

'He's dead,' Thane told him unemotionally.

The bald, sallow-faced printer swallowed hard but looked almost relieved. He licked his lips.

'How?' he asked.

'He fell.' Thane went round to his side of the counter and almost smiled as Kinton backed away, being stopped short as the handcuffs jangled. 'But that leaves you. He told you "That's fixed". What had he fixed?'

Kinton looked away, but stayed silent.

'I haven't time to waste,' said Thane quietly. 'It's your choice, Kinton. The charge can be accessory to murder.' He met Kinton's horrified gaze and nodded. 'Joe Daisy's murder – you're the one he came to, saying he wanted some pirate copies of *The Hanging Tree*, or else. You're the one who passed on the word he could be a problem. Then your little friends went with their hammer and nails to sort him out.'

'I didn't know,' blurted Kinton desperately.

200

'But it happened.'

The man drew a deep, sniffling breath.

'Suppose – suppose I do help you?' he ask hesitantly.

'It would make sense.'

Kinton gave a resigned nod.

'Let's start at the beginning,' said Thane. 'You've done work for Jimbo Raddick?'

'Yes.'

'Why?'

'I owed him.' Kinton was still reluctant. 'He – well, squared things for me once, got me out of a real mess. It was years ago.'

'And you've been on his hook ever since?' Kinton's silence was answer enough for Thane. 'All right, how does he use you?'

'Different ways,' Kinton bit his lip. 'Sometimes he uses Calasan and this address for a mail drop. Or – or I run off print work for him, things like that.'

'The kind of print work other firms would question?'

Kinton nodded, then volunteered, 'That's how Joe Daisy knew I had connections with somebody's pirate video factory. He – a while back, he saw some labels I was printing, for a pirate job. You know, labels for the cases.'

'But that was all he knew?'

Kinton nodded again.

'Then let's talk about Tuce. Why was he here today, what had he "fixed"?'

'His people wanted some special fake labels for *The Hanging Tree*,' said Kinton wearily. He twisted his face into a weak attempt at a smile. 'It's a play on words. The next batch of pirate tapes are being labelled *A Forest Walk*. You know – trees, last walk?'

'Should I laugh?' asked Thane coldly.

'The idea is that if any outsider gets nosey he'll think it's just some nature study video,' said Kinton quickly. 'It was Raddick's notion – he wanted six thousand of them at first.'

'You said at first.' Thane kept his apparent interest minimal. 'You mean that changed?'

'Yes.' Talking was beginning to come easier to the printer. 'Tuce was here to collect them, but they weren't ready – I'd hit a problem. He told me that things had changed, that three thousand would be enough now.'

'Why?'

'He didn't say, I don't ask questions.' Kinton tried to gesture and the handcuff links jingled again. 'The trouble was I needed a special coated paper and it's hard to get.'

'But you've a source?' encouraged Thane dryly.

'I'd arranged for a delivery – I knew I hadn't enough in stock.'

'But you have a source?' repeated Thane. 'The back-door kind?'

'A friend.' Kinton chewed his lip. 'I knew I hadn't enough paper for the job and he'd promised me more – I should have had it here a couple of days ago. But he had his own problems; it only arrived about an hour before Tuce did.'

'That wouldn't please Tuce?'

'No. But he said he'd wait till the labels were ready. That he'd let one of his people know. She would – '

'She?' Thane pounced on the word.

'The woman Raddick is partnering on this,' said Kinton earnestly. He mistook Thane's silence. 'That's how it was – Tuce said he'd have to call her and let her know there was a hitch, because there was no way he could contact Raddick.'

'But she could?'

Kinton nodded. 'She was meeting him somewhere.'

'This woman – ' Thane felt hoarse as he spoke ' – does she have a name?'

'Not as far as I am concerned.' Kinton looked frightened again. 'That's the truth. I just know about her – the odd hint that even Raddick does what she tells him. Tuce was phoning her when – well, when you got here.'

Pann Kinton's story didn't change when Thane took him through it again and he was too frightened to be lying. He knew nothing more, except that the Glassman had had a van parked in the square.

They found the van a little later. By then, more police had arrived, Tuce's body had been taken down from the glass-topped wall, and the small crowd which had gathered had drifted off again, their excitement over.

It was a small Peugeot van and Rome unlocked it with keys he'd taken from the dead man's pockets. The rear of the van was empty but Rome gave a soft whistle as he dragged a cloth-wrapped bundle from under the passenger seat. It was a sawn-off shotgun, and it was loaded.

'Not nice,' he said conversationally.

'Be glad he didn't take it with him,' murmured Thane. He looked at the empty van again. 'Anything else in his pockets, apart from keys?'

'Money and cigarettes mainly – the usual, sir, except for this.' Rome produced a small plastic evidence envelope. Inside it was a bright metal nail twisted into a ring. He grimaced. 'Maybe he liked souveniers.'

Rome's driver came over, stuck his head into the van, and gave Thane a quick nod.

'You're wanted, Superintendent. Our Control says will you call your people, on your own frequency.'

Thane thanked him, went over to the Ford, and used his radio. He was answered immediately, the Crime Squad operator's voice precise and unhurried. A message was in from Campbell and MacDonald.

'They say they have a location, sir. Positive.'

Thane sank back in his seat for a moment, then keyed his microphone.

'DC Felix and DC Craig to meet me at the airport, as arranged. I'm on my way.'

He signed off, saw Rome's lanky figure nearby, waved him over, and wound down the window.

'Can you cope here?'

'If that's the way things are, sir,' said Rome resignedly. 'I'm getting used to mopping up.'

'But you're good at it,' consoled Thane.

They exchanged a grin and Thane set the Ford moving.

*

The helicopter was a four-seat Bell Jet-Ranger with a civilian pilot. It rose from a quiet corner of Glasgow's Airport a few minutes after 3 p.m., scuttled clear of the airport's regular approach routes, then climbed steadily for a spell until the entire Firth of Clyde was spread below like a large-scale relief map.

Sandra was up front, beside the pilot, Thane in the rear with Joe Felix. Before take-off there had been time to confirm that the watch on the Falcon Services depot was being maintained and that Alexis Garrison hadn't left.

Their route was north-west, but with an initial curve which kept them clear of two sections of the glinting water below. Their pilot made apologetic noises over the intercom headphones – neither the Royal Navy in the Gare Loch nor the American base at Holy Loch liked any kind of helicopter traffic over their nuclear submarine pens.

Thane nodded his understanding. Their situation didn't amount to a total race against time, even if that might come later.

Water gave way to dark green hills and the helicopter began beating its way over thick forests streaked with fire breaks. Then more water showed ahead, a long narrow ribbon which was Loch Fynne. They caught a glimpse of fishing boats at work and the old town of Inveraray with its turreted castle, the ancestral home of the Dukes of Argyll.

Their pilot kept up a commentary, mainly for Sandra's benefit, pointing out landmarks, making more apologetic noises when they met the occasional mild turbulence. Joe Felix, losing interest, slept.

Thane hardly listened. He was partly thinking ahead, partly trying to accept and absorb Kinton's belief that Alexis Garrison ranked at least equal with Jimbo Raddick in the pirate operation.

If she did, if she might even run Raddick – he still found it hard to think of her in terms of the rest, with its ruthless brutality.

But it couldn't be anyone else.

He heard the pilot speaking again, then realized it wasn't for their benefit. A moment later the man switched radio channels, spoke again, and gradually the helicopter changed course.

They were still over the hills but losing height. Ahead and to their left, the sea had appeared again as a broad expanse of water littered with islands. The nearest had to be Jura; the long mass near the horizon its mountains topped with cloud, he recognized as Mull.

The helicopter dipped again, its shadow racing over barren, sunlit moorland. They lost their view behind another ridge of hills, the pilot using his radio frequently now, looking ahead, not so much navigating as following instructions.

A few minutes later they sank down to land in a desolate stretch of moorland heather. It was close to a narrow track of a road where two police cars were waiting.

They got out and hurried away from the chunking rotor blades. The first man from the cars to greet them was Sergeant MacDonald. He grinned, waited until the helicopter had taken off again, then led them over to a bulky figure in police uniform.

'This is Sergeant Fraser, sir,' introduced MacDonald. 'We're on his territory.'

'Glad to help, Superintendent.' Fraser, a red-faced man with a soft, lilting voice, shook hands as the introductions were completed. A slight twinkle in his eyes, he considered Sandra. 'The lassie comes too?'

'The lassie damn well better,' Sandra told him frostily.

'Fine, fine.' Unperturbed, he nodded towards the cars. 'Maybe you'll ride with me, Superintendent. Then there's a wee bit walk to where your inspector is waiting.' He sniffed. 'Though how a man with a name like Campbell gets to be an inspector, even in a place like Glasgow, is beyond me.'

In the Highlands, at least, memories of old clan feuds hadn't died.

'Join the club,' said MacDonald grimly.

Then they headed for the cars.

'When we heard what you wanted, it wasn't too difficult,' said Sergeant Fraser as his car bumped and lurched over the rough surface. He swore mildly as a pot-hole deeper than the rest juddered his massive frame. 'This stretch of the coast you're interested in is called the Nathrach by the few folk who live here – it's Gaelic, meaning "of the serpents". Not too many serpents now, sir. Just maybe a wee adder or two minding its own business in the gorse. But like I said, it's lonely. The kind of area where a man could get to know the sheep by their first names.'

'Or the horses?' Thane clung to his seat for support.

'Aye, the horse hairs clinched it.' Fraser chuckled. 'Not many self-respecting horses would live around here.' He drove on, whistling thinly through his teeth for a moment, then gave Thane a sideways glance. 'The folk you want are there, Superintendent. We've seen them. But whatever you've got in mind, it won't be easy.'

'Why?' demanded Thane.

The Argyll sergeant shook his head.

'Best see for yourself, sir. You'll not want to go near the main road, so we'll leave the cars at the head of the glen, then it's just over that wee rise.'

Thane looked at the 'wee rise'. It was a stark black face of rock. But he saw Fraser's face and said nothing.

There were other vehicles parked where they stopped, two of them the Crime Squad cars from Glasgow, the rest Argyll force units. A solitary constable had been left on radio watch and nodded a greeting as the two new arrivals pulled in and their occupants emerged.

'Let me see your feet, lassie,' said Fraser firmly, turning to Sandra. He considered her shoes. 'Aye, they'll do. But just don't go breaking your ankle or anything. You're well enough put together, and I wouldn't like to carry you.'

'Don't put yourself out, Sergeant,' said Sandra coldly. 'I

could always crawl.'

'Not your kind.' Fraser winked at Thane. 'She'd find a broomstick, I reckon, and fly back.'

Sandra scowled. 'What did you do before you joined the force, Sergeant – run a charm school?'

He roared with delight. 'No, I was a colour sergeant in Her Majesty's finest – The Royal Highland Regiment, the Black Watch. Where we ate strong men for lunch and sprinkled wee girls like you on the salad!'

They set off up a savage mixture of naked rock and loose scree. Fraser grunted in the lead, showing the way and setting a pace which left them gasping. Every foothold had to be tested and any loose stone that was dislodged rattled back down the way they'd come, gathering others as it went.

There was gorse and scrub among the thick heather at the top and Fraser signalled them to keep low, off the skyline. Then, before they had a chance to see more, he led them down a gentle slope which had a similar abundance of cover. Eventually, they reached where Detective Inspector Campbell was waiting. He was sitting behind the shelter of a hummock of ground and already had company in the shape of two armed police and a small, grey-haired civilian in patched work clothes.

'Good to see you, sir,' he said laconically. 'Want a look at what we've got?'

'Show me,' nodded Thane.

'Mr Kennedy,' Campbell beckoned to the grey-haired man, 'you're the expert.'

Kennedy on one side, Campbell on the other, Sergeant Fraser just behind, Thane crawled to the top of the hummock and had his first clear view of what lay at the foot of the slope.

They were about halfway down it. A tarmac road ran below, separating the slope from a sweep of sandy foreshore. Tufted with grass, the sand edged a narrow bay formed by two long headlands of rock.

'There,' said Campbell, pointing a boney forefinger.

They were almost directly overlooking a strange, compact huddle of buildings built close to the edge of the sea. On the landward side, they were guarded by a high, rusting security fence. Most of the buildings were small and mere roofless ruins, but two were intact and showed signs of being maintained. The nearest, the remains of a track running to it from the gate in the fence, was a slab-sided structure like a garage block with a corrugated-iron roof, and big sliding doors. Another, stranger building sat behind it, smaller but longer, built on a concrete causeway which projected out into the bay. It had steps to one side leading down to the water, with a dinghy moored at a landing stage. At the far end, Thane could see the remains of an old crane.

'Try these,' Campbell passed him a pair of binoculars.

Thane adjusted the focus and examined the area again. Through the lenses, he could pick out details like the clean metal of the runners on the sliding doors, the glint of glass in the windows of the other building, and the dinghy's smart paintwork.

Something moved on the edge of his vision. He moved the binoculars and swore under his breath as the unmistakable figure of Jonathan Garrison ambled out of the causeway building. Unhurriedly, Garrison went down the steps to the dinghy, put something aboard, then went back the way he'd come and vanished again.

'Know him, sir?' asked Campbell mildly.

'Yes.' Thane lowered the binoculars, puzzled. 'What the hell is this place?'

'The navy built it in the last war,' volunteered Fraser from behind him. 'Lachie Kennedy can tell you more – he's their nearest neighbour.'

'I've just a wee croft down the road,' murmured the grey-haired civilian. 'A few sheep and a wee bit fishing – '

'He's not the Income Tax,' grunted Fraser. 'Just tell it.'

Kennedy grinned. 'The last folk who had it were a daft English couple. He had a yacht, her hobby was horses – she used the garage block as stables. Then he ran out o' money and they left.' He shrugged. 'The place lay empty till these folk arrived. They're not friendly. I only went there once, and didn't get past the gate. Sometimes they're here, sometimes they're not – but when they're away, the place is locked up tighter than a fort.'

Thane nodded and switched his attention to Fraser.

'Know anything about them?'

'Not much,' admitted the sergeant. 'There's a story that they're doing some kind of marine research. They haven't bothered anyone.'

Thane gestured, and they eased back down into the hollows.

'We've seen three or four of them so far,' reported Campbell. 'One could be Jimbo Raddick – he matches the description. There are vehicles in the garage, for sure. They had the door open for a spell.'

A small black beetle was moving slowly over the patch of bare, sandy soil at Thane's feet. He watched it for a moment, ignoring the others, thinking.

Whatever happened now, he knew the responsibility was his. But he was dealing with unknown quantities; he didn't even know how many men Raddick had down there.

He grimaced, watching the beetle vanish under the sole of his shoe then reappear at the other side, still moving unhurriedly. Jimbo Raddick was a man he hadn't seen in years, and Billy Tripp remained not much more than a name and a photograph.

Yet he had come this far in tracking them down – and it wasn't finished. Some of these men were armed; every instinct told him that there would be no easy surrender. Cornered, Raddick would put up some kind of a fight, hope for some chance to escape, however, desperate.

Thane wished he knew more. But he didn't. All he could hope for was a way round it, a way to minimize risks.

A way round. The thought sparked another, wild but just possible. If it worked.

'Mr Kennedy.' He spoke quietly and waited until the grey-haired crofter had eased over to join him. 'You say you fish around here. You've got a boat?'

'Aye.' Kennedy nodded. 'And the name is Lachie.'

'Ever gone fishing in that bay?'

'Often enough.' Kennedy eyed him shrewdly. 'For mackerel mostly, but sometimes I hit something bigger.'

'So they'd see nothing strange in your boat appearing out there – fishing?'

'Fishing.' Kennedy grinned at him. 'Aye, why not? As long as someone pays for the hire o' my boat.'

'Someone will,' murmured Thane.

They'd been overheard. Campbell was frowning; Fraser's broad red face looked anything but happy.

'You're thinking of trying for the back door?' demanded Campbell. His frown became a scowl. 'Sorry, sir. I don't like it. They'd have you before you got near them.'

'He's right,' said Fraser gloomily.

'We could move in,' suggested Campbell. He swore and brushed at his face as something small and buzzing stung him. 'Make a show of strength – try scaring them.'

'And start a war?' Thane surprised them with a grin. 'No. But we need a way to keep them interested in something else. A road accident, for instance – reasonably spectacular, two cars in a crash outside their gates.' He turned to Fraser. 'It means two drivers, the best we've got, to fake it and make it look good.'

Fraser chewed his lip. 'You need one of my lads, Davie MacKinnon. His idea of fun is rally driving. But if you need two – '

'We've got the other one.' Thane thumbed towards Sandra Craig.

'Her?' Fraser swallowed indignantly. 'That lassie?'

'Can do it,' said Thane flatly. He beckoned Sandra nearer. 'You heard most of that?'

'Yes, sir.' She winked at Fraser. 'Woman drivers – you know, what we're like.'

They waited while Fraser fetched his man. MacKinnon, a young constable with a mild, freckled face, arrived out of the bracken carrying a rifle. He grinned at Sandra then squatted down beside them.

'Here's what I want from you.' Thane used a broken twig to scratch a rough sketch on the ground. 'Some kind of collision, exactly at the gates, minor but spectacular.' He looked up at them. 'If one car ended up demolishing those gates, then you two got out and started arguing – '

Sandra and MacKinnon exchanged a glance, as if each were trying to assess the other.

'A half handbrake turn?' suggested Sandra. 'And it's mine.'

MacKinnon raised an eyebrow but nodded.

'That's a dry road,' he cautioned. 'You'll have to allow for it.'

'I will,' she agreed soberly.

One of the men Fraser had left on radio watch with the cars wriggled down the slope towards them. He arrived still out of breath from his climb up the ridge and handed Thane a message slip. It had been relayed from Glasgow. Thane glanced at the scribbled words then crumpled the piece of paper and tucked it into a pocket.

Alexis Garrison had left East Kilbride and was driving north.

'Sir.' Sandra made sure she had his attention. 'We'll work it out. I'll plan on hitting the gate tail-first – that way, it should look convincing enough.'

'It will,' said Thane. 'I'll tell you why.'

He did, and even Campbell began to smile.

Fourteen feet long and clinker built, the old workboat appeared half an hour later, rounding one of the head-lands, turning into the bay. The antiquated outboard motor at her stern muttered asthmatically as Lachie Kennedy, an old cap stuck at the back of his head, steered a course with the relaxed air of a man who had all the time in the world.

Almost in the middle of the bay, he slapped the outboard engine into neutral and it idled, coughing a blue, oily exhaust. Getting to his feet, Kennedy slowly assembled a cane fishing rod, attached a thin wire trace with several hooks, then made a couple of trial casts with the line. Apparently satisfied, he made another cast which left a small blue float bobbing some distance away.

Whistling to himself, nursing the rod, he settled in the thwarts again. The boat drifted, gradually coming further into the bay, carried by the current – and aided by the way Kennedy had the rudder jammed over.

He broke off whistling for a moment and spoke softly, hardly moving his lips.

'You up there. Stay still. Somebody is bein' awful curious from one of those windows with a pair o' binoculars.'

Then he reeled in his line and made another cast.

There were three men lying under the faded canvas heaped untidily at the workboat's bow. They were cramped, damp and uncomfortable, their faces only inches away from the water which swirled along the bottom of the boat as the light swell chunked against her hull.

Colin Thane was in the middle, jammed between Fraser and MacDonald. The Argyll man had insisted on coming, despite his bulk, and the Crime Squad sergeant had been equally keen. That left Detective Inspector Campbell running things ashore, and Thane had seen him wish MacDonald luck for once as they parted. But for the moment, at least, Lachie Kennedy and the way he behaved was more important than any good wishes.

'Boat.' The radio Thane was holding close to his ear gave a tinny whisper. He recognized Joe Felix's voice. 'Standing by.'

He murmured an acknowledgement, swore under his breath as Fraser moved in the semi-darkness and jabbed an elbow in his ribs.

Another few minutes passed. From the stern, Lachie Kennedy stopped whistling for a moment to announce that the watcher had gone. They heard him rise and then the whine of the reel as he tried another cast, whistling again. A contrary puff of wind caught some of the exhaust and brought it stinking in under the canvas.

'Somebody should have changed his socks,' muttered MacDonald, and Fraser quivered with amusement.

Kennedy stopped whistling.

'Now,' he said quietly. 'We're about 100 yards off.'

'Now,' said Thane into his radio.

Aboard the boat, only Kennedy saw it happen. Two cars, both travelling south, swept along the road. One seemed to be trying hard to pass the other, horn sounding impatiently. It began to overtake, then there was a sudden rasp of metal and both cars swerved dizzily.

One ended up broadside on across the road. The other, swinging in a wild but beautifully controlled skid, hit the fence gates tail-on with an awesome crash. One gate tore loose. The other folded back, with the car which had done the damage brought to a halt against the twisted iron, its horn blaring and apparently jammed.

Moments passed. Davie MacKinnon, wearing borrowed civilian clothes in place of his uniform, emerged from the first car and hurried over towards the gate. As he got there, Sandra climbed out of the other car. They stood beside it, arguing, pointing and gesturing.

The car horn wailed on. Figures emerged from the building on the causeway and stood staring. Aboard the workboat, Lachie Kennedy lowered his fishing rod and gently fed the outboard engine a first touch of throttle. The boat's head came round, pointing towards the little jetty and the stone steps.

Then it happened, the final surprise Thane had planned with Joe Felix. The air quivered with a flat blast as six smoke bombs, actuated by a timer fuse, exploded simultaneously in the rear of Sandra's car. Thick smoke belched from the car's open windows and the driver's door, spreading like a dense orange fog.

Hammering and clanking, the outboard's engine rasped to full power. Foam began creaming from her blunt bow while her hidden passengers threw aside the canvas and crouched ready. Ashore, vague shapes appeared in the billowing smoke as Campbell led his force in through the shattered gates. They spread out as they came, the local men's uniforms an immediate identification.

The figures who had been staring from the causeway building scattered, and began tumbling back into shelter, except for one who jumped for the sand and ran desperately along the shore. But none looked back towards the water.

On the workboat they stopped spectating as the engine ceased hammering. Creaming in, the sturdy old wooden hull thumped against the concrete steps and Thane, his ·38 revolver held ready, was first to leap ashore. MacDonald and Fraser followed, Fraser similarly armed, MacDonald clutching one of the Savage pump-guns.

There was a door at the top of the steps. Fraser kicked it open and, as the boat backed off below, they went through into an empty room. A gun barked twice somewhere, then they heard the louder blast of a shotgun. A police whistle shrilled and was followed by the single sharp crack of a high-velocity weapon.

There were two doors in the room. The first led into a small, equally empty washroom. They tried the other, burst through, and stopped, staring.

It was a long corridor of a room, hygienically clean, lined down one side by a bank of electronic equipment. Tiny indicator lights glowed and the air was filled with a rustling, high-speed whisper of sound.

Thane crossed to the nearest panel. As he reached it, there were soft clicks, other lights blinked briefly along the entire bank, and through a glass panel he saw a video cassette pushed sideways by a glinting metal arm. It slid from sight and another quivered into the vacated space, was gripped by a small clamp, and clicked neatly into a slot.

The panel lights changed and the rustling whisper began again throughout the room. One batch of newly recorded tapes ejected and another set of blanks began soaking up the recording coming from some master unit at an incredible speed.

A door at the far end of the room flew open. A young, fair-haired man wearing white overalls came running in. He saw them, his mouth fell open, and he threw up his hands in immediate surrender.

Fraser grabbed him, spun him round, and handcuffed his wrists behind his back. As he was shoved aside, Thane and MacDonald made for the door he'd used.

They faced a hallway, with small, partitioned offices leading off on either side. Down the middle lay opened cartons of tapes and stacked piles of other tapes packaged in glistening new plastic. Thane took another step forward then MacDonald shouted a warning, shoving him hard to one side and down.

As they hit the floor there was a blast. A hail of pellets lashed where they'd been.

Rolling, Thane caught a glimpse of a figure clutching a sawn-off shotgun scuttling from one partition to another. He tried a quick, answering snap-shot with the ·38 and the bullet gouged splinters from a doorframe. Another gun, a pistol, snapped two shots at them from the far end of the hallway.

Swearing, MacDonald brought the pump-action Savage against his shoulder then hesitated, bewildered, as a strange, frantic figure ran across his sights.

'No. Stop, all of you – ' Shouting the plea, Jonathan Garrison headed straight towards the second man's hiding place. His arms were raised, his fists were clenched. 'You promised – '

There was a scuffle. Suddenly Garrison appeared again. He had lost his spectacles, he was grappling with Jimbo Raddick, whose face was contorted with fury.

A single, partly muffled shot rang out. Garrison staggered and started to fall but Raddick seized him, keeping him upright like a shield until he reached another of the doorways. Then he threw his burden aside and ducked into shelter. There was a brief creak of hinges then a crash as another door opened and slammed shut again.

Garrison had slumped to his knees, the sunlight from a

window gleaming on his bald pate. Then, very slowly, moaning, he seemed to fold and finally fell to the floor.

'Wait.' Thane stopped MacDonald from scrambling up and pointed to where the man with the sawn-off shotgun was still hidden.

'You. You horrible little city man in there – ' The bellow, like an enraged bull, came from behind them. Sergeant Fraser strode deliberately into sight and the voice which had terrified untold army recruits roared again. 'You're on your own now, horrible little man. Throw that bloody gun out – now. Or God help you, laddie!'

There was a moment's silence, a sound like a sob, then the shotgun slithered out from behind the man's shelter.

'Out with your hands as high as your kind of ape can reach,' snarled Fraser. 'No tricks, mind you!'

Slowly, reluctantly, an unshaven figure in a sweater and dungaree trousers edged into sight with his hands held high and rigid.

The other two left him to Fraser and ran over to where Garrison lay face down. Gently, Thane turned him over and the one-time scientist's eyes met his own, filled with pain.

'I – I made them promise,' he said weakly. 'No violence. Nobody was to – '

'Easy,' soothed Thane. He could see the blood spreading from the bullet wound below Garrison's ribs, hear the bubbling sound when he breathed. 'We'll be back.'

Rising, he crossed quickly to where they'd seen Raddick disappear. Beyond it there was an outside door and he threw it open, MacDonald crowding out behind him.

They were standing on the concrete walkway which ran round the edge of the causeway building. The shouting and the noise from the front had ended. But in its place they heard the rasp of a boat engine starting up.

Two strides took Thane to where he could see the steps leading down to the jetty. The dinghy which had been moored there was already beginning to move, her barking outboard engine thrashing the shallow water, with Jimbo

Raddick crouched low at the stern.

Thane looked around. Lachie Kennedy's workboat was some distance away, just idling.

The dinghy was moving faster. Raddick looked back at them for a moment, then crouched lower.

'Sir?' MacDonald made it a question, the Savage pump-gun cradled ready.

Thane nodded. Unhurriedly, MacDonald raised the weapon. For a moment, he sighted on a spot between Raddick's shoulder blades. Then he grunted, lowered the Savage a fraction, and squeezed the trigger.

The twelve-bore slammed three times as he worked the pump. One solid shot smashed into the outboard engine which stopped in a scream of fractured metal. The next ripped a gash in the dinghy's fragile hull, and the last punched a fist-sized hole just below the waterline.

'That should do it,' said MacDonald calmly, and the dinghy began to wallow in the light swell, sinking lower and lower as the sea poured in.

'Gather him up,' said Thane curtly.

He went back. Sergeant Fraser was kneeling beside Garrison. Their second prisoner had already been taken away and one of Fraser's constables was standing near. Fraser looked up as Thane came over and gave a slight headshake.

'No chance,' he said softly.

Thane knelt beside him.

'Thane,' Jonathan Garrison's tired, lined face twitched in recognition, 'I – I want to apologize. For all this.' He coughed. 'It was my fault. I designed them – the copying machines.'

'I know an expert who says they're the best,' said Thane quietly.

'They are.' A faint, sad smile touched the dying man's lips. 'But nobody was interested; I tried manufacturers, everywhere.'

'After your breakdown?'

Garrison gave a faint nod. 'Therapy – that's how it

217

began. They're better, faster – '

'Then Alexis took over?' Thane had to ask, had to learn all he could.

'Alexis.' Garrison's voice was weaker, little more than a whisper. 'Don't be too hard on her. She – she just knew people. She meant well.' He looked at Thane, his eyes bewildered and pleading. 'Money – it changes people.'

Another bubbling breath ended in a choking rasp, then his eyes closed and his head sagged.

It was a few minutes later when Colin Thane left the building. A small group of prisoners was lined up to one side, under guard, one of them sitting on the ground with a bandaged leg, another still being given first-aid by one of the Crime Squad men.

Campbell came over, looking pleased with himself.

'Everything's tidy,' he reported, then added almost amiably, 'I hear MacDonald and Sergeant Fraser did fairly well.'

Thane nodded, looking around. They had seven prisoners, including Raddick; two were technicians, the remainder hired muscle, some of them familiar faces.

But Billy Tripp wasn't among them. He was a shape lying covered by a blanket, killed after he'd shot and wounded one constable and had narrowly missed another. Tripp and Jonathan Garrison – two dead and only two. Three of his own men injured, but none seriously.

It could have been worse, much worse. Lachie Kennedy was still calmly fishing out in the bay, hauling in mackerel with every cast.

He saw Sandra and Joe Felix talking to the young Argyll driver, caught Sandra's eye, and gave a slight smile he knew she'd understand. Then he went over to where Raddick was standing. The man's pudgy face was surly, his clothes were still dripping water. But the gold watch on one wrist and the heavy rings on his fingers would have cost about six months of Thane's pay.

'My bad luck,' said Raddick bitterly. A touch of his usual arrogance returned. 'That was a nice stunt you pulled, Thane. You're a Superintendent now, right?'

'Yes.' Thane considered him stonily, keeping a tight grip on the anger he felt. 'You can forget about Spain – you'll be getting your sunshine through bars from now on.'

'That depends on a jury.' Raddick tried to look confident but failed. 'I know my law, remember? You're going to have to prove a lot, not just here.'

'We'll manage,' Thane promised him gravely.

He started to turn away.

'I said it was bad luck,' reminded Raddick almost hoarsely. He gave a humourless laugh. 'You want to know how bad, for free? One last batch of *The Hanging Tree* and tomorrow we were moving out – shifting everything. I've even got the damned packing cases here.'

'And that's why you only took half the tapes from the hijack?'

'What hijack?' asked Raddick sardonically, and spat at Thane's feet.

Cloud drifted in from the west. By early evening, when the big Volvo station-wagon at last purred along the road towards the one-time naval camp, the light was dull and grey, the sea a cold, steely blue.

Everything had been cleared. Only the broken, twisted gates in the fence and the almost submerged dinghy bobbing off shore remained as memorials to what had happened.

Alexis Garrison was nearly at the camp gates before it seemed to register with her that something was wrong. The Volvo slowed and stopped. It began to move again, quickly, then she braked to a halt as a police car appeared ahead, blocking the road. Behind her, another car took up a similar position.

She switched off and waited as Thane emerged at the roadside and walked towards her. Then, as he reached the car, she opened her door and stepped out.

'Hello, Colin.' She studied him for a moment, wryly. 'I did wonder. But I thought – ' She left it there and shrugged.

'It's over,' Thane told her simply. 'Jonathan's dead, Alexis. Your friend Raddick killed him. Jonathan was trying to make him give up.'

'He would.' There was little emotion in her voice. 'And Jimbo?'

'We have him.' Thane stuck his hands in his pockets, seeing the breeze ruffle her hair, forcing himself to discard any remaining memories. 'Why, Alexis?'

She shrugged. 'Jonathan came up with a gold mine. He was too innocent a fool to know what to do with it – and Falcon was barely washing its face.'

'And you knew Raddick.'

'Yes.' She gave him a bitter, half-amused, half-mocking smile. 'You want to know how? It goes back a long time. I met him and I finished with you. It was logical – a lawyer earned more than you did, even with overtime.' She paused and shrugged. 'It didn't last. But when I needed the right kind of help and he knew what I had – well, he came running.'

'Alexis, I – ' Thane checked himself. 'It's formal now.'

'I know.' She stood back from him. 'As I remember it, there's always an arresting officer.'

He nodded.

'Does it have to be you?' The smile crept back again. 'Call it a favour.'

Thane turned. Sandra Craig was standing beside one of the police cars. He beckoned, and she came over.

It was evening of the next day before he could get back to the city and, finally, home. There had been a lot to do and a lot more still remained.

But it could wait.

Mary welcomed him, the dog welcomed him, Tommy

and Kate welcomed him. But they kept him out of the front room until after they'd eaten.

Then Tommy and Kate proudly led him through. There was a video recorder beside the TV set.

'On a week's free trial, Dad,' said Tommy proudly. 'We fixed it. Mum said it would be OK. Then, if you like it – '

He saw Mary eyeing him dubiously and knew what she was thinking. But he was home.

'We got a couple of tapes with it,' said Tommy, slightly worried by his silence. 'Dad – '

'I like it.' He winked at his son. 'But you handle the technical side.'

The telephone rang. Kate answered it then called him through.

It was Doc Williams on the line.

'I heard you were back,' said the police surgeon breezily. 'Thought you'd like to know Francey's getting out tomorrow – being thrown out, more or less, while they've got a nursing staff.'

'Good.' Thane smiled at the mouthpiece. 'Thanks, Doc.'

'One other thing,' went on the police surgeon determinedly. 'That rabbit joke – I'll finish it for you. You remember, there was the old wise rabbit and the young, learner rabbit. Well, they're out for a walk and they see a bunch of female rabbits in the distance. The young rabbit gets excited, right? He says to the old rabbit, "Let's run over and get friendly with a couple of these females." But the wise old rabbit shakes his head. He says, "No, son. Let's walk over and get friendly with all of them." Like it?'

'Good-night, Doc,' said Thane firmly, and hung up.

Then he went through to the video demonstration.

Bestselling Crime

☐ No One Rides Free	Larry Beinhart	£2.95
☐ Alice in La La Land	Robert Campbell	£2.99
☐ In La La Land We Trust	Robert Campbell	£2.99
☐ Suspects	William J Caunitz	£2.95
☐ So Small a Carnival	John William Corrington	
	Joyce H Corrington	£2.99
☐ Saratoga Longshot	Stephen Dobyns	£2.99
☐ Blood on the Moon	James Ellroy	£2.99
☐ Roses Are Dead	Loren D. Estleman	£2.50
☐ The Body in the Billiard Room	HRF Keating	£2.50
☐ Bertie and the Tin Man	Peter Lovesey	£2.50
☐ Rough Cider	Peter Lovesey	£2.50
☐ Shake Hands For Ever	Ruth Rendell	£2.99
☐ Talking to Strange Men	Ruth Rendell	£2.99
☐ The Tree of Hands	Ruth Rendell	£2.99
☐ Wexford: An Omnibus	Ruth Rendell	£6.99
☐ Speak for the Dead	Margaret Yorke	£2.99

Prices and other details are liable to change

ARROW BOOKS, BOOKSERVICE BY POST, PO BOX 29, DOUGLAS, ISLE
OF MAN, BRITISH ISLES

NAME..

ADDRESS ....

....

....

Please enclose a cheque or postal order made out to Arrow Books Ltd. for the amount
due and allow the following for postage and packing.

U.K. CUSTOMERS: Please allow 22p per book to a maximum of £3.00.

B.F.P.O. & EIRE: Please allow 22p per book to a maximum of £3.00.

OVERSEAS CUSTOMERS: Please allow 22p per book.

Whilst every effort is made to keep prices low it is sometimes necessary to increase cover
prices at short notice. Arrow Books reserve the right to show new retail prices on covers
which may differ from those previously advertised in the text or elsewhere.

Bestselling Thriller/Suspense

☐ Skydancer	Geoffrey Archer	£3.50
☐ Hooligan	Colin Dunne	£2.99
☐ See Charlie Run	Brian Freemantle	£2.99
☐ Hell is Always Today	Jack Higgins	£2.50
☐ The Proteus Operation	James P Hogan	£3.50
☐ Winter Palace	Dennis Jones	£3.50
☐ Dragonfire	Andrew Kaplan	£2.99
☐ The Hour of the Lily	John Kruse	£3.50
☐ Fletch, Too	Geoffrey McDonald	£2.50
☐ Brought in Dead	Harry Patterson	£2.50
☐ The Albatross Run	Douglas Scott	£2.99

Prices and other details are liable to change

ARROW BOOKS, BOOKSERVICE BY POST, PO BOX 29, DOUGLAS, ISLE OF MAN, BRITISH ISLES

NAME..

ADDRESS...

....

....

Please enclose a cheque or postal order made out to Arrow Books Ltd. for the amount due and allow the following for postage and packing.

U.K. CUSTOMERS: Please allow 22p per book to a maximum of £3.00.

B.F.P.O. & EIRE: Please allow 22p per book to a maximum of £3.00.

OVERSEAS CUSTOMERS: Please allow 22p per book.

Whilst every effort is made to keep prices low it is sometimes necessary to increase cover prices at short notice. Arrow Books reserve the right to show new retail prices on covers which may differ from those previously advertised in the text or elsewhere.

Bestselling Fiction

☐ No Enemy But Time	Evelyn Anthony	£2.95
☐ The Lilac Bus	Maeve Binchy	£2.99
☐ Prime Time	Joan Collins	£3.50
☐ A World Apart	Marie Joseph	£3.50
☐ Erin's Child	Sheelagh Kelly	£3.99
☐ Colours Aloft	Alexander Kent	£2.99
☐ Gondar	Nicholas Luard	£4.50
☐ The Ladies of Missalonghi	Colleen McCullough	£2.50
☐ Lily Golightly	Pamela Oldfield	£3.50
☐ Talking to Strange Men	Ruth Rendell	£2.99
☐ The Veiled One	Ruth Rendell	£3.50
☐ Sarum	Edward Rutherfurd	£4.99
☐ The Heart of the Country	Fay Weldon	£2.50

Prices and other details are liable to change

ARROW BOOKS, BOOKSERVICE BY POST, PO BOX 29, DOUGLAS, ISLE OF MAN, BRITISH ISLES

NAME..

ADDRESS..

....

....

Please enclose a cheque or postal order made out to Arrow Books Ltd. for the amount due and allow the following for postage and packing.

U.K. CUSTOMERS: Please allow 22p per book to a maximum of £3.00.

B.F.P.O. & EIRE: Please allow 22p per book to a maximum of £3.00.

OVERSEAS CUSTOMERS: Please allow 22p per book.

Whilst every effort is made to keep prices low it is sometimes necessary to increase cover prices at short notice. Arrow Books reserve the right to show new retail prices on covers which may differ from those previously advertised in the text or elsewhere.